"*Going Down* is a very funny and sharply observed picaresque tale of a young woman's struggles in New York, featuring an irrepressible and winning narrator. Jennifer Belle has a gift for capturing the moments of screwball comedy offered up by everyday life in the city, and making them feel not only fresh, but significant."

—Jennifer Egan, author of *The Invisible Circus*

"As credible as preposterous, as glib as painful, *Going Down* works. This only-in-New York gambol deftly conveys the mortification of the world's oldest profession, but as well the persistence of one character's dreams and, too, innocence. Belle chimes in with a ringer."

—John Ashbery

"The best hot-weather bet for hottest new novel...Hilariously endearing...it also possesses the same raw, coltish energy that made bestsellers out of *Bright Lights, Big City* and *Slaves of New York*."

—*Time Out New York*

GOING DOWN

JENNIFER BELLE

RIVERHEAD BOOKS, NEW YORK

This is a work of fiction. Names, characters,
places, and incidents either are the product of
the author's imagination or are used fictitiously.
Any resemblance to events or persons, living or
dead, is entirely coincidental.

Riverhead Books
Published by The Berkley Publishing Group
200 Madison Avenue
New York, New York 10016

First edition: July 1996

The Putnam Berkley World Wide Web site address is
http://www.berkley.com

Library of Congress Cataloging-in-Publication Data

Belle, Jennifer, 1968–
    Going down : a novel / by Jennifer Belle.
        p.   cm.
    ISBN 1-57322-554-1
    1. Young women—New York (N.Y.)—Fiction,   I. Title.
PS3552.E53337G65   1996
813'.54—dc20   95-47918
                                                  CIP

Printed in the United States of America

10   9   8   7   6   5

ACKNOWLEDGMENTS

With thanks to my fabulous agent, Tina Bennett, at Janklow & Nesbit; my editor, Julie Grau; Nicholas Weinstock, Liz Perl, Craig Burke and everyone at Riverhead; my father, and my brother, Matthew.

I am very grateful to the poets and novelists in my writing workshop, especially Doug Dorph, Shannon Hamann, Evelyn Horowitz, Alice Jurish, Anita Lobel, Mary du Passage, John Penn, Robert Steward, Harry Waitzman, and Jill Hoffman at the head of the glass table every week.

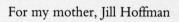

For my mother, Jill Hoffman

Contents

PART 1: A Whale of a Wash   1

PART 2: Blanche's   91

PART 3: The Whale's Footprint   145

PART 4: Going Down   181

PART 5: Manhole   231

"In another moment down went Alice after it, never once considering how in the world she was to get out again."

—*Alice's Adventures in Wonderland*,
Lewis Carroll

A WHALE OF A WASH

1

I WAS SITTING on the bed flipping through the *Village Voice*. I glanced at the adult entertainment section. One ad just said "COED$" and had a phone number. The *S* in COEDS was written like a dollar sign.

I was a coed. I was almost nineteen, with great hair and a new thin body. I called the number. A woman picked up the phone. "Hello."

"Hello," I said. "I noticed that you advertised coeds."

"Oh?"

"I was wondering if you had any escort positions that don't involve sex," I said.

"Excuse me?"

"I thought maybe just escort people, men, rich business-men from out of town, Japanese maybe, to cocktail parties or the theater." The call waiting went off.

"Do you have to get your other call?" the woman said.

I told her to ignore it.

"How old are you?" she asked.

"I'm nineteen."

"What's your name?"

"Bennington."

"Oh, you really are a coed." She thought this was very funny. "What do you look like?"

"I'm thin," I said. "I have long dark hair. I have a gap between my top front teeth."

"How tall are you?"

"I'm short," I said. "I'm very short."

"Petite."

"Right, petite. That's how I like to look at it."

"Who do you look like?"

I hated that question. I didn't look like anybody.

"Valerie Bertinelli," I told her.

"Who?"

"Valerie Bertinelli, you know from *One Day at a Time*." I was so embarrassed.

"Never heard of her. Why don't you come in for an interview?"

"When?"

"Now, at the Chelsea Hotel on Twenty-third Street."

"Okay," I said.

2

I HAD MOVED out of my roommate Andre Singh's apartment on Roosevelt Island the day before.

Andre had come home from his job as a stripper at an all male club carrying two huge duffel bags. He had worked the day shift.

"I made a quick stop at David Good's apartment," he said.

David Good was a fifty-year-old plastic surgeon who had given Andre a free nose job, a computer, and a ficus tree for his bedroom. He was taking Andre to the Four Seasons for dinner that night.

Andre unzipped both duffel bags and started to unpack them. He pulled out forty or fifty CD's, a stereo system, track lighting, a VCR, a Cartier watch and cuff links, a video camera, silver frames, a bottle of Chivas Regal, a tuxedo, and a lot of shirts, ties, and sweaters.

"I decided to steal a few things," he said. "I got these for you."

He handed me four Bob Dylan CD's. "Thank you," I said.

We had been growing apart. He started to hook the stereo up on a shelf in our living room near the Christmas tree we had bought together to try to pretend we were still great friends. He wanted white Christmas tree lights, I wanted blinking colors. We had a huge fight.

Andre's phone rang and he turned up the volume on the answering machine. It was David Good. "Andre, are you there? I've been robbed, can you believe it? My neighbor called the police. They took everything."

Andre and I stood in the living room.

"I'm still at the office. I need you to be with me when I go home to my empty apartment. I'm frightened. What if I'd been at home? The police are there getting fingerprints. I was thinking I could sleep at your place tonight. You've never even had me over. Well, you probably already left for the restaurant. Love you. See you tonight." He hung up.

"How pathetic," Andre said. "I didn't take everything, just what I could carry."

"Why did you do this?"

Andre squinted at me. "I can't believe you're laying all this on me when I'm under so much pressure," he said. "You've changed."

You haven't, I thought. Except now he was old enough to be tried as an adult.

"Maybe you should move out and join a convent, if you can find any nuns who live up to your moral standards. Why don't you just move out."

Andre stormed off to the Four Seasons and I decided to move out before he came home. I felt relieved that our friendship was over. It was time to leave. It was not hard to say goodbye to Roosevelt Island, home of Buddy Hackett. I knew if I left there good things would start to happen.

3

I PACKED MY clothes, my new Bob Dylan CD's, and the few other things I had at Andre's into the two duffel bags and left. I went to the Cauldron of Clams, the bar on West Fourth Street where my father spent every minute of his spare time. My father wasn't there, he was upstate at his country house. The bartender said I could keep my bags in the storage room for a few days.

"Who's D.G.?" he asked. Andre had used David Good's own duffel bags to rob him.

It was already two in the morning and I didn't feel like calling my mother, having her come to the door in a ghostly nightgown with her dog barking, and having to explain about Andre. We still hadn't made up from our last fight.

I walked along Houston Street. I was indulging in homeless thoughts when someone gently touched my back. Even through my long black coat, I have an extremely sensitive back. It is my favorite place to be kissed.

I turned around and was surprised to see Vivian. I had known her when I worked at Millie's Tavern on Bleecker Street, before it closed. She was one of the drunks.

She looked worse, scars on her face, dirty black hair, bright red cheeks. In a bar environment Vivian looked kind of cute. She always did something to fix herself up, like tie a scarf around her neck or put on a pink plastic necklace. She was extremely drunk, which also suited her better in a bar.

I was suddenly happy to be standing on the street under the car wash sign talking to Vivian. The sign had a picture of a round silver whale smiling and said "A Whale of a Wash!" with blinking lights racing around it. "A Whale of a Wash! New Gentle Touch!" Vivian was mesmerized. "I like that fish," she said. "It sounds so nice, a whale of a wash."

Vivian was from Israel but had an English accent. She had been thrown out of an eight-story window by her first husband and set on fire by her second husband. She had been an abused child, she was beat-up.

"I'm tired," I told her.

"So am I," she said. "I can't take another step." She started to cry.

"Where are you staying?" I asked her. "My roommate kicked me out."

"I'm still at the Jane West Hotel." Vivian looked me over. "I suppose you don't want to join me."

"Why not," I said. It sounded fun to spend the night with my old friends from Millie's, sitting up all night talking and laughing. I had never been invited before.

I was aware of an empty brown beer bottle rolling after us like a noisy rat. It followed us to Jane Street and the West Side Highway. Vivian kicked it and we went up the stairs and into the red brick hotel with the strange-shaped tower on top.

4

"KEEP YOUR HEAD down," Vivian whispered. A Japanese girl about my age was asleep behind the front desk. "Don't let her see you."

Vivian pushed a heavy door open and we walked down two flights of cement stairs to a row of lockers. She fumbled with a combination lock for a while. Two pillows fell out of the locker and she handed me one. It was quite nice actually, it said Bloomingdale's and it was fluffy. Then I followed her down a filthy tiled corridor, black with dirt and scattered with a few giant water bugs dead on their backs, and down the metal ladder into the deep end of an empty swimming pool, where we set up our pillows.

As I followed Vivian down the metal ladder into the drained swimming pool I tried not to look shocked. I had the feeling that things couldn't get much worse. It's just one night, I thought. My throat burned and I held my wrist over my nose and mouth, trying to breathe my Norma Kamali perfume.

"Have you ever been down the rabbit hole?" Vivian asked me. "Have you ever been down the laundry chute?"

"It's not so bad," I said.

"Well, think of it this way, there's no place to go but up."

A man I thought I recognized from Millie's was watching a TV attached to a mile of extension cord in the shallow end. When I worked at Millie's Tavern and the regulars said they were sleeping in the pool at the Jane West Hotel, I thought they were using a secret code. I had no idea what they were talking about. "I'll see you in the pool," they used to say but I didn't think they were serious. I didn't think there were rug fragments and pillows, a TV and two easy chairs, a small Christmas tree, a bookcase, and people asleep at the bottom of the pool.

It was very dark but I could hear Vivian next to me, sort of sighing and crying a little, and then taking even, stuffed-up breaths. It was freezing and damp. Dark figures waded in throughout the night.

The smell of mildew and cherry-scented urinals was knocking me out, and I thought, I can just leave this place, I can get up and find another place to sleep, but the idea of standing up made me sleepy. I pictured myself standing up and walking up Jane Street, and my eyes closed. I saw myself calling my mother from a pay phone, apologizing, hailing a cab, and I was overcome with exhaustion. I imagined I was floating on a coral reef and the concrete under me became porous like a sponge.

Before it closed, Millie's had been the oldest bar on Bleecker Street. It had live music. The owner was a man named Sal. He wouldn't let Bob Dylan play there, but he let him sleep on the pool table a few nights. "He's a nice guy but he can't sing," Sal would say. "No talent." I heard a story that one night Bill Cosby pulled up in a limousine and had the chauffeur bring Sal outside, and then Bill Cosby rolled down the window and spit in Sal's face.

Sal stole my tips right off the tables, grabbed dollar bills out of my hand. He was an old man with plaid pants and Coke-bottle glasses tied to his head with a bent piece of wire hanger. One time he bit my finger until it bled. He bit his sister's earlobe off. Everybody hated him.

"How's Sal?" I asked Vivian.

"Dead and buried. We all took a bus to the cemetery and took turns pissing on his grave. Now let me sleep."

People were whispering at the other end of the pool, laughing softly. I thought of Bob Dylan sleeping on the pool table. Lying on the pool table, staring at the old tin ceiling, singing to himself. I lay there thinking about Bob Dylan and trying to remember a worse night than this one.

I am twelve years old, lying in bed at four in the morning. I have a big test tomorrow. I hear the door opening. Dad is home. He is whispering so he is with someone. She is laughing loudly. They are both drunk. The woman is giggling. I hear a spanking sound. Spank, spank, and breathing. The woman is saying, "Oh you're so good, oh you're so good." My body is rigid with fear and rage. My stomach swells with tension. I cough loudly. I throw a book against the wall. I turn on the radio. I say, "I have a test." I sound young, spoiled, ridiculous.

The woman keeps saying, "Oh you're so good." Then there is silence. I cannot breathe. I don't know what to do, I feel my future is in jeopardy. The woman opens my door. She has to walk through my room to get to the bathroom because we live in a railroad apartment. She turns on all the lights. She is very ordinary and young, with blond hair and a parrot on her shoulder. She is naked except for the parrot. I fall asleep at the bottom of the pool, thinking about the parrot-lady.

5

WHEN I WOKE up I felt stiff and bruised. My face was scraped from the concrete. My pillow was gone, Vivian had it. I never thought I'd be able to fall asleep in a place like this. I must have been very tired.

I had almost forgotten about the smell, when one woman started washing a small area of the tiled pool wall with Mr. Clean. "You're a good little poolwife," a man told her.

I was surprised to see that during the night quite a crowd of people had gathered in the swimming pool. I recognized a lot of them from Millie's.

A woman named Frances, also known as Rancid Francid, walked over to me and said, "I thought you disappeared off the face of the earth." When I quit Millie's I left suddenly and never really said goodbye to anyone. I felt bad that I had lied about my age, telling everyone that I was six years older than I really was and in law school. The woman was holding a biography of Sir Francis Drake. "I enjoy to read," she said argumentatively. "I very much enjoy to read."

She was unbelievably skinny. She climbed tentatively up the ladder. The ladder of her ribs showed through her shirt, as if her body were inside out with the label showing. She was completely white, absolutely colorless, except for yellow hair and lavender eyes.

I went after her, thinking she could show me where the

bathroom was. She led me into a large concrete cell with a tiny toilet in the corner.

"This is the bums' room," she said. "Allow me to give you the grand tour. That's the toilet."

The toilet was on a platform and I stepped up, pulled down my jeans, and turned around carefully before sitting down. Without thinking, I started to unroll some toilet paper, when she said, "Other people have to use that too." I wound the toilet paper back, ripped off a couple of squares and put the roll back on the dirt-black floor. I usually use about half a roll.

"Is there a sink?" I asked.

"It's next door in the boiler room. There's bugs."

"I'll wait," I said.

She was leaning towards me and her breath was foul. She reached into an old patchwork leather pocketbook and pulled out an Almond Joy candy bar and unwrapped it.

"Do you want this?" she asked seductively. I hadn't had a bite of chocolate in a long time.

"Yes, thank you." She unwrapped the whole thing and handed it to me. I hoped it wouldn't be the start of my buying some on every corner.

"That candy bar cost eighty cents," she said.

Trying to be nonchalant, I reached into the bottom of my bookbag which was still strapped to me and pulled out my wallet. You only draw attention to what you want to draw attention to. One time I was in a crowded restaurant with my friend Thisbe, and she was hot and wearing too many layers. She actually took off her sweater, took off her shirt, took off her bra, took a sip from her drink and put the sweater back on and nobody noticed a thing because she was so nonchalant.

"Don't worry, no one will steal your money," Frances said. I handed her a dollar bill and she gave me two dimes.

It started to get hard to breathe in the concrete bums'

room. My ankle turned unexpectedly. I was relieved when the door opened easily.

People were beginning to wake up and start talking in small groups. Vivian woke up slowly and sensuously, like this was the Plaza. She zipped and snapped her jeans which had been open all night in a V on her small round stomach.

I said goodbye to Frances and went over to Vivian. She looked harder in the morning, as if she were made of grout. She had interesting eyebrows. Eyebrows can make a person beautiful. "Let's get something to eat," she whispered. We started down the corridor.

"Aren't you going to use the bathroom?" I asked her.

"Here, are you crazy? No way."

We walked up the stairs, I was almost running, and into the blinding light of the poor little lobby. I hadn't realized how dark it was down in the pool.

"Hi Vivian," the Japanese girl behind the desk said. She had a heavy New York accent. "You owe for two weeks." She held a cat up to her cheek. I wasn't allowed to have a pet as a child so I don't even really notice animals. "Are you new?" the girl behind the desk asked me.

"God you're nosy," Vivian said, and she whisked me out of the lobby and into the street.

I will never forget how good the chlorine-flavored water in the quilted diner glass tasted the moment we sat down for breakfast. I felt very self-conscious and vulnerable and kept thanking the waiter for bringing the food and diet Pepsi. I was acting like my rich cousin, Pepper, thanking everybody and apologizing every minute. I sat on the red vinyl bench with my legs pressed together under the table and my hands on my knees.

Vivian hardly said anything at the diner. I paid the check and left a tip, which Vivian put in her pocket the minute I turned my back.

"Where are you going?" I asked her.

"McGovern's Tavern in Tribeca. It opens at eleven. I have a friend, Lars." Her breasts felt like baseballs when we hugged.

"Thanks for letting me crash," I said. I had never used the word crash.

"I want to ask you a favor," she said. People were always asking me favors at Millie's. I was everybody's favor-ite. Vivian started to cry.

"Vivian, what is it?"

"I need to buy a pregnancy test kit," she said. At Millie's I was constantly buying people pregnancy kits.

I handed Vivian a twenty-dollar bill and was shocked by how much the President on it looked like my father. If you want to know what my father looks like, look at a twenty-dollar bill. I looked around Sheridan Square while Vivian buried it in her pocketbook. There's something very soothing about Sheridan Square. The newsstand on the little island and people always talking on the pay phones.

"Will I see you later?" Vivian asked me.

Probably not, I thought. "Probably," I told her. I had to decide what to do.

Christmas vacation had started two days before, but I remembered that a girl in my class at NYU hadn't left to go home to Florida yet and might still be in her dorm room.

Vivian headed towards McKay's drugstore and I kept going along the south side of Washington Square Park to Judson dorm.

6

I BARELY CAUGHT my friend Jennifer before she got into a cab to go to the airport. Her father had come all the way from Florida to help her carry her bags. She saw me coming down the street and started to wave. People always see me before I see them because I have very bad vision.

Jennifer introduced me to her father. I could tell he liked me. I remembered she told me that he hadn't slept with her mother in three years. He had a full head of soft gray hair.

"We had dinner at the Russian Tea Room last night," Jennifer said. I wondered if she'd gone off Nutri/System for the occasion. "It was phenomenal. I saw Tony Randall."

"Jennifer, I have to talk to you about something important," I said.

"Can you call me in Miami? The cabdriver wants to get going."

Jennifer's father got into the back of the cab. He was probably going to try to figure out how much NYU was costing him on a per hour basis.

"Jennifer, I have to ask you something. I had to move out of my roommate's apartment very quickly and I need somewhere to stay for a few days until I find another place."

"Well, I should ask Jennifer Gull first but I think she already left. I haven't seen her in two days." Jennifer Gull was her roommate. At NYU everyone is named Jennifer. "Well, okay." She handed me a single key. "I'll tell the security guard." She walked into the tiny lobby of Judson and leaned against the soda machine. I smiled realizing I had a great place to stay until I could figure out what to do next, and there was a soda machine.

Jennifer's father was holding a huge FAO Schwarz shopping bag on his lap in the back seat of the cab. On my eighth birthday my father took me and six friends to Rumpelmayers for sundaes. Then he took us to FAO Schwarz and let us all pick out something we wanted.

Jennifer came bounding out onto the street and said, "It's all set, I'll call you," and they were gone.

I walked into the lobby and noticed an out-of-order sign on the soda machine, so I turned around and went to the Korean market on Third Street. I bought a *Village Voice* and a six-pack of diet Pepsi to keep in Jennifer's mini-fridge. I decided to pass by the Cauldron of Clams to see if my father was back. His picture is on the Cauldron's "Wall of Fame" with the other regulars', including his wife, Siobhan's. Siobhan (pronounced *Shove-on*) had lived with most of the men featured on the wall.

As I passed by the window of the Cauldron I caught a glimpse of her looming in front of the door to the men's room, holding a dart. She was wearing her big round tortoiseshell glasses that cover her entire face, and she towered over a small man with a mustache, one of her ex-boyfriends, who was known as the Tic Tac man because he was always offering you a Tic Tac. You could hear them rattling in his pocket when he walked. A short time after Siobhan married my father she had an affair with the Tic Tac man and my father punched him and broke his nose.

At first I only saw the infuriating half-smirk on her face, and then I noticed something else. She was huge. Her stomach rolled out in front of her and she was the width of four barstools.

She was pregnant. It was my worst fear, but I knew it would happen.

I stood at the window of the Cauldron a moment too long and Siobhan saw me. She called to my father, who was tensed up in the back playing pinball. I turned and rushed back to Jennifer's dorm room and was amazed when the key worked and I was sitting on her bed in the tiny room. It was unbelievably small, the size of a closet.

I called my brother, Dylan, at my father's apartment.

"Where are you?" he asked. "I miss you. It's Christmas Eve." My brother was going through a very sentimental stage where he was constantly telling me he loved me and missed me. I tried to ignore it.

"Why didn't you tell me?" I shouted. "How could you not tell me? What am I supposed to do about this?"

"I don't know what you're talking about, Benny," he said. He sounded older, until his voice caught on my name and I could tell I was scaring him.

"Why didn't you tell me Siobhan is pregnant?"

There was silence on the other end. I noticed Jennifer's mirror had some pictures taped to it, including one of her with her arm around me. For a moment I wondered if she was secretly obsessed with me and planning to kill me so she could assume my identity. I made a mental note to search her entire room.

I was furious that my brother wasn't answering me. "I saw her. I know she's pregnant."

"She's not pregnant, Benny," my brother said. "She's just fat. Where are you?"

I could hardly talk. I was thrilled. I never saw anyone get that fat. "Don't worry, I'm staying with a friend for a few days," I said. "Dylan, tell me, how could she get that fat?"

"Too many Chicken McNuggets," he said.

After I hung up the phone I lay on my stomach and cried.

I miss my daddy, I miss my daddy, I whispered. I hadn't spoken to him in two years.

When my parents got divorced, the year I was twelve, my best friend, Thisbe, gave me a talking-to in the waiting room of her orthodontist. She had to go to the orthodontist every Friday after school for an adjustment.

We lived in the same building and I looked up to her because she was two years older than I was, beautiful, and had a queen-size bed canopied with exotic mosquito netting like Scheherazade's. She went to the High School of Performing Arts.

"My divorce was not all bad, you know," Thisbe said. She told me about all the things her parents had gotten for her. It was an endless list. "Of course I'm adopted, so they feel doubly guilty," she said.

That night I called my father and said it would be a lot more convenient, I'd feel a lot closer to him, if I had my own phone. My own phone in my room so I could have privacy when he called. The next week a red Trim-Line with my own phone number and a light-up dial pad was installed.

My father told me that he had found an apartment on Eighth Street in the Village and that he wanted Dylan and me to spend the weekend with him. It was Christmas weekend. "It's not much, but it will be fun for us to all SHACK-up here together."

I told him that I needed a drum set because I was thinking of becoming a professional drummer, I needed a Walkman, I needed purple feather earrings, cable television, and my own credit card.

I did not want to spend the weekend in this village. I pictured my father in a tiny shack on the side of a dirt road with chickens clucking and a donkey tied to a post. I didn't know how my father could possibly move to a place called

Washington Square, whose very name suggested a prairie of isolation.

My friends and I had never been to Greenwich Village. Our worlds consisted of the Upper West and East Sides and were connected by the Eighty-sixth Street crosstown bus. Sometimes we ventured downtown to Bloomingdale's or to Times Square to see a Broadway show if someone had a theater party. We lived in townhouses or classic sixes, sevens, and eights. Our apartment had twenty-nine windows. I had my own ballet barre. I awoke each morning to the sound of the doorman's whistle hailing cabs sixteen flights below.

Nobody I knew lived in Greenwich Village. One boy in my fifth-grade class, a chess champion, had lived in a place with the name of a clown, SoHo. SoHo the clown. He jumped off the roof of his building.

My father came to collect us and took us downtown on the No. 1 train. We got out at Sheridan Square, my eight-year-old brother and I absently clutching hands. We went to John's Pizza, my father practically skipping down the street he was pretending so hard to have fun. He ordered me a pitcher of Tab and I began to warm up to this strange village.

After lunch he took us to Washington Square Park and showed Dylan the snow-covered cement hills where he could skateboard in the summer. He took us to the Postermat on Eighth Street where I stood before an entire glass case of feather earrings in every color. He took us to his new apartment, and there, in the middle of the creaky slanted floor, was a pearly Slingerland drum set with Zildjian cymbals.

Soon after that, I moved in with my father, into the tiny apartment on Eighth Street.

My father met Siobhan in the Cauldron when I was sixteen. She was only four years older than I was. I liked her. She was not as smart as I was or as pretty, so, although she was six feet two and thin, she didn't pose a threat. She bought me presents, I borrowed her deodorant and perfume, we went out to dinner together three nights a week when my father had to teach a late class. I was nice to her and I prided myself on not being like those girls on daytime talk shows who hate their fathers' girlfriends. I encouraged her to wear makeup and to have the mole on her cheek removed. I tried to overlook her tattoo, her bad perm, and her incredibly tacky ankle bracelet. One night she got out of my father's bed and wandered through my room to get to the bathroom. She sat down on my bed and said she loved me like a sister. I was so embarrassed for her. She had the worst father-figure complex I could ever imagine.

I liked her until she started to cook and decided there would be a dinner time. She was the worst cook on earth, deeply insecure, always putting raisins in everything at the last minute and then scraping big pots of burnt raisins into the toilet and crying.

"Will you be home at six o'clock for dinner, Bennington?" she would whine, looking up from the marijuana plant she was tending to. She and my father liked to grow marijuana and name each plant, the way some couples get a pet in preparation for having children. This plant was named Potsy. "Dinner will be ready at six o'clock sharp."

I knew at six o'clock sharp she'd be crying and scraping. "I'm not sure, Siobhan, I'm going out with Andre after school." When she cooked, a horrible change came over her, she became a tyrant, spending hours arranging boxes of Jell-O on a shelf.

"I need an answer, will you be home or won't you? I'm making raisin stew. Will you be home or won't you? Will you be home or won't you?"

I would say I would, and then I wouldn't. I'd spend the night at Thisbe's or Andre Singh's or go to *The Rocky Horror Picture Show* and stay out until morning. I would sleep in Washington Square Park with Snake and Kevin, who had lost his thumbs in Nam, and the other bums. Everyone had a nickname and mine was Jailbait.

I would fall asleep on a concrete ledge and wake up to find one of them sitting up and watching me protectively. It was exhilarating to sleep outside, like camping.

My father would leave for work around eight o'clock and Siobhan would go with him because she liked to hang around his office and sit in on his classes. I would hide behind a car and watch them go down into the subway, my father's coffee spilling on his newspaper. He always looked at peace with his hangover, manila folders and books under one arm, pleased with himself.

I would wait until I was sure they were definitely on the train and then I would go back to the park and invite everyone upstairs to shower and eat cereal. Sometimes I would scramble eggs and lend them some of my father's clothes. They sat around the table in towels and bathrobes telling me what kind of cereal I should get my father to buy next. Siobhan always bought raisin bran.

Eventually Siobhan became more secure in the relationship and let my father go to school by himself. She stayed home every morning and my secret breakfast ritual came to an end.

After about a year my father sat me down on a barstool at the Cauldron and said, "Siobhan wants us to get married." At first I didn't know who the "us" was.

"Who's us?" I asked.

He looked at me the way he did when I was a kid, as if he were trying to figure out if I had a learning disability.

"Siobhan asked me to marry her, so I said I would."

Siobhan was sitting at the other end of the bar, looking at us but pretending not to. It occurred to me that this would be a good time to get some money.

"Dad, can I have some money to get some things for school?"

"How much do you need?"

"At least a hundred bucks," I said.

My father looked in his wallet and handed me four twenty-dollar bills. "That's all I have on me. I'll get you the rest later."

My father looked nervously over at Siobhan.

"Now that we're going to be married, we think the apartment is a little small," he said. "We think you'll be a lot happier living with your mother and brother and TED." My mother was living with a man named Tad (short for Taddeus), who my father insisted on calling Ted. I couldn't even really bear to look at Tad, he was a foreigner of some sort with a beard. He wore flip-flops with white sweat socks and he drove a cab.

"I don't want to live with them, I want to live with you and Siobhan," I told him.

"I'm sorry, Benny, it's my turn for happiness now. I need ROOM to start a new life."

I was smiling from ear to ear in an effort to keep from crying. I would have done anything to keep from crying. I smiled like the first runner-up in the Miss America pageant, lips twisted and tortured. I looked over at my brother who had been spending the weekend with us. He was such a trouper packing and unpacking his teddy bear and underwear and toothbrush every week. Now he was innocently playing pinball and talking to a man with no legs.

"Congratulations, Daddy," I whispered. My father gave me a hug and I burst into tears, still smiling. Then he bent over and started banging his head on the bar. "Oh my, oh my," he said. Dylan ran over and the two of us stood there crying while my father banged his head on the bar and Siobhan concentrated on a bowl of peanuts.

When I got home from school the next day my things were packed in boxes—my books, all my clothes, my phone, my debate trophies, and all the things I'd gotten from the divorce. I had never realized before how little stock I had in the world.

How all my things could fit into a dozen Chiquita Banana boxes from the supermarket.

I walked in the door and saw the little pile near the drum set, with Siobhan's compulsive square lettering on the sides of the boxes: BOOKS, CLOTHES, MISCELLANEOUS.

I moved in with Andre Singh on Roosevelt Island. I stood at his front door with my boxes and a copy of *Backstage*. His door was painted red, and the words "Fuck You" that had been carved by a Chinese food delivery boy were still there. Next to the door was a shopping cart filled to the top with dirty dishes, glasses, and pots. He would wheel it over to his mother's apartment so she could wash them. He opened the door and grinned at me and I knew we would live together forever.

Siobhan and my father got married in Ireland on my seventeenth birthday. They dragged my brother there, and in every picture you can see him in an awful plaid sweater, bent over and crying, holding wads of tissues. My father is wearing a kilt and a beret with a pompom, but Dylan refused. He sent me a postcard with a picture of a sheep on it. "They wanted me to wear a skirt!!!" he wrote.

I called my father once when I got my NYU acceptance letter, to see if he would pay my tuition. My father said, "Hello?" and I could hear Siobhan in the background saying, "Who's that? Who's that?" I hung up, determined to pay for it myself.

7

I WOKE UP the next day in Jennifer's dorm room and remembered it was Christmas and I was not a child. I lay in bed for most of the day reading the NYU Spring catalogue. The course descriptions are very humorous pieces of fiction. I drank a chocolate Slim·Fast shake that was sitting on the windowsill.

Everyone had gone home for Christmas, so I was the only one in the NYU dorm. I wanted to find an apartment by my birthday, January 23. Registration started on January 24 and Jennifer would need her room back. I didn't want to live in a dorm and have a hundred girls named Jennifer bursting into my room all the time. It was cheaper and nicer to get an apartment share. I looked at apartment listings in the *Village Voice* and called about a share on Christopher and West Street, right near the Jane West Hotel.

The person who answered the phone turned out to be Joel Shoenfeld, a photographer whose name I recognized from headshot ads in *Backstage*. His ad had a picture of a woman with a big dead fish covering half her face.

When I went to see the apartment that evening I was greeted by two young girls who were vacuuming a bearskin rug. The apartment had a masculine safari theme. There was a real stuffed giraffe and an enormous fish tank with large translucent fish. I can't even eat in a restaurant with a fish tank.

Joel Shoenfeld asked me a lot of questions about myself. I told him I was an actress. Student sounded too flaky and I was really trying to make a good impression. Even with the fish the apartment seemed like a pretty good deal. He showed me his photography darkroom, and said he would make it into a bedroom when he found the right roommate. He said I could live there rent free if I had sex with him every night.

He closed the door to the darkroom and we stood facing each other in the red light. I looked around the room for a sharp object while he explained the arrangements. He would be in the bedroom next door and I would have to make myself available to have sex with him during certain hours. I would also have to clean the apartment. It made living with Andre Singh seem normal.

I told Joel that my friend Andre was waiting for me down-stairs with a few guys and they would wonder what was taking me so long. He grabbed my arm and pressed me against the door. I reached for a tray of clear liquid chemicals and flung it in his face. He let go of my arm. I opened my mouth wide to scream, but just the word "Don't" came out in a tiny whisper. I opened the door and ran through the apartment and down the stairs to the street.

I had been so convincing in my lie about Andre that I half expected to see him standing there in his big white sneakers with his hands in his pockets, but of course he wasn't. He was probably consoling David Good and helping him fill out the theft insurance forms. Outside on the street there were a lot of transvestite hookers. One was wearing a Santa hat. It was a very sad Christmas.

I went to the Cauldron of Clams and looked in the window but my father wasn't there. I got David Good's duffel bags and dragged them to Jennifer's dorm.

When I walked in the door the phone was ringing. "Ben-nington?" It was Joel Shoenfeld, laughing. I had given him Jennifer's number before he attacked me.

"You have the wrong number," I said.

"Bennington, that was water you threw in my face. It was tap water. Why don't you come back and we'll talk about our misunderstanding? I've had a very bad day."

I hung up and lay down on Jennifer's bed. I was hungry. Almost getting raped can make a person starved. I would have to find a diner open on Christmas, or I could go to Abigail's party on Park Avenue. I unpacked my red cocktail dress and fluffed it up. I had worn the same dress to Abigail's Christmas party last year.

The phone rang again but I just lifted the receiver slightly and then hung it up.

He kept calling and I kept hanging up. I looked at the movies in the *Village Voice* and then noticed the adult entertainment section. That was when I called the COED$ ad. I put on my red cocktail dress and took a cab to the Chelsea Hotel.

8

I GOT OFF the rickety wooden elevator, stepping over a pool of what looked like saliva. The elevator door closed behind me and I stopped for a second, trying to pick which way to go. I always feel extremely self-conscious wandering the wrong way down a corridor. I finally found the right door, it had been left open, and walked into a small room with gray carpeting and black Formica furniture. There was a round couch and a black dining room table. There was a desk with eight phones.

"You must be Bennington," a woman said, coming in from another room. She looked exactly the way I had pictured her. She was fat with a beautiful face and a big blond wig. "Sit down," she said. "Can I get you something to drink?"

"Yes please," I said. She reminded me of a woman I knew when I was six years old, named Daphne. She lived on the block where I grew up, Central Park West between Eighty-sixth and Eighty-seventh and I was allowed to go to her apartment to play with her two big white poodles, Candy and Sugar. Daphne gave me ginger ale "on the rocks." She had crazy white shag carpet, tall stools I could spin around on, and a spiral staircase I was told not to climb. Later I found out it was a brothel.

"Here you go," the blond woman said. I took a sip of the diet soda, and she introduced herself. "My name is Holly."

"Hi."

"So, you're interested in working."

"Well, I need some information. I've never called a place before."

"Well, the only information you really need is that we charge three hundred dollars an hour and you keep half, one hundred and fifty plus tip. For overnights you keep fifteen hundred dollars plus tip. You'll make a lot of money with me. My men will love you. Are you a student?"

"Yes, I'm at NYU for acting," I said.

"Oh I have a lot of actresses who work for me. Believe it or not, I went to Bennington." Her voice trailed off as she went into another room. "I'll be right back. Make yourself comfortable."

I was sitting on the couch. I already was comfortable. Make myself comfortable. Comfortable. I suddenly realized what she meant. I slowly unzipped my dress and the elastic straps fell off my arms. I just sat there with my bare breasts exposed like couch pillows. Holly came back in.

"Jesus Christ, cover yourself. What do you think this is, *The Mayflower Madam* miniseries? Put your clothes back on." She was more embarrassed than I was.

"I wanted to show you this. This was me." She held out a framed picture while I zipped myself back into my dress. In the picture she had a big blond beehive. She looked sixteen. "I was a beauty," she said. "I worked myself through. B.J., come out here. I want you to meet Bennington. She's a beauty. This is my husband, B.J."

"Hi, kiddo." A fat man walked into the room holding an enormous wooden bowl. "Caesar salad." He started to toss wildly.

"Bennington's our new girl," Holly said.

"Great!" B.J. said. "Would you like to stay for Christmas dinner? We'd love to have you."

"Thank you," I said.

"Unless you'd rather start tonight," Holly said.

"It's Christmas, Hol. Come on, dinner's ready." B.J. pulled out a chair for me and I sat down in my cocktail dress.

I took a few bites of my salad. "This is delicious," I said.

"Thank you. The olive oil was seventy-five dollars and the anchovy paste is from Balducci's. I have to special order it," B.J. said.

At the sound of the word "anchovy," my stomach began to churn. I couldn't eat it. I tried to swallow a crouton. "It's delicious." I wished I was at my mother's house.

"So, when do you want to start?" Holly asked.

"Next week, after New Year's," I said.

"I'll call you on the second. What's your working name going to be? The name you use. How about Vassar?" She laughed.

"I was thinking of Daphne," I said quickly.

"How about Sarah Lawrence?" B.J. suggested.

After dinner we sat on the round couch and ate chocolate cake and drank champagne while they showed me pictures of their two daughters, who were away in boarding school. When the phone rang Holly answered. "You sure you don't want to do one?" she asked.

"No, I've got to get going," I said.

"All you have to do is play strip poker with this guy. If you win you leave, if you lose you have to tickle his balls with your fingernails for about half an hour. That's all he wants."

"I can't start tonight," I said.

"But you do want to work?" Holly got serious.

"Yes," I said.

She called some girl and gave her the information about tickling the guy's balls. I thanked them for dinner and Holly said she would call me. "Goodbye Bennington," she said. She hugged me and gave me a small stack of business cards with a phone number and the words "A Gentle Touch" in spidery scripted letters.

B.J. insisted on taking me downstairs and putting me in a cab. He gave me a ten-dollar bill. "Bye, kiddo," he said.

Christmas was almost over. The streets were empty. My head ached a little from the champagne. I pictured myself at Abigail's party, talking to her father, talking to her older brother in the kitchen, giving the bartender a warm sympathetic smile, telling Abigail how thrilled I was for her that she got that bit part in the new Woody Allen movie. I got out of the cab and went up to the dorm room. I turned on Jennifer's television.

The news came on so my mind instantly wandered over the events of my day. It was as if the anchorwoman were saying, *Bennington Bloom's top story tonight . . .* and a picture of Joel Shoenfeld flashed on the screen. After the commercials, which I sang along with and watched with great interest, Joel Shoenfeld was on the news again.

"The photographer was shot in the head six times in his own apartment," the reporter said. Then she went on and on about how he had conned many young women by telling them they could be models and offering to take their pictures for free if they would pose in the nude. Then he would videotape them and they would unknowingly appear in porno movies. They showed his living room with the giraffe. "It was probably an angry boyfriend or father," a policeman said. "Any girl who met him was lucky to get away unharmed."

He really did have a bad day, I thought. The phone rang and I answered it. I knew it wouldn't be him. It was B.J. just making sure I'd gotten home safely.

9

HOLLY CALLED EARLY the next morning. I was sound asleep. "I have a date for you," she said.

"A date?" I said. "Oh, you mean for money."

"Of course I mean for money, Bennington. Are you all right? Did I wake you?"

"It's okay. I wasn't going to start until after New Year's," I reminded her.

"I know, Bennington, but I really need you to do me this favor. He's one of my oldest clients. He lives in New Jersey but he has an apartment on Waverly Place just to see my girls." She gave me his name and address. "He'll give you three hundred dollars for the hour and you come here after the session and bring me half. Anything over one-fifty, you keep. Usually, he tips fifty. He knows it's your first time. I try out all my girls on him. I told him your name is Bennington, so just use that for now. He really liked it. Be there at two o'clock and don't forget to bring an umbrella."

"An umbrella?" I asked.

"Yes. An umbrella. You know. A wet suit."

I was silent.

"Protection. Jesus Christ. Rubbers! I don't like to say that on the phone. Bring rubbers!"

"Okay, Holly."

"Call me when you get there at two."

"Should I wear my red dress?"

"It's not Christmas at midnight. It's two in the afternoon. Wear jeans. Call me when you get there."

She hung up. My heart was pounding. One hundred and fifty dollars. I left the little dorm room and walked across the hall to the bathroom, which was disgusting. I sat on the toilet and looked at a sign on the wall that said BEWARE OF RATS. I sat there for a while after I was done, thinking about the sign, thinking about stepping into the NYU shower. I used the last of the NYU toilet paper and was shocked to see that I had my period.

I am always surprised when I get it because I don't keep track. I just know it will come at the worst possible time, and this was it. There was no way I was going to be able to start my new career. It was a sign.

I called Holly. "Hi, this is Bennington. You're not going to believe this, but I can't go. I just got my period."

"You just got it? It just came on in a flash?"

"Holly, I have my period. I can't help it." I laughed.

"Oh really?"

I remembered a gym teacher saying that if Martina Navratilova and Chris Evert could play tennis with their periods, then I could play dodge ball with mine.

"Holly, I'm sorry," I said.

"You have to go. I expect a hundred and fifty dollars this afternoon. Go anyway." She hung up.

I lay back on Jennifer's bed. I needed to start making money for an apartment, first month's rent plus security. But of course I can't do this, I thought. But of course I won't do it. If I get one hundred and fifty dollars, I'll go to La Fondue and have cheese fondue and chocolate fondue. I'll buy some lace socks.

I walked back across the hall to the bathroom and got into the shower. The shower curtain was stuffed in the wastebasket. I don't have to go, I told myself. I laughed, thinking about the conversation I would have with Andre. I would call him up and say, *Oh, nothing much really, got hired by an escort service.*

I could pretend I had never gotten myself into this. I could just get some breakfast at a diner or someplace and think about it. I shaved my legs very carefully. I used a bar of soap with a label on it that said DO NOT USE. Someone opened the door to the bathroom and scared me half to death.

"Someone's in here," I said in a high voice, as if I were in the ladies' room at Lutece.

"Oh, sorry," a male voice said. He shut the door and called from the other side, "I thought I was the only one here."

I got out of the shower. I had brought one little towel in with me. I wrapped myself in it and opened the door. A college boy with a beard just stood there.

"Sorry, we were out of toilet tissue upstairs, so I thought I'd try down here," he said.

I had never heard anyone say toilet tissue.

"What's your name?" he asked.

"Bennington."

"Aren't you at the wrong school then?" He laughed. "My name is Camus. I was Jennifer Gull's boyfriend."

"I'm a friend of Jennifer Gull's roommate, Jennifer Lewis. I'm staying in their room," I said.

"I was her boyfriend," he said again.

"How very nice for you," I said, standing there in my towel.

"No, it wasn't. I just got back from it."

"From what?"

He was standing under another BEWARE OF RATS sign.

"Don't you know what happened to Jenny?"

"I really only know acting majors," I said. "Excuse me." I started to open the door to my room.

"She killed herself. She jumped off the library. I just came back from the funeral."

"I'm sorry, I didn't know," I said.

"She didn't have any friends. So you're in Tisch?" he asked. Tisch is the name of the NYU acting school, pronounced like toilet tish-ue.

"Yes," I said.

"Cool!" he said. "Jennifer Lewis gets all A's because if your roommate commits suicide you automatically get a 4.0."

"Cool!" I said. That was the sickest thing I had ever heard. I really hated talking to him. I felt like I should be getting paid by the minute.

"You know this means that Jennifer Lewis gets all A's next semester, but I'm the one who has to go through hell," he said.

"I'm sorry but I have to get dressed and go to work now."

"What do you do?" he asked.

"I'm a hooker," I said.

"Cool!" he said. I closed the door to my room and listened until he went away. I looked at myself in the mirror in my towel. Boys my own age make me too nervous for words.

I put on pink Capezio dance tights and cowboy boots and a Laura Ashley dress. I put my hair in a barrette. I put on red lipstick and wiped it off.

I left the dorm and went to a drugstore to buy condoms. It turned out to be the most expensive drugstore in New

York. An old lady asked me twice if I knew where the condensed milk was. I bought a conservative three-pack of Ramses, some Certs, and Tampax Super Plus. It was a strange combination to be knocking around in the completely transparent plastic shopping bag. I kept looking at Jennifer Gull's watch. I had borrowed it from her bedside table.

Then I walked up Waverly Place, which twisted and turned in a way I had never noticed, and got longer and longer. It was ten past two when I found the building, an old red brick townhouse with white painted shutters. A plaque near the door read BUILT 1853. I rang buzzer 5B.

"Yes?"

I paused for a moment. "It's Bennington."

10

THE BUZZER KEPT on even after I was in the door and on my way up the stairs to the fifth floor. I was very out of breath, but I tried to keep my cheeks sucked in and my lips pursed. A man stood at the top of the stairs.

"I'm Boyd," he said.

"Hi, I'm Bennington."

"You're beautiful, and so young!"

"Thank you."

"How old are you?"

"Eighteen," I said. I smiled, showing only my bottom teeth. I have a gap on top.

"Petite. Busty. Perfect. Come on in."

"Thank you," I said. He was sort of petite and busty himself, with very little hair.

"Holly says this is your first time. Don't be nervous. All the girls say I'm just like a big lovable teddy bear. Oh, are you a cowgirl?"

"What?"

"The boots."

"Oh."

"Sit down on the couch and make yourself comfortable. Now that doesn't mean take off all your clothes. Holly told me about that." He laughed like Ed McMahon. "Would you like some champagne?"

"No, thank you," I said. I sat on the soft couch. I was pleased that things were going so well. I had planned on being offered champagne and refusing it politely. I looked around the apartment that Boyd kept just for Holly's girls, expecting to see mirrors everywhere and piles of porno magazines. The living room was empty except for the couch, and Boyd had a fire going in the fireplace. The door to the bedroom was open and I could see a big bed with a white down comforter and a TV and stereo on some shelves. On one wall was a framed caricature of Boyd with a small body and an enormous head wearing a chef's hat and a red-and-white-checked apron. There were boxes of Baby Wipes everywhere.

"First thing you have to do is call Holly," Boyd said. "Just press redial."

"Thanks." I called her. "I'm here," I told her. She said she wanted to speak to Boyd.

Boyd got on the phone. "Beautiful. Okay, Hol." He hung up. "Holly tells me you're riding the cotton pony, Bennington."

I looked at him blankly.

"You have your period. It's okay, a woman's sex drive is always highest during menstruation."

"It is?"

"Just get undressed and come into the bedroom. Leave your panties on," he said.

He went into the bedroom. I took off my dress and my bra. My cowboy boots and my tights. I wasn't wearing panties. I stuffed the Tampax string inside me and walked into the bedroom. My palms were ice-cold even though the room was warm from the fire.

Boyd was lying on top of the bed. He had extremely short legs. "Come here, Bennington. I like to cuddle. Give Boyd a big hug."

I lay on the bed next to him and gave him an awkward hug. "Do you like to have your tits sucked?" he asked.

"Oh, yes!" I said. I couldn't believe myself. I was really beginning to get into this. I wished my acting teacher could see this. She'd told me I wasn't really capable of losing myself.

"I'm glad I'm your first," Boyd said. "You'll always remember your first."

I thought of the first time I had sex. I was thirteen. I was in Washington Square Park and I went up to an unlikely guitar player named John Magellen and just said, "Let's do it." I went on a long trip to his parents' house in Far Rockaway, and we lay on some sort of rattan daybed and he said, "I'm thirty, I could get arrested." We had sex and it hurt more than I had ever imagined. When it was finally over, he said, "Want some pizza?" and I said no and he rode away on a bicycle, leaving me alone on the porch. I remember looking at my reflection in the bus window on the way home and thinking I had given myself a present, womanhood.

I bled for a few days and when I stopped it turned out I had V.D. The gynecologist said, "You have a sexually transmitted disease."

"That's impossible, I didn't have sex," I said.

"Bennington, I think you have had sex," the doctor said.

"No, I haven't."

"Yes, you have."

"Doctor, I assure you, I have not had sex."

When I called John Magellen, his mother answered and said he didn't want to speak to me. "I just wanted him to know he gave me V.D.," I told her.

"Bennington, Bennington," Boyd moaned into my ear. Then he went back to sucking like a baby. "Bennington, suck my big hard dick."

I put his little penis in my mouth. He smelled like baby powder. I held it between my fingers like a cigarette and he came in my hand and then jumped up and got into the shower. I washed my hands in the kitchen sink and got dressed.

"Bennington, you were wonderful." He handed me $350. "That extra fifty's for you. Next time I want you to wear your hair in braids."

I left and walked toward Washington Square Park. I had made two hundred dollars in a half an hour. I called Holly from a pay phone. "I'm done."

"How was it?"

"Piece of cake." I thought of my oldest friend, Thisbe, who was the most beautiful girl I knew. She'd told me she wasn't going to be an actress because it made her feel too birthday-cakey.

"Boyd said you were very good," Holly said. "When you girls are so young I don't expect you to be good. I'm very pleased. Put the money in an envelope and leave it with the desk at the Chelsea. I'll call you when you're through with your period. Bye, Bennington." She hung up.

I folded the money carefully into a pink envelope that I found in Jennifer's room and dropped it off at the Chelsea Hotel. I went to La Fondue for dinner. Afterwards, I fell on the sidewalk and scraped my knees like a little girl. I called my mother from a pay phone without thinking. I dialed the number by mistake and she answered. I knew it was her before she said hello. She always picks up the phone and then pauses for a few seconds before saying anything, as if she's trying to find her ear.

"Hello?" she said. "Benny, is that you?" We had gotten into an argument a few weeks before, after Andre had gotten arrested for check forging. He only had to spend three nights in jail, but she wanted me to move out of his apartment immediately. I told her I never would. She wanted me to move in with her and Tad. Tad had a new career of collecting empty cans and bottles and bringing home junk from the street, like couch cushions with cigarette burns. "It's so fun," my mother had told me. "We can all do it together."

"Benny, I've been so worried about you," she said.

"I'm fine, Mom."

"I missed you so much. What did you do on Christmas? Dylan said he thought he saw you in your red cocktail dress."

"I went to Abigail's Christmas party, Mom," I said.

"You wore the same dress there last year."

"No one noticed," I said.

"I had a terrible dream." She started to cry. "I dreamt you went somewhere where there was AIDS and I said, Bennington, don't go, don't go to that awful place, but you wouldn't listen, you went anyway."

"I didn't go anywhere where there's AIDS, Mom," I said.

11

I BOUGHT A cellophane fortune fish for fifty cents in SoHo. The instructions said: *Place on palm of hand, head curl equal jealousy, tail curl equal love, if curl up all-the-way equal passion, flip over equal falseness.*

I placed the fish on my palm and it started to wriggle. The tail curled and the head curled, the fins met each other. It danced in my hand and turned over and over, it flipped onto the floor, it flopped around my feet and static electricity brought it halfway up my leg.

I grabbed it and crumpled it, but it uncurled itself and then flipped over and lay flat.

"I guess you're false," the lady in the store said.

My beeper went off. Holly had given me a beeper. It had been two weeks since my first session with Boyd, and I was working every day and night. At this rate I would have no problem paying NYU a cool nine thousand dollars for the spring semester. I called Holly from a pay phone.

"I have a job for you," she said. "You'll meet a girl named Georgy at a bar on East Twenty-fourth Street, and then you'll be joined by two men. One is a regular client, he'll probably want you, and the other is his friend, a businessman from Texas or someplace. They want to take you to a swing club called Le Tight Rope. You'll each get one thousand dollars and you'll bring me half. If they want you to get together with any other people in the club, they'll have to pay you a hundred dollars for each one you do, which you can keep."

I was exhausted and had trouble writing down the information with an inkless pen. The man at the adjoining phone was listening intently. He had obviously made that phone booth his personal office with papers and a coffee cup and a roll of quarters.

I somehow made it to the right bar. The girl named Georgy was sitting exactly where she was supposed to be, at a table in an alcove. I introduced myself. "Hi, I'm Bennington."

"I'm Georgy. When Holly gave me my name I was mad, but you must be furious."

"It's my real name."

"Oh, I'm sorry. I'm just nervous."

"I wanted to be Daphne or Isabelle or Annette," I told her. "I think Annette is an incredibly sexy name. I also like Sheila." I said it again, "Sheila."

"Well, they're all better than Georgy. I actually lost a client because his brother's name was George."

"Why did she name you Georgy?"

"Because of my English accent. She said it was like Lynn Redgrave in *Georgy Girl*."

"What are you two nice young ladies doing here?" An old drunk approached us.

"We're hookers and we're waiting for our tricks," I told him. Georgy laughed. She was very tall with short blond hair. She had small blue wincing eyes and a very soft voice with a Cockney accent.

"Why are you nervous?" I asked.

"Didn't Holly tell you where we're going?"

"Le Tight Rope."

"For three hours. Do you have a watch?" she whispered.

"Yes."

"Good. Let's try to get out in two and a quarter."

"Okay, Georgy."

Two men came into the bar and walked right over to us. One was short and liked me right away. He did all the talking. He wasn't bad looking. The other was tall with fat thighs. He had a Southern accent.

"What are you going to do while you're here in New York?" I asked him.

Georgy looked miserable. We walked eight blocks to Le Tight Rope. I was wearing high heels. There was no sign on the door. We were frisked. My date wrote our names in a book, Mr. and Mrs. John Winters. The man behind a glass window said it was ninety-five dollars per couple. My date paid for all of us.

A naked man greeted us and ushered us into a coed dressing room. We were the only ones there. We were told to get completely undressed and put our clothes in lockers. I put my condoms, beeper, and watch in my little beaded purse, which I took with me.

We walked into a large room with mats all over the floor, one next to the other. The ceiling was mirrored. In the next room was a small pool with a mosaic of a naked woman on the bottom. She had a triangle of gold tiles between her legs. "Let's go for a dip," my date said and without even thinking I was in the water. I put my head under. The water was cold and felt terrible dripping from my hair.

Another couple came down a spiral staircase. The man was hideously ugly with a huge stomach and hair all over his back and his ass. The woman with him was slim with a Jewish Afro. She was wearing red stockings, a red garter belt, and matching red glasses like Sally Jessy Raphael which looked ridiculous.

My date led me back to the mat room and told me to go down on him. I placed the condom on the tip of his dick and rolled it down with my mouth. The other couple followed behind us and watched.

"You should take lessons from her, she knows how to do it right," the fat man said to the woman, pointing at me.

"Fuck you," she said. Then they started doing it wildly, right next to us. After a while the man said to my date, "Okay, now let's switch."

"Okay," my date said.

"I don't think so," I said.

"Why not?" the woman in red asked.

"Well, uh, I'm just so in love with my man here, I couldn't bear another woman's hands on him," I said.

"Hey, this is a swing club," the man said. "Come on, baby, let's swing."

"You three swing. I think I'll sit this one out."

"This is supposed to be couples," the man insisted.

"She's just a snotty bitch," the woman said. "We're not good enough for her." Two words I have always hated are "snotty" and "snot."

"It has nothing to do with the two of you." This was a typical New York confrontation, like ones on the subway or standing on line somewhere. The thing that made this one different was that we were all lying on a mat naked.

"Look," I said, "if you want to know the truth there's a, well this is really painful for me to talk about, a medical prob-lem. We both have herpes."

"She's just kidding," my date said. He was so confused, his penis kept getting soft, then hard, and then soft again.

"No, honey, it's important to be honest," I told him, then turned to the other couple. "We came here tonight out of a deep sense of anger and frustration. Well, it's a long story but quite frankly we wanted revenge, and now I suddenly realize that it wouldn't be fair to you nice people, but maybe we can exchange numbers and get together when we're in remis-sion."

"We're in remission!" the hairy man said. He had a dry

patch of skin on one side of his mouth, as if he had drooled and just let it air-dry.

"Honey," I said to my date, "let's check out the refreshments." I noticed Georgy was leaning against the drink table.

My date couldn't speak. He was furious. I smiled at him warmly.

The refreshments consisted of a bottle of apple juice, a carton of orange juice, and ham sandwich squares on dry white bread.

"I brought you here to swing. I'm spending a lot of money for this," my date said. Georgy was back in the pool with the Southerner. "Let's go join them in the water."

"Let's see what's upstairs," I said.

We walked up the spiral staircase to an empty corridor lined with closed doors. He opened one. Inside the tiny room was an apparatus that looked like a giant leather motorcycle.

"Let's do it on that," he said.

"Let's go downstairs and join Georgy in the water."

"You're the worst one I ever brought here," he whined.

"You've been here before?" I asked.

We went downstairs. "How 'bout if you, me, Georgy, and Wilbur all do it next to each other on the mat?" he said.

"Oh that sounds fantastic," I said.

We all lay down next to each other and he climbed on top of me and we did it for a few minutes. It was fun looking at his butt go up and down in the ceiling mirror while I made faces.

"Want to go again?" I asked. I liked to ask the ones over forty if they wanted to do it again.

"What are you trying to do, kill me?" he said.

"Your skin is so soft," I said. After the guy comes I always say, "You've got a great body." Or, if there is no way that is plausible, I say, "You've got great hair," and if even that is stretching it, I say, "I love your mustache," or "Your skin is so soft." Sometimes I just say, "Nice apartment."

I read somewhere that women get at least one compliment a day, but men can go years without even one.

Georgy's date was having trouble finishing. "Why don't you and Georgy get it on?" he asked me.

I leaned over and kissed her shoulder. It was like kissing my own arm. I thought I was helping her out but she pulled away.

"Listen we really have to get going," she said.

We got dressed, they paid us, and we left. Georgy and I went to the Abbey Tavern for dinner. We called Holly.

"He said you were terrific. He wants you to go there with him again next Thursday night."

"I don't want to, Holly," I said.

"I'll talk to you later. You know, you're lucky to have this job. I have the best clients." Holly's voice bristled with anger. She hung up.

"I have to go," Georgy said. "I have another trick, Tony, on East Eighty-third Street."

"You see Tony, the man who looks like Dom DeLuise?" I had been with Tony almost every night since I had started. When we were finished he usually sent me into the other room to see his teenage son.

"'Bye, Georgy. It was really nice to meet another girl," I said.

"If you want friends, go to a brothel. Blanche's is good on Twenty-eighth Street. All the girls you ever want to meet." Georgy wrote down a phone number on her business card, which had a picture of her on it, naked from the waist up, talking on a cellular phone. She got into a cab looking miserable.

12

THE NEXT MORNING I was walking by the filthy playground in Washington Square Park when I saw Vivian sitting on a bench. I could tell it was Vivian even though her back was toward me. I recognized her lumpy shoulder pads and the way she rocked back and forth slightly. Her arm was stretched out toward some innocent little kids playing with a sled. There were no hills, they were cross-country sledding. I opened the gate and joined Vivian on the bench.

"I'm getting married," she said. "It's a dream come true."

"Who is it?" I asked.

"The lucky man is Lars 'The Wolf' Wolfson. He's from McGovern's. I can get on his lease at Independence Plaza." She leaned forward and yelled to the kids, "Do you want me to give you a pull?" They ignored her. "We could have a baby if we want to," she told me.

I congratulated her. A mother came up and asked us to leave the playground since we didn't have a child with us. She pointed to a sign that said only children and their guardians were permitted, as Vivian rambled on about the wedding.

"When is it?" I asked.

"Today at two and we change the lease tomorrow. You're invited." Vivian wrote her wedding invitation on a brown paper bag with brown lipstick. She wrote R.S.V.P. without a phone number.

"I can come," I told her.

"I'll throw you the bouquet!" she yelled after me as I left the park. I was a little jealous even though it was only Vivian. I am always jealous when people get married, even if it's strangers standing on church steps I see from the back seat of a cab or characters on a television show. I was even jealous when my friend Barbara Levine married the shortest man in the world. Even though he has bright red hair and is an Orthodox Jew.

I went to a lingerie store on East Ninth Street and bought Vivian a white satiny nightgown. I tried it on and looked at myself for a long time in the tiny cubicle. The saleswoman opened the curtain and said, "It looks good on you."

"It's not for me," I told her.

The wedding took place in the groom's apartment at Independence Plaza, a red brick prison-type building designated for low income housing. Lars was big and square with skinny deteriorated arms and a pregnant stomach. He had a rubber face with beautiful pale blue Norwegian eyes. Someone said he had been a Presbyterian minister and a professor at Columbia. He had once had a wife and daughters and a house in the suburbs. It was hard to picture. He looked like a funny drunk Viking with a caved-in chest. Everyone called him the Wolf.

"He's not well," Vivian told the guests. "He gets blood all over the couch. His asshole bleeds. I want everybody to know I'm just trying to take care of him with some TLC."

"I am not alt-ing my behavior for you, Vivian," Lars said. "I like to sit around in the nude, Vivian, bare buff naked, and you or no other sneaker-wearing woman is going to change that."

Vivian wore a tight white sweater and makeup. She was crying. When Vivian started to cry people just let her. They respected her femininity. An old friend of Lars's came to perform the ceremony.

"Do you, Vivian, take the Wolf to be your lawful wedded husband?"

"Damn yes," she said. They kissed awkwardly.

The apartment already had a feminine touch. Vivian had placed a colorful piece of material on the couch. Everyone admired it. "There's blood stains," she said.

"I look better today in my tuxedo than I did thirty years ago," Lars said.

"It's my day, Lars," Vivian said.

One of their friends brought fried chicken and potato salad from the Food Emporium. "Well, it's not steaks, Joe," Lars said. "I thought we were having steaks. The best man was supposed to bring steaks."

"I wasn't supposed to be the best man, Wolf. Adam was. But he had to go away on business."

Lars held up his beer. "To Adam," he said.

"To Adam," the rest of us said.

The TV was turned on to a football game.

Lars and Vivian opened their gifts. Except for me, all the wedding guests were regulars from Millie's Tavern and McGovern's and residents of the swimming pool at the Jane West Hotel. Each one gave the couple fifty dollars. I gave Vivian the nightgown, and then slipped two twenties and a ten into the card. I always overdo it. Vivian opened the present with girlish shyness. She cried a little when she lifted the nightgown out of the pink tissue paper. Then she went into the bedroom, changed into it, and modeled it for everybody. "Not bad for a day's work," Lars said.

When the football game was over, everyone went to McGovern's and continued celebrating. Vivian looked radiant. She was still wearing the nightgown. I thought about what I wanted my wedding to be like. Not Jewish. Maybe under a big yellow-and-white-striped tent, or in the Rainbow Room, or the Puck Building.

"Can I watch you take a bath later?" Lars asked Vivian.

"Yes," she said, "but you can't touch my breasts."

My beeper went off, and a handsome man with a mustache asked me what I did for a living. "Are you a doctor or a drug dealer?"

"I'm a hooker," I said, smiling like a hooker. The job hadn't made me hate men yet, I noticed. I just liked them more and more. I liked this man, an investment banker called the Judge, who had slipped Lars an envelope with five hundred-dollar bills. I figured he was the McGovern's benefactor. Most bars have one.

My comment had embarrassed him. "You'll learn," Holly had told me about comments like that.

My beeper went off again, and I called Holly. I had to go to an Italian restaurant in midtown to do the chef in the kitchen before the dinner rush.

Vivian was enjoying her day. The Wolf leaned over on his barstool and kissed her neck.

"Cut it out," Vivian said.

13

THE NEXT NIGHT I was having dinner with Holly and B.J. at the Chelsea. We sat formally around the glass dining room table, me in my red cocktail dress, B.J. in an apron that was supposed to look like the front of a tuxedo, and Holly in sweatpants and a big bra. B.J. was carving a rack of lamb. I absolutely cannot eat lamb. He had gotten me a book about how to be a stand-up comic because I had mentioned that at one time I had considered being one. He couldn't let go of the idea.

He asked me to do some of my "act," so I made a few jokes about how much I hated my stepmother, Siobhan. It came out sounding very pathetic and sad and we sat in silence for a long time after my "act." B.J. gave me a big piece of lamb and said I had a little Lenny Bruce in me.

"We had a Siobhan who worked for us for a while," Holly said. "She used the name Fiona. I said, 'You're Jewish, use Barbara or Debbie, something believable,' but she was into this whole Irish thing." Holly got up to answer the phone.

"What did she look like?" I asked.

"Very horsy," B.J. said. "I gave her seven hundred dollars to go back to college because all the men hated her and I didn't know how else to get rid of her. Real father figure complex, that one."

Holly covered the phone with her hand and said, "You should have just said, 'You're a lousy whore, the men hate you, you're fired, now get lost.'"

B.J. laughed and told a story about another girl who refused to shave under her arms and got stopped by Security at every hotel.

I was getting a very bad stomachache. They had a glass dining room table like the one we had when I was a kid and I wanted to lie down under it the way I used to. It was the best place to hide because you could see people seeing you.

Holly was writing an address for me on a Post-it. I had promised to work right after dinner. B.J. excused himself from the table for a minute and I put some lamb back on the serving platter.

He came back with some pictures. "This was her," he said. "She used the name Fiona."

It was a Polaroid of Siobhan, my father's wife, with her hair dyed red, sitting next to Holly on the couch. I couldn't

believe it. It was her. I sat there stunned for an hour, while
they showed me photos of their children.

"We should get a picture of you, Bennington," B.J. said.

I sat there wondering how I could let Siobhan know that
I knew without letting her know about me.

14

I WAS WATCHING Phil Donahue on TV when I decided to
call my father. For some reason I missed him and it suddenly
occurred to me that he wasn't dead, I could just pick up the
phone and call him. I called my father to tell him I wanted
to see him. He said hello and I paused. "It's Bad—it's Bed—
it's Bennington," I finally managed to spit out.

I made a little speech about how Christmas was over and
it was almost my birthday and I thought it was silly that we
hadn't spoken in two years. I reminded him how he had given
me an Indian name one day in the totem pole hall at the
Museum of Natural History when I was little. Holds-a-
Grudge.

"And with my birthday coming up . . ." I said again.

He told me to meet him at the Cauldron of Clams the next
night.

When I got to the Cauldron he was playing pinball. His
dog, Annie, was sitting under the pinball machine. "Hey,
how are ya?" my father said. He looked up from his game
and the ball fell between the flippers. "Good to see ya." He
gave me a wet kiss on the cheek. "How have ya been, Ben-

Ben? Where would you like to go for dinner?" He sounded falsely upbeat, like on divorce weekends.

"Anywhere, Dad."

"How about LOBster?" My father always said LOBster the same way.

"I don't eat fish, Dad."

"Not even LOBster?" That surprised hurt look on his face.

"No, Dad." I always hated fish ever since I was a child and we went to Cape Cod every summer. We would eat fish for breakfast, lunch, and dinner. We had delicious things too, like handpicked blackberries, corn on the cob that we would husk and eat raw in the car, onions from the grill wrapped in tinfoil, and chocolate Dairy Queen with chocolate jimmies. You said "jimmies" instead of "sprinkles" because you were in Massachusetts.

Once, my father caught a huge bluefish, and the lure pierced his flesh. The hook went right through his palm to the back of his hand and the fish was still connected to it. He and the bluefish had to go to the emergency room. Then we ate the fish—my father said he had never enjoyed a meal so much—and I got a long bone caught in my mouth, straight from cheek to cheek. We couldn't get the bone out and my mouth was bleeding. We had to go back to the same emergency room. After that I just couldn't eat fish anymore. My father was surprised every single time I told him this.

"Not even shellfish?"

We walked to a seafood restaurant on Hudson Street. He looked over at the football game on the bar TV.

"Are you reading?"

"What?"

"Do you READ? Are you READing?"

"Yes. A friend of mine gave me a book about stand-up comedy."

"I want to know if you read BOOKS."

"Yes, I do."

There was no more bread and butter, so I went to the ladies' room for a while. When I got back my father said, "Are you still having that bladder problem?"

"No."

"Do you still have a weak bladder?"

"No, I drink a lot of water." I rummaged around in the bottom of my bookbag and found some loose vitamin E pills. The chiropractor said they would balance my water. I took one.

"Are you on another one of those crazy diets?"

"No."

The waitress came. My father pretended to be deeply absorbed in the menu, as if he didn't already know he wanted the lobster. "I'll have the twin LOBsters," he said.

"I'm sorry, we're out of lobster."

"Oh, uh-huh, let's see." He stuck his bottom lip out in a pout.

"Dad, do you want to go somewhere else?"

"No, I'll have an anchovy salad and the mussels. What do you have on tap?" he asked, disgusted.

"We don't serve any alcohol, but you're welcome to bring your own." In a flash, my father was out the door.

I was hoping he would remember to give me a belated Christmas present. At least a hundred dollars in cash. Every time my father wrote me a check he would accidentally make it uncashable. He would write the year as 1776, or make it out to Bennington College instead of Bennington Bloom. There was always a different mistake.

My father came back in. "It's cold out, I forgot to wear my coat." He had three cans of beer with him in a paper bag meant for two. The bag was torn from the rain. He made a pyramid of the beers and craned his neck for the waitress. He looked like a gray swan, drops of water beading up on his sweater.

"How's Fiona?" I asked. I looked at him carefully, waiting for a reaction. There was none.

"Who?"

"Oh, I mean Siobhan."

"Fine. How's your acting coming?"

"Fine."

"Are you IN anything? Any prospects?"

"Not right now."

"Have you just given it up? Have you given UP?"

"No, I'm just not in anything right now."

"Are you using your mind? Do you ever just sit down and do some math equations just for FUN? To stay in SHAPE? The mind is a muscle."

"No Dad, never."

"But do you READ? Are you reading BOOKS? Your brother doesn't read either. He's never read a book in his life."

"Dad, it's still Christmas vacation."

"A vacation from reading?"

My father leaned back in his chair and started hitting his head on the stucco wall behind him. "What happened?" he asked. "How did I fail? How did I fail?" His head was banging on the wall.

He got up to get cigarettes and left me alone at the table again. I remembered shaking my brother once. He spilled something. I yelled, "Dylan, look what you did now! I have to clean this whole place up before Dad gets home." He bent down and tried to clean the mess. I grabbed his shoulders and started to shake him. His head bobbed back and forth like a doll's. "Now look what you did!" I shook him very hard for a long time.

My brother looked at me, terrified. He was small and soft and he cried silently with a hollow-air sound coming from his mouth, my white fingerprints on his bare brown shoulders.

"I'm sorry," I said. I put my arms around him to hug him, and he was crying so hard he couldn't even pull away. "I'm so sorry Dylan, I'm so sorry Dylan," I gasped. I knew I could never make up for this. My father came home and said, "Dylan, you are lucky to have such a good sister."

My father came back to the table and opened up his embarrassing orange knapsack and pulled out a gift-wrapped box. Oh, no, I thought. It was probably something he picked out.

"Merry Christmas," he said shyly. "Benny, I hope you like this. I didn't know what to get you. It's just something I picked out."

"Cash makes a very good gift," I said.

"You know, I've cut back on my course load. I want to spend a little more time up at the house. I'm getting older. Math is a young man's game."

"Thanks, Dad," I managed.

Two years ago, when I finally figured out that I couldn't get my father's attention, I stopped talking to him. I didn't go to the Cauldron of Clams and wait around. I didn't call him from pay phones whenever I found a quarter in my pocket, or stand outside his apartment on Eighth Street looking up at the fifth floor. But I couldn't put him out of my mind. I kept looking over my shoulder. I always thought someone was him, an old man or a woman with a gray sweater. I kept waiting for him to show up. In the seat next to me at a movie, at the dog run in Washington Square Park, at the doctor's. I got a job in a bar around the corner from the Cauldron and worked until four in the morning. I kept waiting for him to appear and grab my shoulders and shake me. I kept thinking he would drag me out of some room and shake me and say, "What are you doing? Stop it, stop it. Listen to me. You're not going to continue doing this. Grab hold of yourself." I waited and waited.

He paid for dinner and we left the restaurant. "I'll walk you as far as the Cauldron," he said.

15

THE MINUTE I got to the dorm room I opened the present. It was a long-sleeved T-shirt from The Gap. It had black and white stripes. It was a size small.

I got compliments on it the whole next day. One client told me to keep it on, he had a prison fantasy. It practically looked like a Chanel suit on me. It looked like I was going to the races.

I couldn't believe how much I liked that shirt.

I called my father and told him how much I liked it. "Siobhan picked it out," he said.

Over the next few days I looked everywhere for the shirt. I couldn't find it. I searched Jennifer's room. I even had Holly call a few clients to see if I had left it behind. My shirt was gone.

I carried a small load of clothes to the laundromat and placed my laundry bag on the big scale. There were beautiful laundry bags everywhere. Jade and mustard Chinese silk that should have been kimonos. The Korean woman walked in from the back. She was wearing my black-and-white-striped T-shirt. I was stunned.

"Receipt?" she asked.

"That's my shirt."

"No, no, no," she said.

"That's my SHIRT." My voice was getting loud. The shirt looked terrible on her. Her skin looked yellow and dirty against the black and white stripes. "That's my shirt, that's my SHIRT."

The woman started screaming in Korean. She was screaming and pretending to cry a little. I just stood there. A man rushed in from the back. He was panting. "You mistaken, you mistaken, miss."

I was not mistaken. You know when someone is wearing your favorite shirt. She looked so guilty in the stolen stripes. I felt so disgusted. That woman had picked through my clothing, Jennifer's sheets, my velvet underwear, my striped shirt.

I grabbed my laundry and left, muttering, "That's my shirt." For the first time, I hated New York.

I went to my favorite restaurant, La Fondue, to calm down. I chose a nice table in the corner. The waitresses were all very old and European and always said I looked thin. Most of them wore enormous wigs. I ordered cheese fondue and a diet Coke. My waitress brought the salad and bread and butter.

There were only a few people in the restaurant. An older couple sat four tables away from me. They were both fat with the same short, thick white hair and they seemed very much in love. They were done with their meal and drinking red wine. I was listening to their conversation when all of a sudden the woman let out a terrible belch from deep in her stomach. It was a disgusting sound, long and drawn out. She just continued to talk, not missing a beat of her conversation. I couldn't believe it.

My fondue came and the woman belched again and then a third time. She never said excuse me or stopped talking. The man didn't seem to care. Then she started belching every twenty to thirty seconds. I thought I was going to throw up.

I told one of the waitresses that I wanted to move and she carried all the fondue equipment to another table. I could still hear faint belches. I got my check and left.

When I walked out of the restaurant it was raining. A delivery truck stopped at a red light and the driver opened the door and said, "Nice titties, mama." The truck was blocking my way so I couldn't cross the street. There was a red rose, like a tattoo, painted on the side of the truck, and the name Nancy's Flower Garden underneath. I rooted around in my bag for a pen and paper and copied down the name and phone number. "I'll give you my phone number, baby," the driver yelled. "I usually like black pussy but it's all pink on the inside, right, mama?"

I went to a phone booth and called Nancy's Flower Garden. When a woman answered, I said, "I own six restaurants in SoHo and I always keep fresh flowers on the tables. I don't enjoy being shouted at and humiliated by your delivery man and I should think you wouldn't want your truck driven by that verbal rapist."

"I'm sorry, ma'am," the woman said, genuinely upset. "What did he do exactly?"

"Well, one thing he said was that black pussy and white pussy are both pink on the inside. Am I speaking with Nancy?"

"Yes, I'm very sorry." She sounded mortified.

"What are you going to do about it?" I was developing an English accent.

"Fire him, ma'am."

"Please see that you do."

I hung up. A cab splashed me and I screamed, "Fuck you." I decided to take the subway. I learned on Sally Jessy Raphael that I wasn't going to meet a man taking cabs. Except a cab-driver. I got on the downtown No. 1 train. It was extremely crowded. I was in the center of a car holding on to nothing. At Forty-second Street, a mob of people got on, including a little Asian woman who was pushing through, clutching a folded-up shopping cart. She jabbed the cart into me, hard.

I reeled around and punched the woman in the stomach without thinking. She doubled over in pain.

"Oh my God, I'm so sorry," I gasped.

"I'm ninety-two years old," she said.

"I'm so sorry," I said again. "It was a reflex action. I wasn't thinking." At Thirty-fourth Street the train emptied out, and people huddled around the old woman. I slithered out as the doors were shutting. I pulled my bag out just in time but I dropped it and it spilled everywhere, tampons and change rolling onto the tracks.

I walked down to Eighteenth Street and Fifth Avenue in the pouring rain, crying. I hesitated at the door of a building and checked some information I had jotted down on a scrap of paper. I have an endless supply of scraps in my bookbag. I carefully buzzed number 3 and took the elevator to the third floor. "I'm supposed to fill out an application," I said to a woman at the desk.

NAME:
Bennington Bloom.

REASON FOR SEEKING PSYCHIATRIC TREATMENT:
Punched a 92-year-old woman on the subway, I wrote.

I tried to make my handwriting look very crazy. The woman reviewed my application. I craned my neck to look down a hallway. There were doors all along it. The chairs and the floor were covered in gray carpeting. Someone was yelling in one of the rooms, "I didn't say that, that's not what I said." The woman took my application into the room with the yelling. What if they wouldn't take me? I closed my eyes and was startled by a hand on my shoulder. "Your appointment is one week from today. Monday, January twenty-fourth at five P.M. with Mrs. Johnson. Is that convenient?" the woman asked.

"Yes, thank you." That was one day after my birthday.

"You'll discuss the fee with Mrs. Johnson." She sounded disappointed that she wouldn't be the one discussing the fee.

As I waited for the elevator, the door to the office opened slightly and a woman about my height, very short, peered at me for several minutes through the crack and then slammed the door.

I hoped I could make it to Monday. I started to walk down Fifth Avenue. Everything looked like black and white stripes and the World Trade Center looked beautiful over the Washington Square Arch. New York is a convenient city to go crazy in. You can always stop and have a diet Pepsi with a malfunctioning straw. You can remember what soothes you and what you must do next. I had a date with a client who loved my young skin and my "gentle touch." It was almost my birthday. I stopped at The Gap. They didn't have any more striped shirts, but when I got back to the dorm, I found it.

16

IN TRIBECA A giant truck with twenty or thirty wheels blocked a whole street. There was no way of getting across, so I crawled under it like a rat. I realized I had forgotten to wear a bra, I was so used to getting dressed without one.

I felt self-conscious with my nipples showing through my Laura Ashley dress and my beeper going off in my coat pocket. It didn't fit with my story about being a paralegal.

I was looking for an apartment share all over New York. Christmas vacation would be over in three days. Jennifer would be back soon, and I had to move out of the dorm.

The first apartment I looked at was covered in white shag carpeting, even the walls and the ceilings were carpeted. Cats ran up the walls and across the ceilings. "A good roommate is a roommate I never see," the woman said. My cowboy boots left black footprints. "I don't think it's going to work out," she said.

One apartment had a loft bed. I cannot sleep if I have to climb a ladder. One place had the words "a whore lives here" spray-painted on the front door. Another had black metal gates over all the windows. An old woman said I could live rent free if I cooked dinner twice a week and massaged her cellulite and swollen ankles.

At the end of the day I took a share on Fifty-third Street and Eighth avenue. My roommate was a miserable middle-aged woman named Rhea. Her voice sent chills down my spine and her neck was stretched out and webbed. "If I didn't have my music, I don't think I could stand the suffering," she said as she pounded out a song from *Fiddler on the Roof* on a small piano. It became clear that I was her best friend.

She wanted to have dinner together right away and collect her security deposit. We went to her favorite restaurant, La Grotesque or something like that. She told me she wrote a newsletter listing sample sales given by famous designers, she could have gotten my dress for twenty-five dollars, she had just gone through six roommates in six months, and she hadn't been with a man in two years. "I'm ready to jump that waiter's bones right now," she said.

The next day I ordered a queen-size bed from Sleepy's and wheeled it around my new bedroom. I made it up with the Ralph Lauren sheets I had stolen from Bloomingdale's. I just couldn't pay a hundred dollars for a sheet. I had my own room in a three-bedroom apartment. I wouldn't meet Brandy, my other roommate, for a few days because she was a flight attendant. I snooped around her bedroom for a while. She had "Prayer for Take-off and Landing" in a plexiglass frame by her bed. Rhea's bedroom door had a lock on it.

Rhea had said I was allowed to use the living room, so I sat on the corduroy couch. What a strange thing to grow up in a city, to spend your whole life there, and end up living in an apartment share with an awful woman and a flight attendant you hadn't even met yet. My stomach started to hurt so I went into my room, lay down on my bed, and looked at my closet, my big white closet with shelves, to comfort myself.

17

HOLLY CALLED AND told me that a client had said I had gained a few pounds. "He said if you lose twenty pounds he'll take you to St. Croix. He also said he didn't appreciate the little lecture you gave him on drugs and alcohol."

I decided to go to a belly dancing class I had read about in the *Learning Annex*.

I stopped at the Chelsea to give Holly six hundred dollars from two clients I had seen that afternoon. I made seven hundred for myself, which was good because I had spent almost that much the day before on a Louis Vuitton train case and a matching wallet. The train case was a small overnight suitcase with a makeup tray and a built-in mirror. I had gone to look at it every day for two weeks. I'd never had anything like it before.

Holly's door was open so I walked in and sat on the couch. I put the train case down. It was heavy with just my cocktail dress in it and some mints and condoms in the makeup tray.

Holly came out of the bedroom. "What's that?"

"I bought it yesterday," I said. I held it protectively.

"Really, Daphne, I didn't think you were the type."

"What does that mean?" She had never called me Daphne before.

"Every new whore buys a Louis Vuitton or a Ferragamo or a Gucci or a Chanel. I thought you were different. But don't get me wrong, I'm glad you did it."

I left quickly and stood in front of a Citibank. I had seven hundred-dollar bills in my wallet. A homeless man pretending to be the Citibank doorman opened the door for me, but Holly had told me not to put my money in the bank because I didn't pay taxes on it. I would keep doing what I'd been doing, putting hundred-dollar bills under my mattress, and spending everything else. I tried to break as few hundreds as possible, with the exception of big purchases like my train case.

"Make up your mind," the homeless man said. "Are you coming or going?"

I apologized to him and kept walking. I went to a boutique on Fifty-fifth Street and tried on a suit. It was actually my third time visiting the suit, but I decided to think about it a little longer. Holly's words were in my head, "every new whore, every new whore." I had to save my money for an apartment without roommates.

I walked up the stairs to the belly-dancing studio on Broadway. People were taking karate in the front. There was a little booth set up with belly-dancing accessories, beautiful beaded bras and scarves with tassels. I bought a card for ten classes from the girl at the desk.

"You have to pick a special belly-dancing name for performances," she said.

I pictured myself in a red and gold costume dancing at Cafe Mogador on St. Mark's Place. "I'm a beginner."

"You'll learn quickly. You have the hair. What's your name going to be? Dig quickly into your subconscious."

"I pick the name Fatma," I said.

"Fatma?"

"Yes, Fatma."

"Well, think about it a little longer."

I wondered if it was a coincidence that all my new ventures involved changing my name. I went into the dressing room and took my clothes off over my leotard and tights. Then I went back to the little booth and tied one of the scarves around my waist, but decided not to buy it. I cautiously entered the tiny belly-dancing room and class began.

The teacher took attendance. They were all old women from the Learning Annex draped in skin and skirts and scarves. "Delilah, Jezebella, Scheherazade, Nefertita . . . Nefertita . . . Is Gladys here?"

"Oh, I'm here."

"And Fatma?"

"Here."

"You're new. Instead of Fatma, I think we'll call you Fatima, or Bulbula. That has a voluptuous round sound."

It was a great class. We mostly posed and then had freestyle, where we all pretended to belly-dance while a man beat on a drum. My hair danced. The teacher said the trick was never to let your feet leave the ground. I loved this kind of exercise.

After class I went back into the dressing room with the old women. They were going to a seminar on organizing their closets.

I decided to buy the scarf after all. I reached into my train case for my new Louis Vuitton wallet, but it was missing. I had moved it from my coat to the cosmetic tray. I emptied everything from the case. It was gone. It had my seven hundred dollars in it, my suit and my scarf money. My apartment money. I told the teacher that my wallet was stolen but almost everybody was gone. I wanted to cry. She told me I could come back for free whenever I wanted to.

"I can't come back here," I said. "And I loved it so much."

The karate class was still in full swing.

I was losing money again. It happened in phases. I knew that I wouldn't stop losing money if I didn't stop stealing. A pair of cuff links on a client's bureau, a ladies' watch on a dining room table, a bottle of Chanel No. 5 from the side of a hot tub. Whenever I stole anything I lost the exact amount of money it was worth.

I called Holly. "Every new whore loses money," she said. "Since we don't pay taxes, the world has a way of collecting."

18

WHEN I GOT home to my new apartment, my roommate, Rhea, was furious. It turned out Brandy, the other roommate, was not a flight attendant at all. Rhea had called American Airlines and they told her that Brandy had been fired three years before. She confronted Brandy who admitted that she had lied but that paying the rent would not be a problem since she was a high-class call girl.

"I am so sick over this," Rhea said.

"It's not the worst thing in the world," I said.

"She's probably brought AIDS into this house."

"They say working girls are the most careful."

"They're all on drugs," she said. "I dated a psychiatrist who told me that all hookers, even if they just did it for one week or one day, it catches up with them and they break down and turn to drugs. I told her to pack her things and leave. What do you have in that big case?" she asked.

I put my Louis Vuitton train case down on the floor.

"Oh, before I forget," she said. "It's very important that you wipe my counter with Fantastik every time you use the kitchen. I wrote you a note." She handed me a six-page letter.

"Is Brandy gone?" I asked.

"She's in her room packing."

Brandy and I shared a moving van. The movers dropped me off at my mother's house and then took her to her new apartment on the Upper East Side. We rode in the back with our things and laughed the whole way. We took turns reading Rhea's letter. "Even tiny droplets of water can stain a counter." I told Brandy I was a hooker too.

"I thought you might be," she said. "When I snooped in your room and saw natural sea sponges and a lifetime supply of condoms, I was pretty sure, but Holly's business card was the clincher."

Georgy had taught me about natural sea sponges. When you have your period you soak them in hot water, squeeze them out, and then stuff them inside you. They soak up the blood and the guy doesn't see or feel a thing. You rinse them between sessions and throw them out at the end of the night.

"I didn't have a clue when I snooped in your room," I told her.

I said goodbye as the movers finished unloading my things in my mother's living room.

My mother greeted me with tea and grapes. "Do you want me to try to cook dinner?" she asked.

"I can't stay for dinner, Mom, I have a date," I said.

"A date!" She was brimming with pride. Tad walked in carrying a child's old chest of drawers with yellow ducks painted on it.

"Hello, Bennington," he mumbled. "Welcome." He made an awkward gesture with his hands and bowed slightly.

"How cute. Look at the ducks," my mother said.

"I just found it. I thought you might like this for your new room," Tad said. I could barely understand him.

"Isn't that nice, Benny?" my mother said. "Taddeus found you this beautiful new chest for your room. Aren't we all getting along nicely?"

My beeper went off and Tad was so startled I thought he was going to dive behind the couch.

"What's that?" my mother asked.

I told her everyone had a beeper these days. I excused myself and called Holly. She said my date had decided to see another girl and I asked her if I could have the night off. She said I could if I worked extra hard tomorrow.

I told my mother my date had been postponed, and I spent the evening with her and Tad and Dylan. We ordered in Chinese and sat around the table eating, Dylan and I mocking the grownups behind their backs, like old times. Afterwards, Dylan went to call my father but I didn't feel like saying hello. I also didn't feel like unpacking.

19

THAT NIGHT, BACK in my old bed, I dreamt that I had a friend. A little Japanese girl named Little Bad Smell. When her parents came to this country they didn't speak English. The woman went into labor, a New York hospital took them in, and she gave birth. She heard the doctor say the words "Little Bad Smell," and she had never heard anything more beautiful.

In my dream, Little Bad Smell had my old Barbie collection with the white fur wedding gown and the stewardess ensemble, and she was very determined, trying to get ahead, despite her name.

When I was a child there were two kinds of girls. The kind who played with toy horses and used words like mare and colt, and the kind who played with Barbie. I had a Barbie townhouse with huge pink plastic furniture and an elevator. I had a Barbie suitcase filled with hand-me-down Barbie clothes from my rich cousin, Pepper, who liked horses. I had three identical Barbie dolls, triplets, with good hair because I never shampooed it.

Each Barbie had her own floor in the townhouse and they would get dressed to go on their big dates and charge men for sex. They mostly changed clothes and had sex, once even in the elevator, but then one left and became a stewardess.

The next night, a client said to me, "You have perfect feet, they were made for high heels."

"Like Barbie," I said. Always on tiptoe, trying to please, feet in the high-heel position. I kept my shoes on when we did it and my legs tensed up like plastic.

My beeper went off. I called Holly while the client took a shower.

"I want you to do one more trick."

"I can't, Holly. I'm too tired. I've done four tonight." It was midnight and I was worried about what my mother would think if I came home too late from my "date."

"How much money did you make?"

"Eight hundred."

"This one will be easy. It's an overnight. You'll get fifteen hundred and it will be easy. Please Bennington, you can't let me down. You didn't work last night."

"I know," I said. "I'm sorry."

"I have a birthday present for you. Oh, and B.J. wants you to come over for a birthday dinner tomorrow. He's going to make cheddar cheese soup and a ham."

"Thank you, Holly, but you know I don't want to work

tomorrow." I couldn't stand the thought of working on my birthday.

"Right. Absolutely. Let me give you the information. His name is Paul Rosenthal and he lives in Trump Tower. He's in the helicopter business with Trump. He'll give you three thousand and a package for you to bring to me."

"Okay, Holly." I wrote down the address and yelled good-bye to the man in the shower. I called my mother and told her I was sleeping at my ex-roommate, Brandy's, house. I was glad I didn't wake her and that Dylan didn't answer.

I went to a high floor in Trump Tower. Paul Rosenthal let me in. He had a huge hook nose. His bedroom had wrap-around windows. I had never seen a view like this. In the middle of his bed there was an enormous bowl of cocaine. There were a few drops of blood on the cocaine from his nosebleed. There was no air in the apartment. I asked for some water, but he said I couldn't go into the kitchen because his two young sons were home. I opened the bedroom door and saw one of them running around in pajamas. I thought about when I used to go to people's apartments as a babysitter instead of a call girl. It had the same feel to it really. Lying on a down quilt or a corduroy couch, getting looks from the father, getting paid.

I asked Paul if we could open a window, but he said they didn't open. Two helicopters came dangerously close. I took off my red cocktail dress and lay down on his bed next to the cocaine bowl.

"Do some," he said.

"No thanks," I said.

"Holly said you would do some."

"Okay." I took a spoon and pretended to do it. He was bouncing on the bed. He couldn't stop moving. The apartment was unbelievably hot. My eyes were closing.

"I feel like taking a little nap," I said.

"I don't mind. We'll fool around later. Keep your shoes on," he said. He was moving so fast, he was blurry.

I stretched out and fell asleep.

20

I WOKE UP at eleven the next morning. Paul was still bouncing on the bed.

It was my birthday. I was nineteen. I jumped up and sort of sang, "It's my birthday, it's my birthday," the way I have always done since I was a kid. "I can't believe I slept like that."

"Baby, baby, baby," he said. "Weeeeeeeeee."

I called Holly. "I slept the whole time. I'm sorry. I couldn't help it."

"It's okay, get the money and my package."

I started to get dressed. "I had a wonderfully relaxed night, Paul," I said. "You have such a nice apartment."

"Did you like the coke?"

"Oh yes, what a treat. It made me really crazy. Well, I've got to go."

"You were great, kid," he said. He handed me three thousand dollars and something wrapped in tinfoil. "You can leave now because my kids went to Little League already."

I took the long elevator ride down. It was so freezing outside, I had to go right into Bendel's to buy a pair of black suede gloves. When the saleslady looked at my red cocktail dress, I told her it was my birthday. I buttoned my coat all the way up.

I took a cab to the Chelsea. "Here's fifteen hundred and the package." Holly was sitting cross-legged on the bed in her sweatpants. She didn't look good.

"Don't tell B.J.," she said.

"Tell him what?"

"About the coke."

"Oh, I didn't really do any."

"You'd better get going," she said.

On my way home I realized what she had meant. I had left Trump Tower wearing a red dress and high heels, carrying cocaine practically all over New York. I couldn't have been more stupid. It was one thing to get arrested for prostitution, but it was another thing to be caught with drugs.

I took a shower the minute I got home. My beeper went off. I called Holly. "I want you to turn in your beeper," she said.

"What does that mean?"

"Fuck you. Don't act like you don't know."

"What, Holly?"

"I know what you've been doing."

"What?"

"I know that you've been lurking around the Chelsea. You were seen lurking around the hotel yesterday. I would appreciate it if you would stop fucking my husband."

"What? Holly, I'm not." I was so confused I started to cry.

"I thought you were different, but you're just a fucking little tramp. You're fired."

"Holly, you've got it wrong. I need this job. Tomorrow I have registration and all the money I've saved goes to NYU. Please, you don't know what you're saying."

"Shut up. I was so good to you. I bought you a wallet for

your birthday to replace the one you said got stolen. Was that a lie too?"

"I never lied to you."

"I want you to leave your beeper at the front desk today. I had you followed so I know your mother's address and phone number. If you don't do it, I'll get you back."

"Holly."

"I'll have you knocked off." She hung up.

Sweat had soaked my sides and under my breasts. I was naked in my room. I started to shake. I stood there for a very long time. I put on my jeans and my NYU sweatshirt. I didn't look like a high-paid call girl.

I went to the Chelsea and turned in my beeper. The boy at the desk gave me a note folded once in half. It said, "Fuck you if you think you're getting your present or your $100 deposit for the beeper. Your second mother, Holly."

21

I LEFT THE Chelsea Hotel and walked down to NYU. I registered and then stood on line at the bursar's office.

"Check, money order, Master Card, Visa, or American Express?" the woman behind the desk said.

"Cash," I said, nonchalantly. I peeled off hundred-dollar bill after hundred-dollar bill, making piles of ten and lining them up, counting and re-counting. Nine thousand dollars in cash.

I signed up for acting, voice, movement, speech, theater

history, and English composition. I was also forced to take Tech, where you have to work behind the scenes. You have to walk around in a flannel shirt and pretend that you're just as happy to build Juliet's balcony as to be Juliet because that is how much you love the theater. You love the theater so much you are willing to get completely covered in paint and climb ladders of any height and carry pieces of wood around. Everybody in Tech loves the theater so much they can barely control themselves.

At five o'clock I went to see my new shrink, Mrs. Johnson. I felt great, I was so together. I was a college student, paying my own tuition, I was going to get another escort job and earn money the most efficient way possible and see a shrink in case there were any job-related side effects. I had everything covered.

Mrs. Johnson was older than I expected. I was shocked at how old she was.

"Are you surprised at my age?" she asked.

"No, not at all," I said. Oh great, I was already lying. Off to a good start. I had promised myself I would be honest with this one. My first shrink, Maurey, had light blond hair. I became obsessed with wanting to know if he was gay or not.

"How old are you," I would ask Maurey.

"Why is that important to you?" he would ask me.

"Are you gay?" I would ask him.

"Why do you feel the need to know that?"

"I just do."

"Why do you ask? Do you want to seduce me?"

"Only if you're gay."

We had this same conversation for months, until one day I was sitting in a cab and I saw Maurey walking down the street looking up at the sky. He was just wandering around holding an open umbrella even though it was perfectly sunny out. He looked like the simpleton in a German children's story. I had wanted someone smart like Freud, and this is who I got, Maurey. I just couldn't go back to him after that.

"Why do you want to end your therapy?" he had asked.

"I think I've helped you as much as I can," I told him.

The one good thing about Maurey was he only charged nineteen dollars.

"Are you surprised at how young I am for my age?" Mrs. Johnson asked. I was enjoying thinking about Maurey in the sleepy atmosphere of the serious little room. It was a comfort just being there.

"How old are you?" I asked.

"Why do you feel the need to know that?"

"You brought it up."

"No, you asked me my age. Listen, I don't know about this, I think we'll have a five-week trial period. After five weeks you'll see if I'm the right analyst for you, and I'll see if I can help you."

I burst into tears.

"But I think we'll work together just fine," she said.

I got up to get a Kleenex from a box on the table. Maurey always had a stack of McDonald's napkins.

Mrs. Johnson got up and grabbed the box out of my hands. "Do you want a tissue?" she asked sternly.

"Yes." I was crying so hard I could hardly talk.

"Then why don't you ask for a tissue? Can you say 'Mrs. Johnson, please give me a tissue?' "

"Mrs. Johnson, please give me a tissue." I was sobbing.

"Here, Bennington, see how easy that was? You have to ask for what you want in life. In here it's my job to take care of you. Now, why don't you lie down on the couch?"

"Okay." I lay down. I was hoping I could.

"Very good. Most of my patients have great difficulty lying down on the couch."

I had no difficulty lying down. I kicked off my cowboy boots.

"No, no, no. We want you to be comfortable, but we don't want you to be *too* comfortable We don't want you to fall asleep. Put those shoes back on."

I didn't think I would fall asleep with her yelling at me. I sat up and put my boots back on. The little room was spinning.

"You know if you miss a session, you still have to pay for it. Twenty-five dollars."

"Okay."

"When you heard I was eighty years old, did you think I would look this young?"

Mrs. Johnson looked very old. She had gray hair and wore a wide-brimmed hat with a feather. She wore a beige pants suit with red plastic rain shoes. She had a large black mole over her lip.

"I really didn't think about it."

"What?"

"I really didn't think about it."

"What?"

"I really didn't think about it."

"All right then. Now, how are you going to pay for your therapy?"

"Well, I was just fired from my job but I still have some money saved."

"Are you going to get a new job?"

"Yes."

"Very good. That's what I'm here for. To help. What was your old job? Why are you crying?"

It took a long time for any words to come out of my mouth. "I don't know."

"Oh come on, you're a smart girl, you can do better than that."

I lay there trying to figure out how much I was paying per minute. I decided to tell her I worked as a receptionist in my grandfather's accounting office.

"I was a prostitute," I said.

"A pharmacist?"

"No, a prostitute."

"What?"

"A prostitute." I was talking as loud as I could.

She looked at me blankly.

"Prostitute!" I screamed.

"What? Did you just tell me that you were a prostitute?"

"Yes, I did."

"Please excuse me." Mrs. Johnson stood up.

"Where are you going?" I asked.

"I'm going to call the police. Don't you think I should?"

"No."

"Do you think I should accept your dirty money?"

I didn't say anything.

"Then let me hear you say 'Mrs. Johnson, please don't call the police.' "

"Mrs. Johnson, please don't call the police."

"Very, very good, Bennington. May I call you Bennington?"

"Yes."

"And what will you call me?"

"Mrs. Johnson?"

"Right. What made you decide to come in for therapy?"

"I punched an old woman on the subway," I said.

"I'm an old woman. Do you want to punch me?"

"No."

"You know, we can express our feelings in this room verbally, but not physically. Do you understand? You can say 'Mrs. Johnson, I *feel* like hitting you right now,' but you can't actually act it out. And I can say, 'Bennington, I feel like hitting *you* right now,' but I can't actually act it out. Do we have a deal?"

"Okay." I could only stop crying with my eyes closed. "So what's supposed to happen in therapy?" I asked.

"In the movie?"

"In therapy."

"I'm not teaching a course here, you know. This isn't Freshman Psych 101."

I cried on the couch, giving up on the tissues, soaking my face and my shirt collar. It felt cool, like when I washed my hair in the rain at theater camp. I cried until she said our time was up.

I said I felt relieved.

"Now wait a minute, aren't you forgetting something? Were you planning on paying me?"

"Oh I'm sorry, here you go."

"Five, ten, fifteen, twenty, twenty-five dollars." She looked into my eyes. "Thank you very much. I like to look into your eyes when I take the money. From now on, I think you should put the money right in my hand when you come in."

"Okay."

"I'll see you next week. At what time?"

"Five."

"Very good. You're going to do very well here."

"Thank you."

"What?"

"Goodbye."

"Goodbye, dear."

I walked out of Mrs. Johnson's little cubicle office past a few people in the waiting room. They had probably heard me screaming that I was a prostitute. I walked with my chin tilted up like the actress in the movie *Beverly Hills Madam*. I went into the handicapped ladies' room and cried for ten minutes. When I looked in the mirror my face was beautiful, relaxed and vulnerable. I always look good after crying or throwing up. I look softer.

I was happy to have Mrs. Johnson. She was very nice. She could be a role model for me. She was eighty years old and earned a good living sitting in a chair and doing nothing. I couldn't wait until next Monday.

22

I WALKED FROM Mrs. Johnson's office through Washington Square Park. A girl leaning on the side of a building in SoHo signaled to me and said, "Hi," in a very high voice. "I'm watching for the police," she said. "I'm selling these lamps." Her voice got higher and higher with every word. She pulled a shade shaped like a sombrero out of a shopping bag and put it on a lamp, angling and cuffing it. She handed the lamp to me. It was made out of straw and faux fur. I really needed one next to my bed in my mother's apartment.

"I make one-of-a-kind lamps and shades," the girl said. "I mean it's not the greatest lamp in the world, I was in a big rush when I made it, but it suits you." She ripped off a thread that was hanging from my sleeve. "My name is Perry Shepherd."

I shook her hand. I instantly liked her. She had frizzy Shakespearean hair and overalls. She looked like a newspaper boy from an old movie. She wasn't too thin. I was tired of thin friends.

"How much is it?" I asked.

"Well, it's thirty-five? but you can have it for twelve or

fourteen? That is if you want it? I can give you my card?"
She handed me a card with her name and telephone number
printed in tiny letters: *Perry Shepherd*.

"I'd like to buy it," I said.

"You can machine-wash the shade but don't put it in the
dryer. You don't have to buy it."

"I want it."

"Really? Well, you can just have it," she said. "It's pretty
demeaning selling them on the street. So you can just have
it, that is if you even want it."

"I love it," I said.

She pulled a man's pocket watch out of her overalls and
said she had to go to her waitressing job at the Broome Street
Bar. She applied red lipstick perfectly. "It was very nice meeting you," she said.

She started to walk quickly down West Broadway, taking
giant strides. I caught up with her and tried to pay her for the
lamp, but she refused. I shoved a twenty-dollar bill in her
pocket and she shoved it back in mine and we did that back
and forth until we got to the Broome Street Bar.

When we went in she got fired. There was a look of anger
and hatred on her face the likes of which I hadn't seen since
I used to babysit for a little girl named Olive.

"I demand to know why I am being fired when I have all
this seniority," she said.

"Because you're a horrible waitress."

I told her about how I got fired when I worked at Haägen-
Dazs because they said I ate all the profits. They claimed I ate
so much ice cream I was going to put the whole company
out of business. This didn't cheer her up. "You have your
lamps," I said.

"I'm an actor," she said.

"I'm an actor, too." We looked at each other doubtfully.

23

FOR SIX WEEKS I went to my shrink, went to classes, watched TV with Dylan after school, and hung around with my new friend, Perry Shepherd. It was too risky to get an apartment now that Holly had fired me, and I had begun to almost enjoy being home. I had even unpacked my clothes into the duck chest and put my old books on the shelves.

My English comp teacher made me write odes to household appliances and kitchen utensils. I got a B minus for *Egg-beater Poem*. I wasn't meeting any nice college boys, mostly fags. Every day I thought about calling Holly and trying to straighten things out. Maybe work one night a week. I missed the money and I even missed the sex, being called beautiful, teasing some poor guy. It seemed strange, telling the truth all the time. I called Holly's number once and got a busy signal and never tried again. Our first exams were coming up.

On Monday I got into a cab. I was running late and I had to get to Mrs. Johnson by five o'clock. It was finally Monday. I heard buzzing. The sound was vaguely familiar. I was wedged into the corner of the back seat because the passenger before me, a Japanese guy wearing a Columbia sweatshirt, had slobbered his wet rainy umbrella over the whole cab.

"Where you from, beautiful?"

"What?"

"Where you from?"

All of a sudden I understood why cab drivers got shot in the back of the head in the Bronx.

"Excuse me?" I tried to say 'Excuse me?' like *fuck you?*"

"Where you from?"

"New York."

"Are you from Puerto Rico?"

"No, New York."

"I mean your parents."

"New York."

"You lying."

"Excuse me?" I took out a pen and wrote his name and license number on a scrap of paper in case I wanted to report him. I closed my eyes for a moment and brushed my cheek with my hand. I felt a terrible, knife-sharp pain in the back of my hand. Oh no, I thought, He stabbed me.

I looked down at my hand frozen in my lap and saw a dead bee lying on it. I screamed. The driver pulled over.

"What's wrong?"

"Look." He twisted around and leered at my hand. "There was a bee in your cab."

"I didn't put it in here."

"You should be careful not to let bees in your cab. Look, my hand is swelling."

"You want I take you to the hospital?"

"No, you've already made me late."

"Look, what you want me to do?" he said.

"Well, when I get into a cab, I don't expect to get stung by a bee."

"I'll take fifty cents off the meter," he said.

"Fifty cents isn't going reduce the swelling."

"Fucking slut."

"Excuse me?"

"Nothing."

"What did you say?"

"I didn't say nothing."

"I'm getting out." I kept my head pulled back away from him. It occurred to me that if there were bees, there might also be lice.

"You know you don't have to get all bent into shape because of a bee."

"I don't know why you have to have the only bee in New York."

"There's a million bees in New York."

"I've never seen one."

"In the park. You go to Central Park you see bees."

"I don't think so." I wrote down his name and information again for the effect.

"Why you do that for?"

"I don't appreciate being called a fucking slut."

"I didn't call you no slut."

"Yes you did."

"I called you fucking stupid."

"Oh. Well, here." I threw five dollars at him and got out of the cab. The bee floated in a big puddle of rainwater on the vinyl seat.

I walked the rest of the way to Mrs. Johnson in the rain. I got there ten minutes late.

"Oh hello, Bennington, I was just calling your answering machine." She was wearing the red rain shoes again.

"I'm sorry I'm late."

"Why were you late?"

"I had trouble getting here. I got stung by a bee."

"You stopped to have tea?"

"No, I got stung by a bee." I started to cry.

"You know if you're late you still have to pay the full amount, so you're really cheating yourself."

"I know, I'm sorry."

"I rushed back here for your appointment from a very nice luncheon with my daughter. She's going through a divorce, we were having a lovely chat. You know, it doesn't matter to me if you're late, or even if you don't come at all, although I'd like the courtesy of a phone call so I can go home early, or enjoy a luncheon, but it's less work for me and the same money. Maybe you wanted to come late."

"No I didn't."

"Maybe you did."

"No, I didn't."

"Maybe we should think about that for a few moments." I was silent. My cowboy boots were soaked through. "Bennington, have you ever heard of the word 'resistance'?"

"Yes."

"Do you think you were 'resisting' your therapy?"

"No, I was just late."

"Maybe therapy is a very low priority for you. Maybe having tea is more important?"

"I didn't have tea."

"Well, what can we do to get you here on time?"

"Mrs. Johnson, I don't want to spend the whole session talking about me being late."

"Well, we can't spend the whole session doing anything because you were ten minutes late."

"Well, the time we have left then. I feel very sorry for myself."

"And angry at Mrs. Johnson?"

"No. Sometimes I think I'm not a very nice person."

"Oh?"

"I get mean to people on the street, or in stores, or to cabdrivers."

"Oh, I hate cabdrivers."

"You do?"

"Yes, it's perfectly all right to be mean to those people."

"It is?"

"Yes!"

I felt better. Mrs. Johnson was right. It was okay. I could

hear her stomach growling. I told her about a dream I had. I was a famous baseball player signing autographs in a nightclub.

"That is a dream about missing your father. You want to impress your father by being a famous baseball player. You need your father. There's nothing wrong with that."

"May I please have a tissue, Mrs. Johnson?"

"Very good, Bennington." She waddled over to the table and gave me the box of tissues. She counted the money I had handed her at the beginning of the session. She had been holding it in her fist. "What else happened in this crazy dream of yours?"

"The usual, I was on the David Letterman show."

"I read somewhere that he wants to have a baby."

"Really?" I didn't say anything for a long time while I lay on the couch and fantasized about having David Letterman's baby.

Mrs. Johnson said, "What?" from out of nowhere.

I hadn't said anything. "I think I am a very angry person," I told her, speaking very loudly so she could hear me. I had done some of my voice exercises from acting class before my appointment. I pictured Mrs. Johnson in the last row of a dark theater.

"Very good. Are you angry at me?"

"No. I'm angry at my father."

"So why don't you call him and tell him that?"

"I can't."

"Well my dear, you certainly have a lot of problems. You know we can't wallow in a twenty-five-dollar fee for the rest of our lives. For one thing we have to get you out and working again. I'll have to raise my fee to fifty dollars a week. How does that make you feel?"

"I can't afford it." I was using tissue after tissue. I hated her so much.

"Then you can come every other week."

"Okay," I sobbed.

"No, I've changed my mind. With your problems, your violent temper and your issues about money, your delusional dreams and your patterns of quitting everything you start, I think you really have to come every week for fifty dollars without fail."

I was crying so hard I couldn't even talk.

"Your time is up. You would have had ten minutes longer but you were late. See you next week. At what time?"

"Five."

"Right."

I went into the handicapped bathroom and cried for ten minutes. Mrs. Johnson thought I should call my father and tell him that I was angry at him. I started to walk down Fifth Avenue in the rain, saying Goodbye to Mrs. Johnson for the last time.

24

BEFORE THE DIVORCE, I used to wake up in the morning and wonder if my mother had committed suicide. I would open the bathroom door cautiously to see if she was in a pool of bloody water, or hanging from one of her long silk scarves. I would look out my window at the sidewalk sixteen flights below. I would look in the oven.

She would lie in bed taking headache medication or she would come into my room and say, "Don't go to school today, don't go to that awful school. Let's go to Bloomingdale's, two girls together," and we would buy our winter wardrobes and eat at Chock Full O'Nuts.

It was strange to be living with my mother again. I woke up in my old captain's bed and listened to her talking on the phone. It was Saturday, the first day of spring break, and I had wanted to sleep late. Midterms were over. I had done well in everything except Tech—we were learning costume design and I accidentally sewed the costume I was making onto my skirt—and I was tired.

I had a 10 A.M. breakfast date. It was a blind date from the *New York* magazine personals. It was the only personal ad I had ever answered. It read: PRINCE CHARMING, SWM 40, MILLIONAIRE, SEEKS SPECIAL CINDERELLA FOR FUN, ROMANCE, AND EVENTUALLY A ROYAL FAMILY. PHOTO A MUST.

I had sent a postcard of the royal family that I had gotten in London, with a cut-out picture of my head pasted over Princess Di's. He called and we set up a date.

I got all ready to go.

"Here's some nice tea," my mother said. "Where's your date?" I was wearing my purple Laura Ashley dress and cowboy boots.

"He's a few minutes late."

"Maybe he stood you up." My mother was always sure I was being stood up. "Where did you meet this man?"

"I met him at school."

"How old is he?"

"He's not a student, he was just walking around campus." The buzzer rang. "He's here," I said.

I told the doorman to have him wait in the lobby and I went down to meet him. I stopped and stared at him. It was Boyd. The same man who was my first trick with Holly.

"I guess you're surprised to see me," he said.

"On the phone you said your name was Barry, which is it, Boyd or Barry?"

"I'm pleased you remembered my name. I didn't recognize

you at first from the picture you sent, but I knew it had to be you because of the name Bennington.''

"In your ad you said you were single.''

"Well times are getting tough now. I can't spend as much money on call girls. Maybe once a week, not every day anymore. Last night I went home and I said to my wife, 'Tell the cook to make pasta for dinner. We don't have to have filet mignon or lobster every single night. Let's do vegetarian, let's have pasta and sauce,' and she said, 'That sounds like fun,' and the kids liked it too. So we're even changing our eating habits for this recession.''

"Wow, you had pasta for dinner.''

"I know, it's so interesting finding out about each other.''

"You were supposed to take me out to brunch,'' I said. This whole time we were just standing on the street outside my building, with my mother leaning out the window and waving at us.

"Who's that, your crazy roommate?'' he asked.

"Yeah.''

"Well, I'm up for anything except pasta. I had that for dinner last night. But of course you already know that. What's good around here?''

"We could go to Tavern on the Green or Cafe Des Artistes,'' I said.

"That place on the corner looks nice. Let's try that place.''

I followed him into the Greek diner and sat down in a booth away from the window. The manager made us move to a tiny booth for two.

"You know I only got two responses to my ad in *New York* magazine. I was shocked,'' he said.

I shuddered. I felt a hive break out on my stomach.

"Is that your only dress?'' I was wearing the same Laura Ashley dress I had worn on my first day as a prostitute.

"Well if I had known it was you, I would have worn my hair in braids.''

"You have a fantastic memory," Boyd said. "Were you shocked when you found out?"

"Found out what?"

"You didn't hear?"

"I don't know what you're talking about."

"About Holly."

"What about Holly? I haven't had anything to do with her since my birthday, January twenty-third." It was already the middle of March but I thought Boyd might still give me a cash present.

"Didn't you see it on the news?"

"What?"

"Holly killed herself. She put a gun in her mouth and blew her head all over the Chelsea Hotel. They showed a picture of her. I knew she was a blonde. I always wanted to meet her but I never did. She's been sending me girls for thirteen years."

"When did this happen?"

"A month ago. End of January. B.J. called me. He burned all the books and left the Chelsea. They had a big estate in Connecticut and he went up there."

I couldn't say anything. I just sat there and listened to Boyd. I felt like he was my best friend and we had been through so much together.

"I know it's unbelievable. She had sent me a new girl that morning. Bennington, I was thinking, I'm sort of interested in settling down. Now that Holly's gone things are different. I can't get the quality girls. I could set you up. The apartment on Waverly Place could be yours and I could give you money. I could buy you clothes. Here's a hundred dollars to start you off. Buy yourself an outfit." He put five twenty-dollar bills on the table.

"What kind of outfit do you think I could buy with a hundred dollars?" I asked. "An outfit would cost ten times that."

"How much could an outfit cost? It's a start." He leaned over the table and tried to kiss me.

"I don't kiss on the first date. Goodbye Boyd, or Barry, or whatever your name is." I got up and left the diner.

My father always said that my actions had consequences. One night could change my life, one action, one deed. I should think before I did something, think it all the way through to the end. But my father was wrong once again. I would not be punished. It was like I had never done it.

Holly was dead. If I ever became a famous actress Holly would not appear on *Geraldo* and talk about me. The books were burned. The men would never talk. Boyd would never speak publicly about it. Things *could* get undone. It was over and done with.

I stood on the corner and watched a mailman open a mailbox and stuff letters into his sack. Two letters blew away and he ran after them down the block and then gave up. When you mail something to someone you don't expect it to just blow away. Boyd walked out of the diner, got into his silver Jaguar, and drove off. My only mistake was not taking the hundred dollars from him.

25

I WAS QUICKLY using up the money I had saved working for Holly, pretending to be a normal college student and hanging around with Perry Shepherd. We did scenes together in Washington Square Park and sold her one-of-a-kind lamps and shades at the Twenty-sixth Street flea market. I'd bought a dozen of them and would turn them all on when I got home to my room in my mother's apartment. Only one caused a small fire.

Perry and I ate grilled cheese sandwiches and chocolate egg creams because she was a vegetarian, ushered in theaters so we could see the plays for free, and constantly bought each other presents. We were going to one day: take her lamps to Barneys, get an agent, buy a Chanel suit and take turns wearing it, find great men to marry and have kids with.

I was so busy going to school and trying to like it, and following Perry Shepherd around like a lost sheep, that I forgot all about working. For a while. Then Perry got a part in a show on Martha's Vineyard, and NYU started to seem extremely dull.

PART 2

BLANCHE'S

26

THERE IS NOTHING more humiliating than throwing up in New York. You don't make friends throwing up in a garbage can. I wiped my face with the palm of my hand. I was shaking and my legs were weak, but I started to walk quickly, only stopping to look at some handmade jewelry on the street. I could be on my deathbed and muster up the strength to buy something on the street.

I found the brownstone on Twenty-eighth Street and walked up the steps. I looked up into a camera. Before I could knock on the door, a woman opened it. She was wearing Chanel earrings as big as my fist. "My name is Bobbi," she said.

"Hi, I'm Benny."

"Bennington, I know. You should have called from the corner. Everyone has to call from the corner."

"I'm sorry, I didn't know." The first floor of the brownstone was small. Another woman sat behind a desk looking at me. There were two small chairs, a mirror, and a closed door.

"You cannot come in here scraping the boots all over the floor," the woman at the desk said in a thick French accent.

"I'm sorry." I took my boots off and held them.

"That is okay. You must forgive my moods, I am pregnant. My name is Monique."

"Come on, Bennington." I followed Bobbi up two flights

of stairs into a very large bedroom with pale yellow walls and a high white ceiling. I sat down next to her on a big bed with just a sheet on it. "So you said on the phone you were experienced."

"I've never worked in a place. I did Escort."

"Who did you work for?"

"Holly."

"In the Chelsea?"

"Yes."

"Oh." Bobbi was silent.

"It was very good."

"I've heard." She sounded genuinely impressed.

"Is this your place?"

"No, it's Blanche's. She's not here because she just had a baby. Everyone gets pregnant at the same time here."

"How did you avoid it?" I said.

"I wouldn't let anything stand in the way of wearing this fabulous suit. I have to run downstairs for a sec, so you just get comfortable and I'll be right back."

I sat on the bed and listened to the sound of her Chanel heels clicking around outside the door. There was a little mini-kitchen in the corridor between the two rooms. I heard a motor like a blender or a vacuum cleaner. I noticed a large vibrator on the bedside table. She walked back into the room.

"Didn't you hear me tell you to get comfortable?"

"Yes, thank you, I am."

"No, I mean get completely undressed. I have to check you for needle marks. Everything off." She smiled and left again. I took off my clothes and looked in the standing mirror. It was old familiar me in this strange room, standing naked waiting to be checked for needle marks.

Bobbi came in holding a drink. "Banana shake. We have a blender in case you want to go on a liquid diet." She took my hands and looked at my arms and the backs of my legs. She asked me to lift my hair off my neck. "Okay," she said, "you're hired. The day shift is ten to five, and the night shift is five to twelve. I only have three night shifts available, is that good?"

"Okay."

"We charge one hundred and thirty-five dollars for the hour and you get sixty-five dollars. The house gets sixty-five and the phone girl gets five. You can also tip the phone girl five dollars per session. Most girls do. Actually, it's required. You can get dressed now."

I put on my tights, my bra, and my sweater-dress and clutched my boots in my arms. On the stairway we passed a man.

"*Who* is this?" he asked.

"John, this is the new girl." Bobbi put her hand on his back and turned to me. "This is one of Blanche's oldest and dearest and, may I add, cutest clients."

"Hi, I can see that," I said. He was a fat Irish-looking man with a little bit of white hair.

"My, my, my, did you check her ID? She looks like jailbait. What's your little name?"

"It's Daphne," I said.

"Daphne, Daphne, Daphne, can I see you right now?"

"I'm not working yet," I said.

"Bobbi, please let me see this little Miss Daphne right now."

"I don't know, John, she just came in for an interview and there are a lot of clients who want to see her."

"Please, Bobbi, I want to be little Daphne here's first so she will always remember me."

"The thing is, John, she's a little nervous. She came here because she needs the money for college, but the truth is she's a virgin."

"I'll give her four hundred dollars." John had become very businesslike.

"Well, it's really up to her. Ben—a—Daphne, would you like to see John now? It's up to you."

"Well I don't know," I said.

"I'll be real gentle, sweetheart."

"Okay."

"Isn't she a doll, John? You'll be in room number four where we just were, and I'll buzz you in an hour. John, go on up and make yourself comfortable. Daphne will be right there."

"All right, Bobbi." He heaved himself up the flight of stairs.

"That was good," Bobbi said. "Here." She handed me two condoms. "After the session you give Monique sixty-five dollars and her tip. You get to keep the rest of the four hundred. For the next few weeks tell all your tricks it's your first day. If they'll believe it from anyone, they'll believe it from you. I'll see you back here tomorrow night. Wear something sexy. Garter belts and stockings required, stockings, not thigh-highs."

I went into room number 4 and John was lying on the bed. "I've never done this before," I said.

"I know, sweetheart."

I took off my tights, my bra, and my sweater-dress.

"Don't you wear panties?"

"No."

"Sit on Daddy's lap."

I sat on his lap. We were on the edge of the bed facing the mirror. His clothing lay in a pile. There were four hundred-dollar bills on the bedside table. *I am who I always wanted to be*, I thought. I lay on my back and added four hundred minus sixty-five plus five. Seventy plus three hundred and thirty. Sixty-five plus sixty-five plus five. One hundred and thirty-five minus sixty-five plus five. John was on top of me. I was hoping this wouldn't take an hour because I had a class and I needed twenty minutes to get to NYU.

"Does it hurt, does it hurt?" John asked.

"Oh yes," I said. Sun was streaming in between the slats of the vertical blinds. The blinds were like the car-wash skirt I saw on a TV morning show, the one thing to get for spring. It was a waistband with sheer strips of material swishing around your leggings. Sixty-five plus sixty-five, sixty plus sixty is one hundred and twenty, five plus five is ten, equals one hundred and thirty, plus five is one thirty-five. My legs were getting crushed under him. All I could feel was his weight, and then something really disgusting started to happen.

Little drops of his sweat were falling on me. On my face and neck. His sweat dripped on my breasts. It was horrible. His huge stomach was slick with sweat. His forehead was a watering can. He came and collapsed on top of me. When he finally rolled off me, I got right into the shower.

I used a handful of Softsoap. I rinsed off quickly, there were two doors to the bathroom and I had only locked one of them. I didn't want anyone walking in on me in the shower. There was no towel so I dried off with the bathmat. I drank a sip of water from a Dixie cup and went back into the room.

"Was there any blood?" he asked.

"Oh yes, a lot," I said.

"That's okay honey, you're a woman now."

"Oh thank you," I said.

"I'm going to come back and see you. Do you do two-girl sessions?"

"I think so."

He handed me the four hundred dollars from the table. I got dressed quickly and we went down the stairs. I escorted him to the door. I'd been told to give money to Monique, but there was a different girl at the desk. "My name is Josie," she said. "You're the new girl?" She was very aggressive with a harsh voice.

"Yes. I'm Bennington. Daphne."

"Okay, sign in here next to your name."

I handed her one of the hundred-dollar bills and she gave me change. "Where's Monique?" I asked.

"She quit."

"Why?"

"She's afraid of getting arrested, especially when she's so pregnant. If the house gets busted, they'll let you girls go, or you might spend one or two nights, but being a phone girl is a felony. It's considered pimping. If one of you dumb girls makes a mistake with a cop, I take the heat. Right, Angelica?" She said "Angelica" very loudly.

A Spanish-looking girl came out of the small living room off the reception area. I could see two couches and a few other girls. Angelica had large breasts and wore a tiny Spandex tube dress. I thought she was very beautiful and then very ugly.

"What you want?"

"Angelica caused us plenty of problems, didn't you, Angelica?" Josie said.

"Shut up."

"Anyway Daphne, you look reasonably intelligent, so I look forward to seeing you tomorrow at five o'clock."

I just made it to my class on time. I slipped into the lecture hall with 799 other hopeful freshman acting majors, unnoticed.

27

THE NEXT NIGHT I went to the brownstone and was buzzed in. Josie was sitting at the desk. Her hair was the same color as the carrot juice she was drinking. She had an unfortunate Pippi Longstocking appearance. Which is why she worked on the phone, I figured. "You're late," she said.

"It's not even five yet."

"The shift starts at five o'clock, which means you have to be here at four-thirty."

"I'm sorry, I didn't know."

"Go upstairs to room three and change."

Room 3 was across from room 4. There were two girls in it. One was sitting on the big bed putting on eye shadow. She had an enormous tray of colors. "It's my art," she said.

"Ooooh do me, Jackie," the other girl said.

"You can do yourself, you just stripe."

"Hi," I said. "My name is Daphne."

"That sounds fake, what's your real name?" the other girl asked.

"Bennington."

"Better stick with Daphne. My name is Candace and this is Jackie. Is this your first time?"

"I did Escort," I said toughly.

"For who?"

"Holly."

"I worked for C'est Magnifique."

I clutched my bookbag to my stomach. I had been up all night terrified of meeting the other girls. I had made a secret place in my purse for my money. I thought it would be like a women's prison.

"You're going to like it here," Jackie said.

"Thank you. Candace, I like your outfit," I said. I thought it was a good idea to be complimentary in a situation like this. Candace was wearing black velvet leggings and a black velvet bustier. I was thinner than she was.

"Well, we're really not supposed to wear pants but Blanche says I'm allowed to, because I have the legs. Hey, why are you staring at my pit?"

"I'm not."

"What, do I need a shave?"

"No, I wasn't staring." I was so embarrassed, I was trying not to stare at anything else. I hate when people say pit instead of underarm. I put on my red cocktail dress. I didn't feel like brushing my hair.

"Don't you wear any makeup?" Jackie asked.

"No."

"You're lucky."

"That's a great dress. It hides your thighs," Candace said.

"Thank you."

"C'mon."

We went downstairs to the little living room. Josie stopped me. "Daphne, that dress is ridiculous."

"Why?"

"The clients like to see what they're getting. Bring something else next time."

There were a total of six of us in the living room, facing each other on two little couches. There was a Chinese screen blocking a washer and dryer, a little table with bottles of liquor, and a mini-refrigerator. All the women were very different. Angelica was there, sitting next to a short girl with a heart-shaped face named Maryanne, and a girl with punk fuchsia hair who wore a weird ruffle around her stomach.

"Hi, I'm Heatherly, I'm seven months."

"Hi, this is my first day."

"We're deciding what to name him." She was writing on a pad. Her legs were crossed primly and she looked like a secretary.

"Name who?"

"My baby."

"You're pregnant?"

"Yes, seven months."

"Oh my God, you're thinner than I am."

"I know. The guys can't even tell. What's your name?"

"Daphne."

"*Love* it!"

Jackie started playing with my hair.

"We can't decide what to name him. It's down to Dylan, for Bob Dylan, Bruce, for Bruce Springsteen, or Tom, for Tom Waites."

"My brother's name is Dylan," I said. I immediately regretted it. I wasn't going to say anything personal about myself.

"You have a brother?" Maryanne whispered.

"Actually we ruled out the name Bruce because we found out that it was Pyramid Dick's real name, and besides it's kind of faggy," Candace said.

"I can only hope my baby turns out to be a fag," Heatherly said. "The only men I have any respect for are fags."

"Who's Pyramid Dick?" I asked.

"One of the tricks here. His dick is gruesome. You can't keep a rubber on him. The base of his dick is very wide, but the head is pointy like a triangle. The rubber just rolls off and it really hurts when he fucks you. Jackie likes him."

"I do not."

"You do, too. Jackie likes everybody," Candace said. "But

we're all allowed a couple of guys we refuse to see. They put your name on his Rolodex card next to his code and they have a Won't See list. Almost everyone won't see P.D. I also refuse to see Indian guys. You smell like curry for a week."

"I don't want to see any Hasidic Jews," I said.

"Oh, we have a lot of them. They're really gross. It's against their religion to bathe. Or tip."

"You look so familiar to me," Maryanne whispered. "Do I look familiar to you?"

"No."

Josie opened the door to the living room and stuck her head in. "We have a Will Choose coming in two minutes." The girls all put their high heels on.

"What do we do?" I asked.

"A Will Choose means he doesn't have an appointment with any particular girl," Heatherly said. "We just sit here and he comes in and gawks at us and chooses. And then the lucky girl goes upstairs with him for a mere sixty-five dollars, and that's it."

A man walked into the room and sat on a canvas director's chair. He looked us over very carefully. I looked him over. He had long brown hair and dark skin. He was good-looking, thin and young. Young guys make me too nervous. He said his name was Michael. Jackie introduced us. "I'm Jackie, and this is Angelica, Candace, Maryanne, Heatherly, and Daphne. Can I get you a drink?"

"You have beer?"

"No, just *cock*tails."

"I'll have a crotch and soda," Michael said. He laughed and looked at me. Jerk, I thought.

Jackie stood up and walked behind the screen, exaggerating her hip movements. Her legs looked like tree trunks. Josie stuck her head in again. "Who's it going to be, Michael?"

"The flamenco dancer."

"Oh, you must mean Daphne. I'm sorry about her outfit.

Michael, tell me the first initial of your last name and your birthday . . . Okay, so your VIP code is Michael R. 10/13.''

"I want to put this on my credit card."

"Okay, no problem. Daphne, you're in room number two at the top of the stairs."

I started up the stairs and he followed me. He put his hand under my dress. The room was big and airy like the other rooms. The walls were painted light blue. The sheet on the bed had fat roses and stripes. "Make yourself comfortable," I said, and left the room. I went downstairs to the living room.

"Pour yourself a diet Coke, Daph," Jackie said. "Good luck." They were looking up at me. I opened the mini-fridge and pulled out a green plastic bowl of melted ice. I poured flat diet Coke into a Dixie cup, took a sip, and put it on a little table. Heatherly put her cigarette out in it. "Sorry, if I didn't put it out right then, I would have kept going all night."

"Daphne, what the hell are you doing? Get your ass up to room two NOW!" Josie screamed.

I stepped over everyone's high heels and went back to the room. Michael was standing in the middle of the room naked. His body was thin and hard. He had a huge hard dick sticking straight out. He looked like a hatrack. I couldn't think of anything to say. I was nervous. My hands were ice cold. I could feel a white hive on my breast. I unzipped my dress and let it fall to my feet. I was wearing a black garter belt, black stockings, and red panties.

"Do a flamenco dance," Michael said.

"Let's dance together lying down," I said. I couldn't believe myself.

"How does it feel to be a hooker?" he asked.

"I love it, it's like a fantasy."

"Bullshit. It must feel terrible to be a whore." He sounded nasty. He looked into my eyes and then at my mouth. I played with the religious medallion around his neck. "Don't touch that, my mother gave it to me. My mother was a hooker. She did men in our house and I watched. She did ten men in a night sometimes. That's why I understand you. I understand whores. I want to marry you and save you."

"That sounds too good to be true," I said.

I felt really sorry for this guy. He looked sort of sad now, a little scared. "I don't want to fuck you," he said.

"Okay," I said. I was very relieved. I touched his long hair.

"I want to make love with you."

"Oh," I said. He got on top of me and fucked me hard for forty-five minutes. I couldn't find a focal point, I couldn't catch my breath, I couldn't keep the numbers straight in my head. Sixty-five plus sixty-five is one hundred and thirty, minus five, equals one twenty-five. Sixty-five plus sixty-five. Sixty-five plus sixty-five. Sixty-five plus sixty-five.

"You're beautiful like my mother."

I felt a sharp pain in my stomach and I froze while he finished. He kissed my forehead. "You were wonderful. Do I have time for a quick shower?"

"Sure." I handed him a towel. I wrapped the rubber in a stack of tissues and threw it in the wastebasket. I put a new sheet on the bed, violets with green stems and a small bloodstain in the corner. I wrapped the used sheet and his wet towel in a ball and we walked down the stairs.

"Daphne, put the sheets in the washing machine," Josie said.

When I came back to the reception area, Michael was gone.

"Okay, now you give me sixty-five dollars and sign next to your name," Josie told me when I came back down.

"He paid on credit card."

"What!" Her voice was shrill and loud.

"He told you he was paying on a credit card."

"He never said that. I would have taken the card before he went upstairs."

"He didn't pay me. He said he was paying on credit."

"Daphne, it is your responsibility to get the money up front. You are responsible for giving the house sixty-five dollars."

"I don't have it."

"You will by the end of the night. I have appointments booked for you."

I was so angry, I almost started to cry. "He was such an asshole." I was as red as my dress.

"Go upstairs and pull yourself together."

I went into room number 4 and lay on the bed. Angelica came into the room and lay down next to me.

"Don't worry, it happens to everybody. Once," she said.

"I'm so angry."

"Josie is a bitch."

"It was her mistake."

"Josie is a cunt."

"It was such a hard session, I worked so hard."

"She's a cunt with herpes."

Jackie walked into the room. "Don't feel bad, Daph, it happens to everyone once. C'mon, we'll all go out for a drink later."

"Really?"

"I can't go because my son is at home and he'll worry about me," Angelica said.

"The rest of us will go."

The night went by quickly. I saw an obese man who had a fantasy that I was a TV anchorwoman and he was performing oral sex on me behind the desk while I delivered the national news. I had to read copy that he had handwritten about a woman who was raped by five black men. His penis was the size of a grape, buried in the folds of his stomach and thighs.

I saw an Irish man who took my temperature with a baby rectal thermometer for an extra hundred. I had a slight fever.

I saw a Hasidic Jew named Sammy who picked me even though I scowled at him in the living room.

I saw Pyramid Dick, and clutched the rim of the condom so it felt like I was punching myself while he fucked me.

At the end of the night I had made four hundred dollars and I gave Josie sixty-five for the first guy. I went to Cafe Society with Jackie, Candace, Heatherly, and Maryanne, and drank frozen margaritas and danced. There was a flamenco band with musicians whose ruffled sleeves were bigger than their instruments. Candace showed me her tattoo in the ladies' room. Heatherly invited me to her baby shower. I had never loved a group of friends so much.

28

OF ALL THE girls I met at Blanche's, I liked Angelica best. She was forty, with a thirteen-year-old son and a seventeen-year-old boyfriend who was still in high school. She was from Honduras. She had short brown hair and very bad teeth which usually had lipstick on them. First her lips would purse and her eyes would narrow into slits, and I would think, If I were a man I would choose Angelica, and then her mouth would widen into a smile and her teeth would show, and I would think, If I were a man I'd choose Libby or Heddy.

Libby and Heddy looked alike and told the clients they were twins. They did a lot of two-girl sessions and they were very hard to compete with. They had long blond hair and flat-chested Swedish bodies with very large nipples. "My name is Libby, as in women's lib, in which I very much believe. And this is Heddy, as in she gives excellent head. Heddy used to be a waitress in the old Playboy Club."

"Not a waitress, a hostess," Heddy said. "I used the name Twinky. That way I could say, 'Hi, I'm your hostess, Twinky.' "

"What was the color of your bunny costume?" I asked.

"I don't know, blue. We didn't get to choose, they were assigned."

I got my period in the Playboy Club in New Jersey when I was twelve. My grandfather was a member and took me and my brother there to play in the pool. Every time I finished my pink lemonade it was immediately refilled by a beautiful bunny. Then one came over to me and asked me to go to the ladies' room with her. I followed her, imagining myself in the full costume, trying to choose what color I would wear.

"You have your period," she said. "Is this your first time?"

My bikini bottom was soaked with blood. She rinsed it out in the sink and I waited, wrapped in a towel, for her to return with a sanitary pad and a pair of ears for me to wear. "You're a woman now," she said.

I spent a lot of evenings in the living room of Blanche's brownstone with five other girls waiting to get picked. We talked about how smart we were to have a job where we made so much money. How we had the time and the money to do the things we wanted, unlike our friends who weren't in the business. How we were free and liberated and adventurous and we didn't hate men.

Or we would talk about how much we hated men. How what we were doing was perpetuating the problem of men seeing women as sex objects and how sore we were at the end of the night.

No matter how much we talked, when a man walked into the room we would arch our backs and cross our legs at the thigh and happily introduce ourselves. It always came down to this: We were making two or three hundred dollars a night and if we didn't do it, somebody else would.

A Will Choose came into the living room and didn't want any of us. He walked out.

"We'll have six different girls tomorrow," I heard Josie say as he walked out the door.

"You can go to Donna's Dungeon and get paid for beating the guys," Libby said.

"That sounds good to me," Heatherly said.

"I think those dominatrixes are the most submissive of all," I said.

"How's that?"

"They do exactly what the guy wants, they play out his fantasy. I don't. I don't do anything. I think you have to be very submissive to piss and shit on a man just because he wants you to. If he didn't want you to, it would be different."

"You are obsessed with women's lib," Heddy said. "Are you a feminist or an actress?"

"I'm an actor."

"You shouldn't wear that necklace here," Heatherly said. "We could get robbed. There's a lot of lunatics who like to rob whorehouses at the end of the night 'cause they know we're loaded and we won't call the police."

I didn't say anything for a long time. It was my grandmother's diamond lavaliere that I never took off. I felt my grandmother in the room with me, hovering over me. I felt her watching me working, sleeping with man after man, sitting on the toilet after, wearing her necklace and her ring. "It's fake," I finally whispered. I walked upstairs and hid it in an old shoe in the closet. I went back down to the living room and Josie opened the door.

"It smells like an ashtray in here." She sprayed half a can of lilac air-freshener into the room. "There's a client coming.

I don't want another walk-out. You girls look terrible. You look like a flock of crows, you look like a nest of beetles, you're going to scare the client. Why did you all decide to wear black today? You girls do not understand this business."

29

THE BUZZER RANG. We put our high heels on.

If I were a man I would come to these places all the time. I would spend a long time in the living room choosing. I would want a girl who was thin, with very big tits. I would say tits or melons or headlights. I would pick two girls, one with big tits and one with small tits, just to see how the two of them got along. I would want them to get into different poses, bend over and look at me between their legs, arch their backs, stick their asses in the air. I would leave a big tip.

The client walked into the room and sat in the director's chair.

"What's your name?" Heddy asked.

"Uh, Joey."

"Hi, Joey, I'm Heddy, and this is my twin sister Libby, and that's Daphne, Angelica, and Heatherly."

"I thought there was supposed to be a black girl," Joey said.

"She's busy."

"How long have you girls been working here?"

"Oh, we don't work here," Heddy said. "We're just hanging out together. Hey, I really like your mustache." She said mustache to point out to the rest of us that he was a cop. "Would you like a drink?" Cops couldn't drink on duty.

"No thanks. You girls have condoms, right? Because I didn't bring anything."

"Why would we need condoms?" Heddy asked, looking right at him.

I sat frozen, wedged in between Angelica and Heatherly, like three ice cubes stuck together.

"I'd like to go with you." He was pointing at me. I knew he would choose me because I looked the most scared and naive. I stood up. There was a certain pride in being picked, even if it was by a cop. Heddy winked and put her wrists together, like she was wearing hand cuffs. The cop followed me up the stairs to room number 1.

"Make yourself comfortable," I said.

"How much is it?"

"How much is what?"

"The sex."

"Sex, I don't know what you're talking about, sex. Make yourself comfortable." I walked out of the room and shut the door. Josie signaled to me and I went down the stairs. "If you get me busted, I'll kill you," she said. "No mistakes." I poured myself a diet Coke and walked back upstairs and into the room. The cop was standing behind the bed. He was naked. A cop isn't supposed to get undressed, but this one was. He had a small waist and muscular thighs.

"What kind of condoms do you use?" he asked.

"Condoms?" I asked blankly. I walked around the bed and saw that he was wearing socks. Long black socks. "I think we have a terrible misunderstanding," I said. "I'm sure you don't mean to insult me, but I have to say, I have never been more humiliated in my life. I hope you don't mean to imply, sir, that I would in any way sell any kind of intimacy for any kind of money. My father, may he rest in peace, was a police officer, one of New York's finest men in blue, and I'm sure he's turning over in his grave as we speak. I'm sure you're just trying to be amorous, but that is, of course, out of the question, and I think you owe me an apology. I'm sure this is just an embarrassing misunderstanding and we can still be friends." For some reason I had started to talk in a Southern accent by the end of the speech.

He picked up his pants and reached into his pocket. I stared at him and he stared back. "This is my first day hanging out here," I said.

"This place is too weird, I'm leaving," the cop said.

"I understand, sir. I'm sorry." He got dressed and stormed out, saying, "Nice job, girls," as he passed the living room.

I walked down the stairs, swinging my hips. "You were brilliant," Heddy said. "We heard the whole thing. Josie had the intercom on and she taped the whole conversation."

"You're a pervert, Josie," I said. "Do you listen to all the sessions?"

"I just love you, Daphne," Josie said. "Another cop came in here once and asked Angelica what kind of condoms she used and she said Ramses unlubricated and we both went to jail for two nights."

"Shut up," Angelica said.

"But the truth is, if they want to bust you, they bust you. No matter what you say or do."

"This is some job," I said.

"You know any job has its dangers," Heddy said. "A nurse can get AIDS, or a cabdriver can get shot in the back of the head, or a store can get robbed. Once a Playboy bunny had to go to the hospital because her circulation got cut off."

Heddy listed every job she could think of and its dangers.

"Anyway, working girls are the most careful. I know hundreds of hookers and they've never gotten a disease or AIDS. We're the smartest and the safest."

"A stewardess can crash," I said.

"That's what I'm saying. Flight attendant: one of the most dangerous jobs of all."

I was still shaking but I put my high heels on because a client was coming in. He sat in the director's chair and carefully looked at each of us.

"Hi, my name is Daphne," I said confidently.

"I want you two." He chose Libby and Heddy, and the rest of us kicked off our shoes and sank into the couch. I knew that different guys liked different types, it was nothing personal, but I felt rejected and fat.

"If I was a man, I would pick you," Angelica said.

"Thank you. Would you tip?"

"Shut up." She covered me with a blanket. I closed my eyes and listened to Angelica tell Heatherly how much she liked to do it with her boyfriend when she had her period, and, "Ooooh, didn't everybody?"

As I was leaving, Heatherly said, "Don't forget your necklace," and I ran upstairs to get it.

I carried these women around with me in my head. They floated around with the dollar signs behind my eyes. We went together up and down the stairs and changed places on the beds and loveseats. What a club, I thought. What a crazy tea party.

30

SOMEWHERE IN THE East Village I sat on a fire hydrant that had been painted metallic silver. I stared at a flyer that was glued to a lamppost. On it was a drawing of a Victorian girl, with judgmental eyes, making a moue with red lips. Above her was written, LIPS THAT TOUCH LIQUOR WILL NEVER TOUCH MINE. I had to laugh. She looked exactly like me.

For some reason I was comfortable on the fire hydrant, perfectly comfortable, I could almost have fallen asleep. Dogs walked by and looked at me. I felt like a queen on my silver throne. I threw up in a matching silver garbage can. I always pray when I am throwing up, like a reflex action. I whispered the words *thank you*.

A bum wearing the zip-out lining of a Burberry raincoat told me not to worry about throwing up in the garbage can, he already had what he needed. He was carrying clear plastic garbage bags filled with soda cans.

I looked in my pockets for a tissue or a napkin. I wiped my mouth on my sleeve. My stomach felt a little better but my body was shaking, my eyes were tearing, and I was light-headed. "Can you give me some money to buy some con-doms with?" the bum asked me. I pulled the beaded purse out of my bookbag and handed him a strip of condoms wrapped in shiny foil. It looked like the strips of lollipops my father used to let me buy in Provincetown when we would go square dancing on the pier. "You made my day, you made my day," the bum said. "Now I'm not gonna throw my cigarette in your bag."

I started to walk uptown looking for a street sign. I hit Third Street and turned to walk west. I twisted my usual ankle. I thought maybe I could find a dark cafe and get a mint tea and sit for a while. I could think of someone to call on a pay phone, make a plan. I noticed a church in the middle of the block, squeezed in between crumbling tenements. The stained glass windows stood out from the surrounding vertical blinds, For Rent signs, and plastic flamingos displayed in the other East Village windows.

I went up the stairs and into the low-ceilinged church. I walked down the aisle and sat on a pew in the front row. Even in church I like to be in the front row. I put my bookbag on the floor at my feet. I looked through the reading material in front of me and took off my jacket which had been buttoned wrong. I cried for just a few minutes. I wiped my face on a pamphlet about St. Anthony.

What's wrong with you? I asked myself. You are a happy person. You are an up-beat sort of person. Men smile at you on the subway, women ask you what shampoo you use. Cheer up for Christ's sake, I told myself, relax, you're fine, be happy, Girl. When I talk to myself I call myself Girl.

"Hello," a young priest said to me. "Do I know you?"

"I don't think so." I looked at him warily, thinking he might be a client.

"You look so familiar to me. Maybe I've seen you at the Veselka."

"Maybe." I did go to the Veselka for cabbage soup once in a while.

"I love the matzoh ball soup, when they have it," he said. He was staring at me. He must have been able to tell I was Jewish. "I have to close up in a little while, but take a few more minutes."

"Thank you," I said.

I picked up my bookbag and went to the altar to look for a place to leave a tip. An image of myself flashed before me. Was there someone who looked like me sitting at the end of the pew? With my bad vision I am always in a funhouse, seeing things. I can never believe my eyes. Sun streamed through the stained glass, turning my skin golden, blinding me. I moved closer to get a better look, and there, on the wall of the church, was a life-sized painting of me in my red cocktail dress covering Jesus' feet with my hair. Fishnet stockings were carefully stenciled on my legs, one black high-heel shoe lay under a geometrical pear tree. One finger, with my grandmother's heart-shaped ring on it, was held up to my lips, *my* lips, *my* smile, *my* eyes, *my* eyebrows. Above the tree, three angels were painted in blue and gold with my head between their winged shoulders. Each played an instrument and had a different one of my expressions—judgmental, worried, up-beat. My face was everywhere.

I yelled for the priest. "Sir, Father, are you there?"

"What is it?" he asked, appearing from a side door which was covered with a painting of me as one of the three wise men wearing a mustache, a beard, and a crown.

"Who did these paintings?" I asked.

"A wonderful artist named Perry Shepherd. I'm the first wise man. Father Thomas is Joseph in two places . . . So *that's* where I know you from," he said, laughing.

Before Perry moved to Martha's Vineyard she had told me she was sleeping in a church for a few weeks in exchange for light painting work. I had no idea she was painting us as saints over the double church doors. I am on one side, she's on the other, and Frieda Kahlo is in the middle with a monkey on her shoulder. We are eternal friends, holding hands and smiling.

On my way out I passed a girl with her head wrapped in a scarf coming in. It was Maryanne, from Blanche's. She seemed upset to see me and unsure about going in, as if the whole thing were now ruined. We walked by each other without saying anything. She always said I looked familiar to her.

31

I WENT FOR a massage on the Bowery. A hippie with huge hands rocked me back and forth. My eyes were closed and I started to fold in on myself, deeper and deeper, until I was like a dandelion stem swaying in the grass. Hairless, headless, outfitless, weightless.

"You retain a lot of water," my masseur said. He was strange-looking and I was beginning to wish I could have chosen from five or six masseurs. "You have to drink water to flush out the poisons."

"Mmmm." I meant to say yes, but just a little moan came out. I was embarrassed.

"Water retention is half your problem." I felt like an ear of corn in a tight-fitting dish of butter. "You should take nettle juice. It flushes you out, it eats the fat," he said. "You have very good feet."

"I took ten years of ballet when I was a kid."

"Really?" He sounded doubtful.

My mother and I were both very proud of our feet. "You and I have very beautiful feet," my mother would say. "Chinese women went through torture to achieve feet half as lovely as ours." My mother taught me to love myself. When

I came home from school she would say, "How many compliments did you get today, Bennington?" We kept track. If
I didn't get any, I made them up. Once, when I was seven,
a boy in our building was having an all-boy super-hero birthday party, so I wasn't invited. My mother called his mother,
furious that I was left out. I was told I could come as Wonder
Woman. My mother and I had no idea what Wonder
Woman looked like, so she put me in a black leotard and
covered me in silk Chanel scarves pinned on with diamond
and pearl brooches. We admired the costume in the mirror.
I was glad I was a girl. I felt sorry for boys.

At the end of the party I made the birthday boy show me
his penis. "Show it to me. You have to," I said. We crouched
under the desk in his bedroom and he pulled it out. I looked
hard at it. It looked like a little yellow piece of Silly Putty.
Not the furry cat's tail I expected. I said it was nice, but his
chin trembled in fear and humiliation. I felt guilty. I should
have just left his penis alone. It's his, I thought. After that he
didn't talk to me again.

"Turn over," my masseur said. I turned over onto my back
and felt my breasts and stomach flatten. I felt cold and the
sheet was still a little damp. He had a strong smell, not a good
smell. We were in his art studio and I looked around at the
paintings on the walls. All red squares on white canvases.

"I love your art," I lied. I was so glad I was an actress and
not an artist. At least there were no terrible performances
hanging all over the walls.

"I call them boxes of pain."

"Wow."

He started to massage my breasts. "You have such a great
body. Your body is the exact opposite of my wife's." Now I
was uncomfortable between the damp sheet and his fingers.
My skin became sensitive to the constant rubbing, kneading,
stroking. It felt raw. The tiny muscles around the top of my
breasts hurt. I stiffened.

"That's where you hold your anger, in your chest. When you feel that anger, put it in a box. Put the lid on it and let it go."

I sat up quickly, irritated, and wrapped myself in a damp Mickey Mouse towel. I didn't want to be my masseur's good time. *I* was paying *him*. I thanked him and told him what a great masseur he was and how relaxed I was.

I left and went to a health food store to buy nettle juice. The store smelled disgusting, like vitamins and health food. In fifth grade, I sat next to Chloe Seaver who took ten gray vitamins every day at lunch. She smelled like vitamins and she had very bad breath. I got her to read *The Sensuous Woman* by J with me behind our math books. I told her masturbating was when you stroked any part of your body for two minutes or longer.

"I don't think so," she said. "It's a certain part of your body."

"No, any part." I didn't know she had cancer then.

When I got the nettle juice I was so happy to think of it eating my fat, I walked down Spring Street smiling. I came across a long line of people, all my age.

"Is this an audition for something?" I asked a girl. She looked a little bit like me.

"No, we're waiting to meet Greg Brady from *The Brady Bunch* and get our books signed." She was holding a book called *Growing Up Brady*. The line was two blocks long outside the bookstore. My whole generation was on this line, the Brady Bunch-TV-Prostitute generation. I stood on line for a while feeling in, a part of something.

Usually I am threatened when people are like me, my age, young, female. I can't watch TV anymore because I keep thinking I see Tatiana, a girl in my acting class, in every commercial, soap opera, and sitcom, even though I know it isn't her. I even thought she was the model handing the Oscars to the presenters on the Academy Awards. Even if the person doesn't look anything like Tatiana I think it is her and a vise clamps my kidneys and I feel blinding anger and jealousy. It fills my chest and jaw and my stomach becomes swollen. If Tatiana ever became famous, I would swell up and burst. I would burn up and my ashes would scatter all over New York. I stood on the line thinking about how much I hated Tatiana, and wishing I were tall.

32

THAT NIGHT I lay in bed and watched David Letterman. I rubbed Clinique Dramatically Different Moisturizer onto my cheeks. I was agitated, itchy all over. I fell asleep with the TV on. I felt tugged, scratched, bitten, eaten, clawed. I slid my hand into my panties, brushed my hand over my pubic hair, and started scratching. I opened my eyes and pulled off the sheet, turned on the light, pushed down my panties, and examined myself. Almost immediately a hideous bug was on my finger. I knew it was a crab because it looked exactly like a miniature huge crab. I had crabs. I got a little hysterical and rocked back and forth on my bed. I knew I needed Quell, I remembered hearing Heddy talking about Quell, but it was two in the morning and all the drugstores were closed. I was going crazy thinking about those crabs drinking my pubic blood. I didn't know how I was going to make it to morning with all those huge crabs.

I put on my purple Laura Ashley dress, slipped out of the apartment, and took a cab downtown to St. Vincent's hospital emergency room. I wanted to go to a hospital in another neighborhood. I gave the black woman at the glassed-in reception desk a fake name and address.

"Why did you come to the emergency room?" she asked, clicking a computer.

"I have crabs," I said.

"What!" She looked up, "You came here for crabs? You need Quell."

"All the drugstores are closed."

"Oh my. Wait over there."

I remembered a girl I knew from ballet class named Quell—no, her name was Gwenn. She came back from camp with her hair cut off because of a bad case of lice. She couldn't wear a bun anymore and eventually dropped out of ballet.

I sat on an orange plastic chair. I heard someone screaming, "It hurts, oh it hurts." A sad man sat in an orange chair across from me. I was only wearing one contact lens. I felt very sorry for myself and I was going crazy itching. I decided, after thinking about it a long time, that I would go into the little chapel, but the door was locked. I pulled on the door. I used the opportunity for a little scratch while my back was to the sad man. I told myself to remember what feeling this miserable felt like so I could use it in my acting. I was trying not to scratch and the sad man was trying not to cry, until we both couldn't stand it anymore and just let loose. Finally someone said, "You can come in now, Miss Strasberg." I looked up to see a young guy in a white coat standing in front of me. He was just a kid.

"Are you my doctor?"

"I'm an R.N."

"What's that?"

"A registered nurse."

"Where's my doctor?"

"It says here you have crabs. I'm going to take care of you."

I started to cry. "I have a very bad case. I think I should see a doctor."

"We're very busy here. All you need is Quell. Follow me." He led me into a small room which was tiled from floor to ceiling. There was a drain in the middle of the floor, and a showerhead and knobs on one wall.

"Take off your clothes and put them in this bag," he said, handing me a white plastic garbage bag.

"You're going to examine me in here?"

"We're very busy tonight, Miss Strasberg."

He left the room and I took off my clothes and put them in the garbage bag. I was scratching my entire body. After about a second I heard a knock.

"Come in."

I was standing naked on the tile floor. I felt like I was about to get gassed. He got down on his knees in front of me, and shined a flashlight on my crotch. I looked down at the top of his curly head.

"Is it bad, nurse?"

"Call me Steve."

I didn't think so. Holding the flashlight in one hand, Nurse Steve started parting my pubic hair with the other, examining each individual hair for a long time. After a while I said, "This seems a little unusual."

He stood up and was now looking down at me condescendingly.

"You only had one crab."

"Is it still there?"

"No, I removed him."

"*Him?*"

"Here." He handed me a bottle of Quell. "Turn on the shower and wash everything. I mean everything. Leave the Quell on for five minutes before rinsing. Quell up everywhere, the hair on your arms, everything."

He left the room and I felt a little insulted. I was very

sensitive about the hair on my arms. I turned on the shower, making it very hot, and Quelled absolutely everything I could Quell. I stood under the water for an hour. I noticed a pile of white hotel-type towels in the corner of the little room and I wrapped one around my head like a turban and used eight more to dry off. There was a knock and Nurse Steve opened the door just wide enough to stick his arm through with a shopping bag. I noticed that he didn't have any hair on his arm. "You can't put your clothes back on, so here are some from the emergency relief room."

"I don't understand."

"People donate clothing, mostly for burn victims or people whose clothes get too bloody."

I looked in the bag. It was kind of exciting, like Christmas. I pulled out a pair of Sergio Valente jeans with red piping on the back pockets, a black turtleneck, and a pair of boy's penny loafers. The jeans were tight and I rolled up the cuffs above my ankles. Braless, the turtleneck looked sexy, and the shoes were a few sizes too big. It was that new dykey look. I liked it. I had been meaning to start wearing ties. I walked out of the shower room feeling fabulous, holding my white garbage bag of clothes.

"You'll have to throw those out," Nurse Steve said.

"I can't, it's my favorite dress."

He handed me six bottles of Quell. "Wash them in this, then," he said, "and use Quell for the next couple of days."

"Thank you, nurse."

"What do you do?"

I was surprised by the question. I was tempted to tell him the truth, that I was a hooker, because it seemed so appropriate with the crabs and everything, but I said, "I'm an actress." He looked doubtful.

I walked through the waiting room. The chapel door was open and the sad man was gone. I walked out on the street. It was six-thirty in the morning and someone whistled at me.

I wheeled around to give the person the finger and a dirty look and was embarrassed when it turned out to be Nurse Steve. I smiled at him and got a cab home.

I took one more shower, changed my sheets, and got into bed. I dreamt that it was my birthday and Nurse Steve forgot to give me a birthday present. I woke up that afternoon, furious at my father.

33

A JAPANESE GIRL named Yuki walked into the tiny living room at Blanche's and sat on the couch across from me. She had a long black ponytail. We were alone in the living room. There were six girls working and all four rooms were full.

She looked familiar but I couldn't place her. She was examining her leg and didn't say one word to me. I was sure I had seen her before.

When you live in New York long enough you get to know everybody in the whole city. There are days when I recognize everyone on the street. Sometimes I see people two or three times in one day in different parts of town, first sitting at the next table in a restaurant, then admiring the same pair of shoes in a store window, then later that night sitting at the next table in another restaurant.

"I'm in no mood to boink," Yuki finally said. When she spoke her face moved like rippling water, as if an invisible koi had suddenly splashed across it. I was surprised by her New York accent.

"Why don't you go home?" I said. She was a size two, and I was sure the men would pick her over me even though she was flat as a board. Some men like that.

"I tried. I said it's the first day of my period and I'm bleeding like a pig. I called in sick last night so she said I had to come in today."

I studied some takeout menus.

"I went out on a blind date last night," Yuki said. "I let my mother fix me up with the son of a woman she met on a plane. She was so excited about the date that she lent me her pearls."

Yuki told me all about the date. He was staying at the Plaza Hotel for three days and he sounded nice on the phone. They decided to meet in his hotel room and then go to the Rainbow Room for dinner. She was embarrassed because she had never been to a really fancy place for dinner, just Elaine's once with a client, and he had asked her to take her panties off under the table so he could finger her. Elaine was sitting at the next table.

She got into the cab and said, "The Plaza Hotel," and she was excited thinking, It's Saturday night, I'm young, I have a great date. She had a rare feeling that something nice was actually going to happen. The last time she had gone to a hotel she'd been doing Escort and was stopped by security guards at the Inter-Continental. They brought her to an office and took Polaroid pictures of her and told her that she was not welcome there ever again. She had to take a week off to recuperate.

She walked into the Plaza and went right to the elevators. She knocked on David's door and he opened it wearing a suit and tie. He was good-looking. They talked about how embarrassing blind dates were and he said, "My mother didn't tell me you were this beautiful," and he asked her if she was hungry. She said she was.

The next day her mother called and woke her up and wanted to hear everything that happened on the date.

"We went to the Rainbow Room," Yuki said.

"Tell me everything that happened," her mother said. "Are there rainbow lights? Does the dance floor really move, does it really rotate right under your feet while you're dancing?"

Yuki said she didn't know if the dance floor really rotates. She was so happy, she was floating on air. Her feet never touched the ground.

"How are the pearls?" her mother asked.

"That's the last time I ever let my mother fix me up," Yuki told me. He had ripped off her clothes. He had stuffed a towel into her mouth and thrown her on the floor on her stomach. He raped her. He did it over and over again. He couldn't seem to get comfortable, he kept moving her around the room from the bed to the floor to the desk to the chair to the toilet. When he finally stopped she was able to grab her shoes and her skirt and a towel. She put on her ruined skirt in the stairwell and wrapped the towel around her shoulders. She ran down eight flights of stairs and straight through the lobby and into a cab.

"How *are* the pearls?" I asked.

"They're history."

"Why didn't you tell anyone?"

"What for?" Yuki said. "What I should really do is work. The best thing I can do tonight is make five hundred dollars. The men will probably get off on these bruises. Are you ordering food?"

"Definitely." I felt sick. I thought I was going to throw up.

"Did you ever stay at a place called the Jane West Hotel? You look so familiar to me," she said.

"I stayed there once," I said. I remembered her then. It

seemed like a hundred years ago. "You were behind the desk."

"I was the bookkeeper there. Small world."

I told her all about Vivian marrying Lars and moving to Independence Plaza and we laughed and talked while the other girls on shift occupied the four rooms. Finally Josie told us we could leave since we weren't making money anyway.

I took Yuki to the Old Town Bar for a drink and then took a cab to the Angelika movie theater to see what was playing. I stood on a long line to get a cappuccino behind two men who turned out to be women in seersucker suits. I got on the escalator and was descending into the blue pool of the lower lobby when I doubled over in pain. My stomach was filled with blue fire. It was swelling up. I felt like I had swallowed the chandelier. Sucked on the blue neon tubes and swallowed the gas. I stepped off the escalator and moved around to the side, leaning against it, feeling it vibrate. I sank to the floor and watched people rushing past me, diving into the long narrow theaters. I watched intimate couples divide up strategically to get good seats. I was so lonely, burning up on the floor. I wanted to get to the ladies' room but I just couldn't. I couldn't stand. I couldn't seem to get down low enough on the floor. And my eyes were closed. I couldn't get to the ladies' room with my eyes closed.

34

I OPENED MY eyes in a hospital bed. I decided to try to move my legs. I wondered what would happen if they didn't move. They moved. A doctor came in and stood over me. "You're a lucky young lady," he said. "What's your name? You didn't have any ID."

I didn't carry ID because if I ever got arrested I could give the police a fake name. I told him my name which I immediately regretted since I didn't have insurance.

"You have a perforated ulcer," the doctor said. He went on and on about it. I blocked out the details.

"Am I okay?" I asked him. "Can I still have a baby?"

"Did you think you were pregnant?"

"No. I mean in the future."

"Yes."

"Can I get a phone and a TV?"

"Yes. When you passed out you hit your head, but we got that stitched up." I put my hand on my head.

"I hope you didn't have to shave anything."

"Just a little patch."

"Oh my God! I never signed anything for that." I started to cry. "How long am I in for?"

"This isn't a prison."

"Then can I leave now?"

"No, you'll have to stay a few days."

"Please call my mother," I said.

My mother came to visit me in the afternoon. She had a bouquet of tulips and a Lord & Taylor shopping bag. She handed me the tulips.

"Aren't they just the most beautiful flowers you've ever seen in your life? Five ninety-nine. I was thrilled when I saw them. They're exquisite."

"Thank you. What's in the bag?"

"A new nightgown. I'm so tired of sleeping in an old rag." She took it out and put it on over her clothes. "Eighty-nine dollars on sale. I really need it but I got a terrible headache spending the money. A terrible bum came up to me and I gave him a dollar, but then I realized it was a twenty-dollar bill and I grabbed it back and I didn't have a dollar bill so I gave him all the change I had, three pennies, and he called me a bitch." She thrust her hand toward my stomach to give me a pinch. "Who's my baby girl?"

"Mom, be careful, I have a bleeding ulcer."

"That's just too horrible to imagine. My stomach muscles are killing me from Stretch & Tone. And that's with a hot bath." She took two aspirin with the water by my bed. "How are you feeling, Benny?"

"I'm very shook up." The minute I said the word "shook" I felt like crying.

"What happened to your hair?"

I started to cry and so did my mother.

"I feel shook up too," she said. "This whole thing has given me a headache."

We just sat there and cried and she got into bed with me, climbing over the metal rail. "Here we are, two girls together," she said.

The doctor walked in. "What do we have here?"

"Doctor, I have to talk to you," my mother said. "Should I take a Midrin for a tension headache or an Anaprox?"

"Are you a patient here?"

"She's my mother," I said.

"I'm her mother."

The doctor looked at my chart. "Visiting hours are over. I'm sorry, you'll have to leave."

"Oh, that's okay, I'm going to stay. I spent a lot of money on a cab plus tip."

"You can come back tomorrow."

"I carried her in my womb."

"Mom!"

"I did. Did your father visit?"

I told her he hadn't.

"Oh, isn't that interesting. I guess I'm the better parent."

"I think you and Dad should get back together," I said. The doctor left. "Dad told me he wants to get back together with you." I always told my mother that my father wanted to get back together with her and my father that my mother wanted to.

She blushed. My mother likes the idea of anyone being in love with her, even the janitor in the building across the street, even my father. "Your father is a sick pervert who makes me want to vomit," she said.

She handed me a pill as if it were a family heirloom. "Here," she said, "you can sneak a Midrin. Get some rest. Think of this as an expensive vacation. This is wonderful. You'll probably lose ten pounds in here. I love you." She handed me my velvet pillow. I can't go to sleep without touching velvet.

35

WHEN I WOKE up I felt extremely sorry for myself. My TV hadn't been turned on yet and my stomach hurt. I had to call in sick for work. I lay there for a long time thinking about what I would tell Josie. I decided to tell her I was going away on a vacation. I didn't want to worry her and the other girls. I called the brownstone and Josie answered. "I'm not going to be able to work this week. I'm sick in the hospital," I told her.

"Jesus, Daphne. Don't give me this bullshit. I can't take you girls anymore. What happened, did you meet a man or something? You're in love and you can't come in? You have a responsibility to be here now. I have three clients booked for you." She said the word "clients" as if she were the CEO of a Fortune 500 company.

"I'm in the hospital. Someone else can see them."

"Look, Little Miss Ivy League or whatever your name is, if you were the only one out it would be one thing, but Heatherly called in sick and Maryanne's in Bellevue again."

"In Bellevue again?"

"She didn't come to work and she got very noncommunicative and then she didn't answer her phone at all. I kept calling and finally someone answered and said they were taking her away in a straitjacket."

"In an actual straitjacket?"

"Yes, an actual one. If you're really in the hospital let me speak to a doctor right now," Josie said.

"Oh, sure," I said. "I'll just ask a doctor to get on the phone and explain to you why I can't come to work in the brothel this evening. Maybe you can send my 'clients' here. I'm sorry Josie, I'll let you know when I'll be back. What's the number in Bellevue?" I asked quickly. She gave me the number for the pay phone on Maryanne's floor, suggested I check into Bellevue myself, and hung up.

I didn't even have a ginger ale or a plastic dish of fruit cup. I wrapped my arms around myself to see what it would feel like to wear a straitjacket. I looked at the number Josie had given me. My handwriting looked strange, not like my own. Lately it was different every time I wrote something.

I called and a female voice answered, "Hello, looney bin, may I help you?"

"Is Maryanne there, please?" I didn't know her last name, or, for that matter, her real name. Maryanne was the name she used. I was about to hang up, when the woman said, "She's in her room."

"Can you get her, please?"

"Maryanne, Maryanne . . ." She was screaming the name down the hall. It got farther and farther away.

Then I heard Maryanne's tiny voice. "Hello."

"Hi it's Daphne, how are you?"

"Fine thank you. How are you?"

"Maryanne, are you okay in there?" I asked.

"Yes I'm feeling better now, thank you. I was having illusions. I had an illusion that you didn't like me anymore and is that true?"

"No, that's not true. I like you very much."

"I had an illusion that the bad man in my building hypnotized me and is that true?"

"I don't think so."

"Well, I know he worships Satan. Maybe he hypnotized you too and that's why you wanted to kill me. Is that true?"

"No Maryanne. Do you need anything, food or a nightgown?"

"They issue pajamas. I'm a small. Do you know what happened to my cat?"

"No I don't. When did you last see him?"

"Her. I took her to the welfare hotel across the street. Do you think the bad man got her?"

"No Maryanne. Why would he want your cat? A nice kid is probably taking care of her."

"I hope she's okay. I'm very very frightened. I'm very scared. When you have those illusions it comes at you from all angles. You go to the movies and instead of seeing the screen the movie fills up your whole mind. The doctor said I got so high I almost exploded. I burned up. I could have another attack. Do you think it's safe for me to watch the TV?"

"Yes. Maryanne, can you live with your parents?"

"My father can't handle me in Florida and my mother's a ward of the state. I don't want to go back to my apartment."

"We'll find you an apartment. You know, nobody's perfect. Everybody has something like this to deal with."

"That's true. Are you calling me from your apartment?"

"No, I'm in the hospital too."

"Bellevue?"

"No, I have an ulcer."

"Did I shoot you in the stomach?"

"No."

"I had an illusion that I shot you."

"That's a coincidence."

"And is that true?"

"It's true that it's a coincidence."

"It was a hell-ucination. Is that true?"

"Yes."

"Are you going to die?"

"No I'm not."

"I have to go. I can't stand up with this medication."

"I'll call you soon, Maryanne. Goodbye."

I used to wonder if I was retarded and nobody told me. I would constantly wonder about this when I was a child. I was friends with a girl in my building who was emotionally disturbed. She could recite *Alice in Wonderland* from beginning to end without stopping. Sometimes she would just scream for hours, going up and down in the elevator. I liked her a lot.

I felt very sad thinking about Maryanne in a size small straitjacket.

36

MY FATHER APPEARED in the doorway.

"I came as soon as I heard. I didn't get the message until this morning. I was terribly TERRIBLY frightened. I love you, girl, you know that."

"Thanks Dad." His skin was wrinkled and gray. His eyebrows looked thin and drawn-on, like a worried cartoon character's. Mine were arched and I could shape them with my finger for different effects. They could look perfect and Oriental or wild and off-balance.

"I brought you something." He took a white food container from a brown paper bag. "It's sushi."

"Thank you, but I don't eat sushi."

"You don't like Japanese food?"

"I don't eat fish."

"But this is RAW fish."

"No thank you," I said.

"No? I'm sorry. I would have brought you a shrimp dish or something."

"I don't eat shrimp."

"No shellfish?"

"No."

"I brought you the *New York Times*."

"Thanks, Dad."

"Do you read the newspaper? Don't you have to read the NEWS to be a stand-up comic?"

"I'm not trying to be a stand-up comic anymore."

"Why? Did you just decide to give up on it?"

"Yes."

"How come?"

"I couldn't think of anything funny to say."

"That's funny." He laughed. "Heh, heh, heh." With his mouth tight and his tongue flat and wide sticking out between his lips like a third lip. My father started talking about Jeffrey Dahmer, who had been in the news for cutting people up and keeping them in his refrigerator. I had seen his parents on TV saying how sorry they were, the mother wearing enormous false eyelashes. All I could think about was that this woman's son had killed dozens of people and she had put on false eyelashes to go on TV. "What do you think about it?" my father asked. "Do you think he's insane? I think . . ."

My mind wandered off. The other bed in my room was still empty. When I was in fifth grade I used to fantasize that Andrew Lippman and I both got a rare and terrible disease and we had to be quarantined together overnight in a hospital room. Sometimes I fantasized that there was a new law: Fifth graders had to get married. We would get married in the school gym and there would be a class trip-honeymoon in

Disney World. Then my face would burn when Andrew Lippman walked by.

"What do you think?" My father was still talking.

"I don't know." I hadn't heard a word he'd said.

"A man who CUTS people up in little pieces . . ." My father was eating pale pink pieces of sushi with chopsticks. "Eats their FLESH . . ." Little neon orange eggs wrapped in seaweed. "Heh, heh, heh." A piece the color of his flat tongue. "How are you feeling?"

"Sick."

"The doctor said he had never seen an ulcer bleed like this one and you're very very lucky. He said you're tense. Are you TENSE, Girl? Are you NERvous? Have I RAISED a nervous girl?"

"Dad, you're making me tense."

"You can't live your life nervous and afraid. I've always taught you to take risks. I've always taught you not to be afraid of DEATH."

When my father's mother died he cried like a baby. "I'm an orphan," he wailed. "I'm an orphan."

"Did I tell you what happened to me? I rented a car to visit Siobhan's parents and the car went over a little bump and the airbag inflated and knocked me out. I crashed into a concrete wall. How's your mother?"

"Fine."

A Filipino nurse walked into the room and gave me pills in a little cup. "How are we doing?" she asked.

"We're fine," I said.

"Who is our visitor today?"

"This is our father."

"Hello."

"Hello," my father said. She left.

"That nurse woke me up twice last night to give me sleeping pills," I told him.

"You could have been a stand-up comic. But you quit, you QUIT."

I remembered one of my clients telling me that when he went into the hospital for a triple bypass, a nurse came into his room every night and offered him a massage and a hand job for twenty-five dollars. He loved being in the hospital.

"Are you READing?" my father asked me.

"No."

"What do you do?"

"Watch TV."

"I can't stand that stuff. God, I hate it. What do you watch?"

"*Cheers* and Geraldo Rivera."

"Did you hear that when they were interviewing jurors for Jeffrey Dahmer's trial they needed people who didn't think there was anything wrong with cannibalism and murder, and the only person they could find was Geraldo Rivera?" He laughed. "What's that?"

"It's my pillow."

"Do you still have that problem?"

"I can't sleep without velvet, what's wrong with that?" Once when I was a child, my father had me see a psychiatrist who told him that touching velvet wasn't hurting anybody.

"Give it up, will you? It's sick, SICK."

"You always complain that I give up on everything."

"I never complain. I just want to make sure you use your mind. You're a very smart girl. Do you exercise your body?"

"Not here in the hospital. Those pills made me sleepy, Dad."

"I'll let you get some rest." I thought he said, *I'll stay with you while you rest.* "I love you, sweetheart." He kissed my forehead and left.

I started to cry. I cried with my mouth open, my jaw stretched as wide as it could go. My face screwed up into a fist.

37

WHEN I GOT out of the hospital I had a long vertical scar on my stomach. My doctor said I did not have the normal tension level of a young girl. He suggested meditation and Tai Chi. He suggested acupuncture. Nothing made me more tense than the thought of meditating and taking Tai Chi, except the thought of acupuncture. I broke out in hives in his office and was given a sedative.

My acting teacher at NYU had said I would never work on the American stage because I had too much jaw tension. No one at NYU had ever seen a jaw so tense. They prodded and poked around my ears where my "hinges" were, they massaged the back of my neck to loosen the base of my tongue, they pulled on my chin and rolled my head and chastised me for holding in my stomach. They told me to think of myself as a giant cavity, to let the breath drop to the base of my spine. They said all my emotions were locked in my jaw. I saw my emotions as a school of small sharks darting past clamshell teeth and the rigid tongue reef.

"Breathe into your vagina," my acting teacher told me. She had a mouth bigger than Carly Simon's. "Your jaw is connected to your vagina," she whinnied.

When the stitches in my stomach came out I signed up for an acting class, outside of NYU, one night a week after school. The first day the teacher punched me in the stomach to help me feel real pain. I lifted up my shirt to show him the scar from my operation.

"Excellent," he said. "You're not afraid to be private in public." I hated his beard and his Italian Jewishness. I hated all the kids in the class, especially the girl who ended up becoming my partner for the "Meisner Repetition Exercise." We had to repeat the same line back and forth to each other. She started it.

"I hate your sneakers."

"You hate my sneakers."

"I hate your sneakers."

"You hate my sneakers."

"I hate your sneakers."

"You hate my sneakers."

We had to do this until an organic change took place, but it never did. We were supposed to do it in front of the class and between classes. I couldn't stand my partner. Her name was Maureen Frank but she made everyone call her Morty. "I'm going to invite you to my Morty-gras party," she said.

When the class was over, I dashed down the three flights of creaky steps and into the street. The rest of the class was going next door to Dunkin' Donuts—"Are you going to Dunkin' Donuts?" "Am I going to Dunkin' Donuts?" "Are you going to Dunkin' Donuts?" "Am I going to Dunkin' Donuts?"—but I told them I was in a big rush to get somewhere. I didn't know how I was going to go back to that class. I had been determined to stick out the month because I had paid in advance and Mrs. Johnson had said I had a pattern of quitting everything.

I went to a lingerie store and tried on a Merry Widow. It covered my scar with black lace. I wouldn't have to take it off, it was crotchless. If I was careful I could work a few shifts and make some money. I got dressed and paid for it.

I started to walk uptown to Blanche's. A gray-haired man sat in the glass storefront window of Le Beautiful Nail having a pedicure, his suit pants rolled up to his knees. Two geishas wearing surgical masks were kneeling at his feet.

I went to the door without calling from the corner first. "I want to come back to work," I told Josie.

I stood on the bed in room number 2 and showed Josie and the girls who weren't busy my scar. They examined it closely. Everyone said I was lucky to get to take so much time off work.

I had one session and almost made back what I had spent in the lingerie store and I started to relax a little bit. I would have made a lot more if I had agreed to do anal.

"I'll give you fifty extra for your ass," he'd said.

"No, I'm saving that for my wedding night," I told him. I cherished that virginal part of myself. I had never thought about it until the day we were sitting in the living room talking about what parts of our bodies we liked the best. Heatherly said she liked her ass because she'd never had a dick up it.

All through the session he kept offering more and more.

"I'll give you five hundred for your ass."

When I went downstairs, Josie said, "Here, Blanche wants you to have this." She handed me a Xeroxed sheet of paper.

"No matter what you wear, you look like a flamenco dancer," Josie said. I was wearing the red spandex dress they kept in the closet in case someone forgot to bring work clothes. "You look like you should work in a brothel in *Gone With the Wind*."

"Thank you."

"You look like you should sit on a red velvet divan."

"Thank you." I walked into the living room and sat on the couch with the other girls. They were solemnly reading their Xeroxes.

A GOOD HOSTESS . . .

Shows up on time

Collects up front

Doesn't get herself or the phone girl busted (Angelica this means you)

Doesn't hustle for tips (Angelica this means you)

Keeps a neat appearance

Feels comfortable with her sexuality

Smells good

Has a positive attitude

Doesn't drink or drug at work

Doesn't have a pimp

Wears finger and toenail polish (I've seen some of your feet they're disgraceful)

Doesn't wear perfume

Doesn't have "private clients"

Doesn't gossip

Wears a garter belt and stockings

Doesn't let personal problems interfere with her work

"Daphne, fold the sheets in the dryer," Josie yelled from the other room. We could hear her talking on the phone to her boyfriend, Ned, about how he wasn't just her boyfriend, he was her soulmate. She told Ned that she worked in a psychiatrist's office. "Oh, Ned," she sighed. She was like a New Age Nancy Drew all grown up, using her detective skills to lead a double life, lying, working in a whorehouse.

I took the sheets and towels out of the dryer and put them into a plastic basket. I learned how to fold a sheet at Blanche's. I had to be careful not to knock the Chinese screen down or Josie would come in screaming that we were all a bunch of bulls in a china shop. For a moment the small figures painted on the screen came to life. Women carrying baskets trudged up a steep hill in wooden slippers.

"Why do we work here?" I asked.

"Why do we work here?" Libby repeated. "Because we have low self-esteem."

"Low self-esteem?"

"Low self-esteem."

The tiny living room started to close in on me. The noise from the washing machine became deafening. Everybody looked suddenly hideous, all rotting teeth, flesh flattened into tight elastic dresses, bottoms of feet filthy black through stockings, garter belts like polio braces, deforming, excruciating, humiliating. Smiles were false with tense jaws and puffed lips, stomachs held in, fake breasts held high. I was tired of breathing in the smoke and nail polish remover, cocoa butter and sperm, tired of the taste of condoms.

"I'm going to quit," I said.

"You should work at Gail's, it's a lot better," Libby said.

"I'm going to quit the business."

Josie came into the room. "Daphne, I need your social security number."

"Why?" It didn't sound like a good idea to hand over my social security number to a phone girl in a whorehouse.

"For taxes."

"Taxes!"

"Yes, all the girls have to pay taxes now. Hurry up, you

have an appointment in five minutes."

"I'm not up to it. I think I'm going to go home."

"You can't, he wants to see you. We're trying to run a business here, the client comes first."

"I'm leaving."

"That's very irresponsible."

I looked around at Angelica, Jackie, Libby, Heddy, and Heatherly. They looked like moths comfortably resting on an electric zapper. Counting condoms, reading their Xeroxes, writing down their social security numbers for Josie.

"Come with me," I said to Angelica.

"No way," she said. "I have low self steam."

I pulled on my jeans and my coat and left Blanche's for the last time. I had a test the next morning in Theater History which I was pretty sure I was going to fail. I had some money in my pocket. Mrs. Johnson would be happy to know I wasn't cured of my pattern. I was quitting my job and my acting class in one day. I was also going to quit NYU.

I had an audition the next day for an off-Broadway play called *Freddy's Funeral*. The play that puts the "fun" in funeral. The play takes place in a funeral parlor and it's all improvisation with the audience as fellow-mourners. Tickets cost sixty-five dollars each because after leaving the funeral home the cast and the audience walk a few blocks to Mama Carmella's restaurant for food to ease their grief. Then some actors playing waiters (*there's* a stretch) bring out trays of Chef Boyardee spaghetti and iceberg lettuce and the whole audience pounces on it to get their sixty-five dollars' worth.

With all these great auditions coming up, I really didn't need NYU. It was only April 1 and finals weren't until the middle of May. I didn't want to go back there.

I stood on the sidewalk and looked up at Blanche's brownstone. I remembered that I'd left a pair of high heels in the closet. I knew I wouldn't walk down this street ever again. There were quite a few streets I couldn't walk down—Manhattan was getting smaller and smaller.

PART 3

THE WHALE'S FOOTPRINT

38

I WAS RANSACKING my father's apartment on Eighth Street. I was looking for the Exxon stock certificates I got when my grandmother died. I knew they were somewhere in the apartment and I really needed the money.

I was alone with Annie, my father's dog, an enormous Irish setter. My father got her as soon as he and Siobhan kicked me out because the apartment was too small. The dog spent most of her time at the Cauldron of Clams, but just my luck now she was in the apartment.

"That's a good boy," I said, patting her with my finger. I guess it was more of a poke. There was a certain amount of sibling rivalry between me and Annie. My father was always saying how smart she was and how pretty.

Once, when I was in fifth grade and had a Farrah Fawcett haircut, my father told me my hair felt like Brillo. I had to get ready for school but I kept looking at myself in the mirror and touching my hair. I had a big pimple on my face which I covered with a Band-Aid. At school, Steven Shore asked me if I cut myself shaving and said I wasn't fooling anybody.

I thought about the present Steven Shore gave me at my twelfth birthday party. It was a mirror with Ziggy on it, and the words "Hey Good Lookin' " in a red heart.

I called information and asked for Shore on West End Avenue. The minute before the operator gave me the number I remembered it, as if I were reading it from the margin of my loose-leaf notebook. I dialed the number and Steven's father, Mr. Shore, answered. He had obviously been asleep.

"May I please speak to Steven?" I asked.

"Steven?" He sounded surprised.

"Yes, Steven Shore."

"He's at Yale."

"Oh, that's wonderful," I said. I sounded like a crazy psychotic killer.

"Who is this?"

"A friend from school," I said.

"From Yale?"

"No . . . from elementary school," I said.

I hung up quickly. My heart was pounding. They would know it was me. They would call Steven in a few days and laugh about it, this crazy girl calling in the middle of the night, and Steven would say, *It's probably that girl—what was her name? something weird—Bennington, Bennington Bloom. I heard she's always trying to get in touch with people.*

I *was* always trying to get in touch with people. Why couldn't we all get together again?

On Valentine's Day in the fifth grade we went ice skating at Wollman rink in Central Park. We gave each other carnations. We drank hot chocolate and rented skates with pink pompoms. I didn't know how to skate, so everyone grabbed me and dragged me into the middle of the rink where a huge red heart had been painted on the ice. I just sat in the middle of the heart laughing and thinking: This is happiness, right this second, this is it.

I walked through the bedroom of my father's apartment and into the kitchen. Siobhan had put a bowl of large shells in the middle of the kitchen table. They looked like the skulls of her latest victims. She had covered the whole apartment in pale yellow wallpaper which was now filthy. I read somewhere that yellow causes feelings of intense panic. The whole place was squalid and smelled like the dog. It was a railroad flat, just three rooms—a living room, a bedroom, and a kitchen, all in a row, with thin yellow doors connecting them. There was a shower in the kitchen and a tiny toilet room where you had to sit down, then close the door, and then pull a chain with a wooden handle to flush.

I found three twenty-dollar bills in a mug in the kitchen. I took one.

I gave Annie some dog biscuits. My father was always calling me Annie. It wasn't her fault. "What will we do when our father has another daughter?" I asked the dog.

She barked as if defending him, just like my brother.

The living room had a desk, a futon, and wall-to-wall bookshelves. Siobhan had a few dolls propped up on the shelves. I pulled two dolls off a shelf and several books, looking for my Exxon stock. I searched the desk. Then, at the bottom of the last desk drawer, I found an S & M magazine with a glossy centerfold of a man hanging from a big piece of machinery being fucked by another man with a black leather mask over his eyes.

Once, my father came home drunk and said that Ben, the super of the building who lived on the top floor, had tried to kiss him. I had brought Ben pizza and orange drink from Ray's on Sixth Avenue because he was dying of AIDS. We had the same name. We always called each other Ben a lot.

Looking at the picture of the two men was exciting me, making my heart pound, making me feel pinched and hot. I put my hand between my legs and touched myself through my jeans. Annie wagged her tail. She could kill someone with that tail. I picked the magazine up and saw something wrapped in a white plastic bag. I lifted the bag out of the drawer and a tiny pink dildo rolled onto the floor. Annie ran to it and brought it to me in her teeth. It looked like a little dog biscuit in her mouth. She dropped it on my lap. It was wet from her saliva. The slimmest little dildo I had ever seen.

I pictured my father wearing Siobhan's enormous high

heels, leaning over the desk with the little plastic cigarette up his ass. His lips tight over his teeth, his forehead with seven deep creases, moaning softly, anxiously.

It's hard to respect a man who can't even take a bigger dildo.

I played fetch with Annie for a while using the dildo until it was a little chewed up. Then I found my stocks in a shoe-box, on the top shelf of the closet, under Siobhan's sweaters from Scotland. I put the stock certificates in my bookbag and straightened the place up a little. Out on the street, I felt bad that I hadn't said goodbye to Annie.

39

ON JUNE 27 I ran into Perry Shepherd on Fourteenth Street. She was carrying enormous khaki duffel bags, antique suit-cases with stickers all over them from other countries, a small metal luggage cart which was piled with straw baskets and canvas artists bags, and her grandmother's crocodile purse. Her hair was flying, the ends were wet, and her breasts were flattened into a white handkerchief blouse. I thought she was on Martha's Vineyard.

"I've decided to stay there for a while," she said. "I just came back to pick up some of my stuff. I didn't have time to call you. Here." She handed me a garbage bag. I walked with her, trying not to drag the garbage bag on the street.

"My bus leaves in fifteen minutes," she said. There was no way she was going to get to the Port Authority in time. Pennies poured out of a hole in her jacket pocket. "Why don't you come with me? You can stay with me at my aunt's house."

"I can't, I don't have any clothes."

"I just gave you a whole bag of stuff." I opened the garbage bag and pulled out a lavender dress with torn lace dripping from it.

I thanked her and gave her a hug, throwing my arms around her and the suede knapsack strapped to her back. I put her in a cab with her things and watched her speed up Eighth Avenue, her skirt stuck in the cab door, her head bobbing as she gave the driver specific instructions.

I stood on the sidewalk thinking about what to do next. I pictured myself taking a cab to the Angelika and waiting in line to see a bad movie, having a bowl of Hangover Tomato Soup at Finelli's, maybe going down to McGovern's and buying Vivian a frozen margarita with salt or taking her to a drugstore and buying her a lipstick or some pantyhose. I could go to the zoo by myself. I love doing things by myself. I wished I could call someone to go with me.

I hailed a cab and got in after pushing Perry's garbage bag onto the back seat.

"Port Authority," I said.

"Shit."

We drove through the plant district past the palm trees standing in brown paper bags. We got stuck in traffic. The bus was probably leaving.

When I got out of the cab the bottom of the garbage bag tore and a white girdle fell out on the street. I didn't stop to pick it up, I just ran into the Port Authority thinking everyone I saw was her, on every ticket line, crumpled in every corner. I was about to turn and leave, when I heard my name called out in a high screech, and there she was, going down an escalator, red-cheeked and sweaty.

"I'm going with you," I yelled and ran to the escalator like a crazy person. When I caught up to her she was already on the bus and having a conversation with the bus driver. I paid for my ticket and we sat next to each other, talking about how amazing I was for doing this and how I was the best friend anybody could ever have, which was true, and sharing a bagel with cream cheese.

At a rest stop in Rhode Island we ate several doughnuts and jammed into a photo booth. We fed dollars into the machine and laughed hysterically, our cheeks pressed together. The strips of photos fanned out of our jacket pockets like cigars.

Perry gave the bus driver a vintage chauffeur's cap and a red paisley scarf with fringe from one of her bags.

The trip took forever. I was full of regret, remembering past trips that had seemed like a good idea at the time. After the bus, there was a ferry. We sat on the deck exhausted. I felt anxious looking at the black water and the black sky. Perry cried when her straw hat blew away. She said she could hear it getting shredded under the boat.

We were going to have a wonderful time, she said. There was a wonderful place for apple crumb cake tomorrow morning, a place to pick baskets of flowers, a carousel and gingerbread houses, a friend with a boat, a friend with a horse, a friend with a brother, a friend with a theater and parts for both of us, and I was welcome to stay with her at her aunt's for as long as I wanted.

Finally there were tiny lights and toy boats on the horizon. A horn blew.

When we got to the house we woke Perry's aunt. "Perry, may I speak to you alone for a minute?" she said. I sort of curtseyed and stepped out into the corridor which was lined with antique photographs in round frames. "She can only stay one night," I heard her aunt say. "You can't just bring a guest, this isn't some flophouse for your poor actress friends. She's going to have to shower outside."

"She said you can stay as long as you like," Perry told me.

I spent the next morning looking up airlines in the Yellow Pages and calling for flight information while Perry sulked.

"You know there's a hundred other places we can stay on the island," Perry said.

"Doesn't the word 'island' make you feel claustrophobic?" I asked.

"Manhattan's an island."

"Not really. There are bridges."

"Well, I'm sorry you're having such a horrible time and you can't bear to stay even one more day. I'm sorry it's such torture to spend one more minute on this claustrophobic little island." She sucked on a marshmallow. I was counting twenties to see if I had enough for plane fare. I did. "Where do you get all your money?" she asked me.

"I saved this up."

"You always have so much money on you." Her tone softened.

"Then I can buy breakfast."

"No, I want to treat."

We shared the last piece of apple crumb cake at the bakery. Perry insisted on paying. "I dragged you out here," she said. She ended up giving the woman behind the counter a painted wooden bracelet instead of money. We saw Carly Simon walking down the street.

"I'm having a great time," I said. It was always a big mistake to leave New York.

40

I HATE HITCHHIKING. It's much worse than prostitution. I considered suggesting to Perry that she work at Blanche's for a while and buy a car. Make some real money. Then I could tell her why I always had so much money in my pocket and that she could too. She would just have to sit on the couch at Blanche's a few days a week.

But I didn't want to be the one to put the idea in her head. Once you get an idea like that into your head it's hard to forget it. And once you've done it, you can't undo it. You're a garter-belt-wearing member for life. She wouldn't be good at it, anyway. She would want to help everybody. She would cry and give discounts, or believe them that they just had to go to their bank machines but would be right back. She would think about them and buy them birthday cards and bake them cookies. She baked a cake for her doorman on National Doorman's Day.

We spent the whole day standing on the side of one dirt road or another, hitchhiking. I thought I saw Lars and Vivian in the back seat of a car that zoomed by us. I was getting delirious. I tried to hail a big van that said "Adam Cab" on it. There was a picture of a blue whale on the side and the words "A Whale of a Cab." It was the third one that had passed us. I would have paid any amount to get someplace.

When a car finally pulled over, we would get in and go wherever they were going, and Perry would tell them exactly how to get there or how they should have gone. Most people wouldn't let Perry into their cars. She had gotten a bad reputation on the Vineyard as a back-seat driver.

Finally a tourist picked us up and Perry forced her to take us to Gay Head. We walked on the beach and gave ourselves mud masks from the clay cliffs. We passed two naked women doing yoga exercises and a pregnant woman who had dug a hole in the sand for her stomach. Perry went swimming in Calvin Klein panties and I collected shells.

I'm materialistic. I like to have something to show for my experiences. If I go to the beach, I get shells: if I work a double shift at Blanche's, I buy a new pair of shoes.

We went to a restaurant called the Black Dog, which I recognized because everybody in New York wears the T-shirt with a drawing of a black dog on it. I went to find the waitress so I could buy one, and there, sitting at a quaint table by the fireplace, was Vivian arguing with Lars. I couldn't believe it. Lars was wearing a tuxedo and Vivian had on a nubby black skirt, a white blouse, and pink plastic troll earrings. The two of them looked completely out of place, like boats in the sky.

I remembered Vivian mentioning that Lars's daughter was getting married on Martha's Vineyard. Vivian kept going on and on about how she was so nervous because it was the first time she was going to meet Lars's family, his mother, his daughters, his ex-wife. At the time I thought she was just having a crazy drunken fantasy.

"I *know* it's her day," Lars was saying. "But the father of the bride looked pretty damn good." His speech was slow and exaggerated and he was leaning to one side. He was drunk.

"But Lars, it's her day," Vivian said. She was also drunk, talking loudly in her angry English accent.

"Hi, Vivian," I said. She turned around quickly but didn't seem at all surprised to see me.

"I *know* it's her day," Lars said. "All I'm saying is I looked very good in my tuxedo."

"But Lars, it's her day," Vivian said.

"I *know* it's her day. All I'm saying is I looked great. You looked great, Vivian, when I took you to Atlantic City to hear Frank." Lars turned to me. "Did I tell you we went on a luxury bus?"

"No you didn't," I said. I tried to imagine what a luxury bus was. "What are you doing here?"

"Trying to get a goddamned drink," Lars said. "Waitress!" The waitress came over and explained to Lars that they didn't serve alcohol in Vineyard Haven. "I'm just talking about a beer," he screamed, "or an Irish coffee. Once you put the coffee in, it's not a drink anymore. Maybe you think my lovely wife here is underage."

"Shut up, Lars," Vivian said.

"It's a dry town," the waitress said. She said "drytown" as if it were one word. As if she said it a thousand times a day. When I worked as a wench at the Renaissance Festival I had to tell people where the privies were all day long. It was humiliating.

"It's a what?" Lars said.

"A drytown," the waitress repeated.

"A *what*? This *is* called The Black Dog Tavern, isn't it? The Black Dog *Tav*-ern! I believe Mr. Webster defines a tavern as a place where I can get a goddamned drink!"

The waitress said they were welcome to go to a package store a few miles away and bring beer back. "Jesus Christ," Lars said. "It's a special occasion. Today I walked my lovely daughter down the aisle on her wedding day . . ."

"It's her day, Lars," Vivian said.

"I *know* it's her day. All I'm saying is that I looked *très* elegant in my tuxedo."

"But Lars, it's her day."

"I *know* it's her day."

I walked over to where Perry was sitting with her back to the window with the oceanview. A man was repairing a boat on a scaffold. A few of her friends had joined her at our table and they were deeply absorbed in a conversation about an upcoming production of *Peter Pan* which Perry was going to direct. Perry would be an excellent director. She would also have made a great Peter Pan except that her breasts were too big.

"You're going to be Tiger Lily," Perry told me. I was disappointed. I remembered Mrs. Johnson saying that nothing ever satisfied me, no school was good enough, no friend, no shrink. I got up from the table and said I'd be right back.

"You're not going to call your answering machine again, are you?" Perry asked me. "Bennington is having a miserable time," she told her friends. I explained that I had run into some people I knew and I had to talk to them for a few minutes. I went back to their table.

"But Lars, it's her day," Vivian was saying.

"I *know* it's her day. I walked my daughter down the aisle today, on my arm, in my tuxedo, didn't I?"

"But Lars, it's her day."

"I *know* it's her day. I'm just saying even though I got there so late, and people were nervous . . . Why do you have to wear those earrings?"

"I'll wear whatever I want to," Vivian said. "You're not my boss."

"I bossed you around pretty good on the dance floor today. We were the best dancers there."

"Lars, it's her day."

"I *know* it's her day. I'm just saying people noticed I danced good. Come on, Vivian, let's go."

"Lars, wipe your nose."

"I looked so good in my tuxedo, everyone was taking pictures."

"But Lars, it's her day," everybody in the restaurant said.

"I *know* it's her day. Come on, Vivian let's find a real bar."

"Where are you staying tonight?" I asked Vivian.

"We're getting a bus home from Provincetown. Lars's friend is taking us to the bus stop from the ferry. He drove us up from New York but we're taking the bus back. Do you want to come with us?"

"My friend rented a Lincoln Town Car for the occasion," Lars said.

I glanced over at Perry. She was alone at the table now, sulking over a vegetarian sandwich. Where were all these cute guys she was going to introduce me to?

"I can't," I said. "I have a big part in a show here this summer. I probably have a rehearsal to go to tomorrow."

"A fellow thespian," Lars said. "I'm an actor too. Vivian, show her my model shots." Lars had been asleep at a booth in McGovern's one afternoon, and a photographer from *New York* magazine came in and took a picture. In the picture Lars was asleep in a corner of the bar with his mouth open.

I bought Vivian a T-shirt and they stumbled off.

Perry convinced her aunt to let me stay one more night, and the next day we hitchhiked to the noon ferry.

Perry stood on the dock waving dramatically. How fake, I thought.

I headed straight for the snack bar and got a napkin and pencil so I could write down some sort of plan. I flirted with a man who turned out to have a wife and kid, and they drove me from Woods Hole to Provincetown. I stood on the wharf and considered taking one of those dumb whale-watching boat rides. I was lonely and I wished I were home. I wished I had taken the bus with Lars and Vivian. I wished I had just stayed home. Perry Shepherd was one of the most unreliable friends a girl could have.

41

"Is this yours?" a man asked me, holding up a plain brown T-shirt that could have belonged to anyone.

"No, it isn't," I said. I turned around reluctantly. I had never been on a whale-watching boat before and I was trying to look for whales. I didn't want to miss a single one. The man smiled at me. He had blue eyes and a chin. I was having trouble seeing him, the sun was in my eyes. I couldn't tell what he looked like. All I could see was what you see when your eyes are closed very tightly, shapes moving, paisley patterns, floating colors.

I was thinking about my father. He used to take me on fishing boats, those summers on Cape Cod. He would spend the whole time below, sick, vomiting over and over, curling up on a bench. No matter how many times he got sick on those boats, he would never remember it the next time.

"Dad, you always get seasick."

"What are you talking about? I've never been sick on a BOAT. I'm a fisherman."

"Give me money for the snack bar."

He'd give me a ten-dollar bill. "Here's your change, son," the dumb guy behind the concession stand would say to me.

"I'm a girl. Look." And I'd show my tiny ring, a thin gold band with a pearl between two green stones.

The man with the chin asked me if I knew where the Lost

and Found was. "Just keep the shirt," I said. "There might be money in the pocket."

"I would never do that, would you?" He took a picture of the sunset and put another roll of film in his camera. Then he made jokes about all the fat people on the boat, saying he just saw a whale, another whale sighting. He said we had picked the right boat, the sunset was so nice.

I didn't think I'd really see an actual whale, until Diane, our Naturist, said over the PA system, "Movement at eleven o'clock." And I saw a spout. I remembered how one summer my tiny ring slid off my finger when I was playing in the surf, and how I thought, if I had to lose it, I was glad it was there on the bottom of the ocean, on a mermaid's pinky.

Everyone on the boat stood silently focused on the eleven o'clock position, waiting. I was concentrating like an Indian boy in the woods.

"There's a footprint at nine o'clock," Diane said. "If you look you'll see a glassy patch on the surface of the water caused by the whale's tail movement."

I looked for the whale's footprint.

"It's there," the man said to me, pointing. And I saw it, a perfectly smooth patch in crushed velvet, a small dance floor.

"Nine o'clock," Diane said. And out of the ocean came a huge whale with a fin, arching up over the water and then back under. The boat was rocking harder than any boat I'd ever been on.

"What we just saw was a fin whale estimated at seventy feet and about seventy-five tons. Bigger than any dinosaur that ever roamed the face of the earth."

I couldn't believe I saw a whale. I felt like jumping up and down, diving in, but I stood frozen on the deck with my eyes glued to the water. I was looking at the water, but I wanted to look at him. Eyes on the whale, I told myself, you see men all the time.

"I got a picture," he said.

I looked up at him. "I've never seen anything like that in my entire life."

"I'm glad I took a Dramamine," he said.

We watched the fin whale spout and come up out of the water three times.

"We're very lucky," Diane kept saying over the PA system. "The fin whale is an extremely elusive and evasive mammal, however, they do need air every fifteen minutes. The whale can no better swallow salt water than you or I."

I stood on the deck at the nine o'clock position concentrating on the water. Whales are so out of place in this world. They live in the water but they can't drink it. And they can't breathe in it. They have to come up for air over and over again. Sometimes I think breathing is an effort, I tell myself to relax and breathe, and I suck the air in with little grasps of my lips until I get enough. I have to wake up in the night to breathe or my body gets overheated like a kettle.

"Here, I thought you could use this." The man handed me a cup with a triangle neatly ripped out of the plastic lid. He cleared his throat. In New York if a man likes you, he makes a phlegmy noise in the back of his throat. Sometimes he'll also do you the honor of spitting across your path on the sidewalk. "My name is Adam," he said. "I think you're very beautiful."

"Am I supposed to give A-dam?" I said, laughing. He laughed back but I couldn't believe how stupid I was to say that. I liked him. He looked like a bronze Buddha. He was so clear-eyed and open. His thoughts were written on his forehead. I took a sip of the hot chocolate he brought me and I felt myself spinning like a skater on Wollman rink.

The boat had turned around and was heading back to Provincetown.

"Would you like to have dinner with me?" he asked.

"I had a late lunch before we got on the boat," I said, but

I wished I hadn't. I had nothing to do by myself in Province-town that night.

"I know, I saw you eat a hotdog." I had wolfed down a foot-long hotdog with mustard and sauerkraut at MoJo's on the wharf.

"I hope you're at least twenty-five," he said.

"I hope you're thirty-five at the most."

Diane's voice came through the tinny speakers. "As we sail into Provincetown, I would like to thank you for choosing the Spout Route Whale Watching Cruise. We had three extremely successful views of the fin whale, an extremely elusive and evasive mammal. Bigger than any dinosaur that ever roamed the face of the earth."

When the boat docked we walked over to where a small crowd had gathered. An old man was giving a lecture on whaling and Adam and I sat close together on a bench. The old man was saying, "Thar she blows!" and talking passionately about scrimshawed valentines a crewman would send to a woman he might not see for fifteen years. A sperm whale, he said, can go under water without coming up for air for an hour and a half. It can dive down thousands of feet and grab a giant squid in its teeth and kill it by swimming up towards the surface, because the whale can stand the change in pressure but the giant squid can't. I don't recommend going to a lecture on sperm whales on a first date. The word "sperm" was said more than twenty-five times.

"What's your name?" he asked me. "You haven't told me."

"Bennington Bloom."

"That's an unusual name."

"Not really, Bloom is quite common."

"I mean Bennington."

"Actually it was one of the two most popular names the year I was born."

"What year was that?"

"What's your last name?" I asked.

He laughed. "My last name is Brown, so if you marry me you'll have two college names, Bennington Brown."

"I wouldn't do that."

"Marry me?"

"Take your name."

"Why not? I think if we like each other this much in a year we should just get married." He looked at his watch. "It's June twenty-ninth. We'll do it one year from today. It's natural, I think we're the only two straight people left."

There were hundreds of gay couples walking around us on Commercial Street. Each couple looked like identical twins. Two women with frizzy hair and John Lennon glasses wore matching shirts—one said "Top" and the other said "Bottom." Two wore shirts that said "STRAIGHT" in big letters and "not!" in tiny letters underneath. Two were topless. Adam took a picture, he certainly seemed to be enjoying himself.

We stopped in front of a public restroom. Adam handed me a guidebook with a restaurant circled. He asked me to call and make a reservation. He went into the men's room and I called from a pay phone.

"Brown for two."

"Okay, Ms. Brown, see you in a half hour."

I wondered if I would recognize him when he came out of the men's room. There were so many people. He had blue eyes and blond hair. I had never dated a blond man before. He had thinnish lips and a round chin. He was dressed like the fisherman on the frozen fish-sticks boxes, sort of wide and baggy. He was wearing a pink jacket. And wasn't he spending an awfully long time in the men's room?

Adam's gay, I thought. Of course he must be, there were so many clues. For one thing, I liked him. For another thing, he was wearing a pink jacket. He kept pointing out gay T-shirts. And he was alone in Provincetown.

Adam walked towards me and I recognized him.

"You're staring at me," he smiled.

"I just noticed that your hair is brown."

"Very observant."

Our fingers touched when we walked. We went into a hammock shop and he tried out every hammock. I pictured him as a child chasing a butterfly with a net.

"Bennington, try out this hammock with me." He was sprawled out with his head on a big green pillow. I don't recommend getting in a hammock with someone on the first date. "I'll take this one with two pillows," he said. "It's for my house," he told me.

"I'm from New York City," I said, disappointed.

"I live there too but I have a country house upstate."

He was from New York! I was hoping that he wasn't gay, just a straight guy with an interest in gay T-shirts.

42

ADAM TOOK ME to a restaurant on Commercial Street. He ordered steak au poivre and I picked the chicken special. The waitress described it at great length but I couldn't understand one word she said. She had a thick Boston accent like my short Aunt Minnie. I had no idea what I had just ordered, but I didn't want to spend too much time choosing. I didn't want to seem obsessed with food. I hoped I would get just a slab of chicken with no bones or skin. There's nothing worse than having a chicken chopped in half on a plate in front of you.

Adam was looking at the wine list. "I feel like choosing this wine is one of the most important decisions of my life," he said. "It should be really great."

It was amazing how alike we were. Perfectionists. I felt exactly the same way about the chicken.

"I like red," I said. Why was I so bossy and pushy? I should just keep my mouth shut and let him choose.

"I've only been in New York for ten years. When I got out of law school, I thought I'd sort of take a bite out of the Big Apple," Adam said.

He told me he was from Iowa and I said I had never heard of it. When I like a man I have to ruin everything, I have to be coy and stupid, and yet with Adam I got the idea that it didn't matter what I said. Nothing could spoil it, it was a done deal. I had chosen him even though he had approached me.

I pointed out that he pronounced "red" like *rid* and "pen" like *pin*.

He had a hurt look on his face. His hair was mussed. "Are you making fun of my accent?" he asked.

"No, I love your voice. You have a great phone voice."

"We've never talked on the phone."

I pretended to become absorbed in a flyer about whales. I didn't know what to say. I had heard his voice on the phone because there was a credit card receipt with his phone number stuck in the guidebook he'd handed me before he went into the men's room. I had called eight times and listened to the answering machine to make sure he wasn't married. It just said, "Hi, this is Adam," and a regular message. It said, "I can't come to the phone," not "we can't come to the phone," and, "I'll call you back," not "we'll call you back." Each time I called, it seemed more original than the time before, and so sexy and masculine but at the same time soothing and steady.

It was worth listening to the whole message over and over just to hear him say, "Thanks, 'bye."

"I just imagined that you have a nice phone voice, since it's so nice in person," I said.

The waitress brought our food. Mine was a large chicken ball smothered in a cream sauce. "What is this?" I asked her.

"It's the chicken stuffed with . . ." I couldn't understand her. Adam told me to taste the wine. It made me want to take off all of my clothes.

"This is the best wine I've ever tasted," I said.

He smiled. He took a bite of steak after scraping his knife across his plate. "I shouldn't be eating like this," he said. "It's loaded with fat. I should just cut out red meat." He was eating the steak so fast, scraping, cutting, and eating. "I really shouldn't be eating this."

I sipped red wine and looked at his forehead. There was something about it that made me want to tell him the truth. It was high and interrupted by a thinning V of hair which looked soft and brown. He lined up his knife and fork neatly on his plate. "How's your chicken?" he asked.

"Would you like to try it?"

"Are you finished?"

Somehow he put his empty plate in front of me and put my full one in front of him, whisking away silverware and anything else that got in his way.

"This sauce is loaded with cream," he said. "What do you do?"

I had decided to tell him I did office temp work. "I'm an actress," I said. "I was just on Martha's Vineyard auditioning for a show."

He loved that.

"I was going to drive back to New York tonight but it's already so late. Let's get a room in an inn here and I'll drive you to the city tomorrow," Adam Brown said.

Adam and I lay in separate beds at a place called the Driftwood Inn. I hoped he would drift over to my side of the room, but he stayed well-anchored. I listened to his quiet breathing and the foghorn from across the dunes in Truro. The blaring horn, every fifteen seconds, brought back summers lying awake, while my brother Dylan slept in the next bed, scratching his eczema and mosquito bites and poison ivy.

I lay in bed thinking about how I used to be a hooker. How it was all in the past. When I got back to New York I could do office temp work. Adam would never know. Just when I was convinced that Adam would never find out about it, the foghorn would sound, telling the whole world.

43

ADAM AND I woke up late and had breakfast in a little place across from the Driftwood Inn. Adam ordered something called "two pigs in a hole" and I ordered matzoh brei and told him right off that I was Jewish. I once had a bad experience with a comedian I'd dated a few times. One night I watched his act at the Comedy Cellar on MacDougal Street. He walked me home, and after kissing for a long time, we started talking about religion. I told him I was Jewish and he wiped his mouth and never called me again.

It was almost night by the time we decided to make the long drive to Adam's country house in upstate New York, then head back to Manhattan. I threw my bookbag into the trunk and the two dozen loaves of Portuguese sweet bread I'd bought. I always like to re-create the tastes of my childhood. I reached back in to get a loaf and pulled my hand out just before Adam slammed the trunk closed.

"What do you need?" He sounded agitated. I began to think it wasn't a good idea to take this long drive with someone I hardly knew. Men are insane in cars. They always want to "get on the road."

"Do you need to get something out of the trunk?"

I shook my head and stood in front of the passenger door waiting for Adam to open it. I learned to do that from watching *Love Connection*.

"Let's get the show on the road," Adam said, taking off his jacket and getting into the driver's seat. He leaned over and unlocked my door and I got into the car. He buckled himself in and made several small adjustments, like a pilot getting ready to fly a complicated plane. The phone in the rental car was broken and kept ringing spontaneously and Adam answered it, pretending it was a different woman each time. "I told you, DeeDee, I can't see you tonight. Or your twin sister, either. I met another broad . . ." He looked so cute on the car phone.

I sat next to him feeling very womanly because I had bought a bag of peaches and washed them in the ladies' room of the restaurant. I always admired my mother for doling out grapes the minute we got into a car. Soon I would say, *Would you like a peach?* and he would say, *Yes*, and *Delicious*. He was a man and I was a woman, an adult woman with fruit.

His arm hair was bristling in the air conditioning. I really liked him.

"Could you stop jiggling?" he said. "I'm trying to drive."

I had been waiting for the right moment to ask him when the next rest stop was. "Maybe I should just try to stop breathing," I said. I made a lot of comments like that for a while.

"Could you lower the air conditioning a drop?" I asked.

"I like it cold when I'm driving," he said, moving the air

conditioning lever a fraction of an inch. "It keeps me awake."
I better not touch the back of his hair, I thought.

I unzipped my dress and slid out of it. Adam kept his eyes
glued to the road. I unhooked my bra and got up on my
knees in the passenger seat. I leaned over to him and kissed
his neck. He pulled over.

"Do you mind? I'm trying to drive," he said. "I think you
should respect the driver."

"Most men would feel happy if they had a naked woman
in their car."

"Well, I'm not most men."

We sat in silence for a long time. It was much harder getting into my clothes than getting out of them.

"Would you like a peach?"

"Love one."

I handed him the biggest, softest peach with a brown paper
towel from the ladies' room.

"Delicious," he said.

All the way to Adam's, my boyfriend's, country house,
sitting on the freezing leather seat, holding it in, keeping track
of the moon and his moods, I had the sensation of incredible
luck. After hours and hours, we hit Lee, Massachusetts, and
drove for a long time looking for Adam's favorite diner, open
twenty-four hours, seven days a week. When we finally found
it, it was closed. We watched the sunrise and ate Portuguese
sweet bread in the car.

I thought about how lucky it was that I had met Perry
Shepherd, because if I hadn't gone to Martha's Vineyard with
her I would not have met Adam.

As we drove, everything looked flat from far away, a stripe
of sky, a stripe of sheep on a stripe of grass. Close up, the
sheep looked like marshmallows on a green paper plate. Adam
pulled over and we got out and stood at a wooden fence
watching them. One fluffy sheep walked right over to us.
Adam touched it with his hand. I couldn't believe it.

"Go ahead."

"I've never touched one."

He took my hand and put it on the sheep's back. It was like touching the chest hairs I had glimpsed when Adam changed his shirt in the car. I poked my finger into the sheep's wool.

"His fur is so fluffy."

"I think it's a she."

"How can you tell?"

"It's a sheep. You don't know much about animals, do you?"

Adam kissed me. It took me by surprise, even though I had been keeping my lips moist with my tongue for hours and sucking breath mints. I hadn't kissed anyone in a long time. I never kissed the clients on the lips. I would twist my head and neck around like a wooden dragon toy from Chinatown. There was a moment before the kiss when his mouth was close to mine and I could feel and taste his breath between us, maple syrupy and hot and masculine. He kissed my neck, and over his shoulder I noticed that two small sheep had gotten into the back of the rented Lincoln Town Car.

"You're a beautiful ripe plump blackberry," Adam said. I wondered what he meant by plump. He took my hand again, and we walked to the car. "Do you want to drive for a while?"

"I don't have my license."

"That's okay. Just for a little while."

"You don't understand. I don't know how to drive."

"You are over eighteen, aren't you?"

"I grew up in New York City."

He pulled me around to the driver's seat, pushed me in, and slammed the door. Then he went around the back of the car, shut the back door and locked himself into the passenger seat. He put the key in the ignition and turned the car on. The car phone rang automatically. This time I answered it,

"He told you he already has a woman, so don't call here again. He's taken." Adam laughed but looked a little nervous. He told me to press one of the pedals with my foot and the car lurched forward. My heart was pounding.

"Maybe you need a phone book so you can see over the dashboard."

"Shut up."

With all four of our hands on the steering wheel, we moved forward down the empty country road in little lunges.

"Shouldn't we bring the sheep back, Adam?" I had never said his name before.

"Keep your eyes on the road."

"Are you getting nervous?"

"No, it's a rental."

There I was, behind the wheel of a big blue Lincoln Town Car with a great-looking man by my side and our two sheep sound asleep in the back seat.

We traded sides and Adam sped through a town and down a private road and pulled up next to a dilapidated red barn with a broken window and some sort of fake brick siding. So this was it. The big country house. The grand estate. It looked like it was about to collapse. Adam was already emptying the trunk. We walked past the old barn and then I saw it, the beautiful white house set back behind some trees.

"Home at last," Adam said.

I opened the car doors, and the sheep jumped out and started eating grass.

44

I WENT UPSTAIRS to the bedroom and took off my clothes and arranged myself on the bed in a seductive pose. I waited for Adam, adjusting an arm, arching my back, waited for him to come upstairs and make love to me.

"Come upstairs," I finally called.

After a long time I heard Adam's footsteps up the stairs and into the bedroom. My heart was pounding. He stood there looking at me on the bed.

"Did you brush your teeth yet?" he said.

"No." I got up and went to the bathroom to brush my teeth and when I got back, Adam was lying on the bed naked, in the same pose I'd been in. I lay on top of him and kissed his neck, which made him very shy. He rolled on top and I sucked in my breath. His weight felt good on me.

When I worked, I tried to stay on top. I had better control that way. A working girl knows never to end up with her legs over a man's shoulders. Knees are her best self-defense. My eyes wandered to the digital clock. I don't have to keep track of time, I told myself. I liked his butt and the hair on his chest. He had big arm muscles.

He managed to put on a condom and we did it. I made a lot of noise and he said it was good we were in the country. I felt awkward and young. And after I sort of came I burst into tears. For a while he didn't even notice I was crying, and then he handed me his white cotton underpants to blow my nose in and he held me tight until he fell asleep.

When I cry I always think about my father. Even if I start crying about something completely unrelated, like sex with a man, I end up thinking about my father. I had called him from Provincetown when I was waiting for Adam to come out of the men's room, to see if he wanted me to bring him any salt water taffy, and he ended up hanging up on me. He said he thought my brother should consider going to work at a fish cannery in Alaska for a year to get some real life experience instead of going straight to college, and I told him you always see people on Geraldo who lost an arm at one of those places, and he hung up on me.

The next morning I woke up clutching Adam's underpants and called his name but he wasn't in the house. A note on his pillow said, "Went for milk, please make coffee." I had no idea how to make coffee, so I took a very quick shower and snooped around in his closets and drawers for a while. I examined the medicine chest. There was a bottle of green and yellow pills with a label that had been ripped off. I put one in my pocket to have analyzed at a lab later. I stayed wrapped in a big white towel. I look better in a towel than in anything else. I always used to tell them at Blanche's that they should let me work in a towel.

When Adam got back, he made coffee and I went out on the back porch in my towel. His phone rang. I could hear him talking. "Just calm down," he said. I saw him write something down through the screen door. "Everything's going to be fine, Vivian," he said.

"We have to go back to the city," he told me. "My friend Lars is in the hospital."

"I know Lars."

"You know the Wolf?"

"I know Lars and Vivian," I told him.

I knew at that moment that it was in the cards, we were

supposed to be together, and nothing that I could do, no stupid thing I said, would ruin it.

I told him about working at Millie's Tavern on Bleecker Street, about the night I had spent with Vivian in the pool and how I had gone to their wedding. He told me about his friend the Judge and how they hung around at McGovern's and how Lars had asked him to drive him to his daughter's wedding.

We got on the road, headed for Adam's apartment on the Upper East Side. I was relieved to be leaving the country.

The trip was smooth and quick and easy and I kept my clothes on the whole time.

45

LARS WENT TO the hospital in the middle of the night, naked and wrapped in a sheet. They thought he was DOA. His condition was critical. They hooked him to an IV. His body shook for three days without alcohol.

Vivian stayed with him in the hospital. "I'm his wife, goddammit." She wouldn't leave. She spoon-fed him vodka. Then she brought fifths with the kind of straw that bends. When the nurses confiscated it, she said, "Don't worry, Lars, they've got vodka in that IV bag. Clear cold vodka. Stoli's." Lars was calmed by the thought of alcohol running into his arm.

"The nurse complimented my strong arms," he said.

The doctor came to his room often despite no insurance

and no job, and despite Vivian. "If you take one more sip, just one more drop of liquor, it will kill you instantly," he said.

Adam and I visited along with some of the regulars from McGovern's. "No more drinking, huh Wolf?"

"Oh, no," Lars said. "The doctor said that was up to me. He suggested moderation, but it's up to me. When I get back, drinks are on me. My painting's still hanging, right? You put your heart and soul into a work of art, you expect to get a little recognition and some cash for Christ's sake. If it makes one person smile I'll be happy. That's how I used to feel about my sermons.

"They've got a lot of cute little nurses around here, let me tell you, but Vivian has nothing to worry about. I'll be faithful to Vivian even while I'm here on vacation. I really miss her.

"My daughter came to visit me—she's still here, she just went to get some decent food for us. She said when she has a son she'll name him Lars. If she has a daughter she'll name her Vivian.

"When am I going to get out of this place? Didn't anyone bring me any . . . Yup, the doctor said I could just have a few drinks in the evening.

"Beer is fine. I can have all the beer I want, but he said with food. So I can have a big steak with French fries and a beer, or some chili. He said I was looking pretty good for an old man. I'll tell you, I don't know what we're supposed to do for sex around here—Vivian's shy here in the hospital. When I get out we're going to have a big party—steaks and homemade fried chicken, potato salad, cornsticks, mashed potatoes, lemonade, and my little girls will come, my two daughters, and we'll go to the park. They can play the video games at McGovern's—the kids love that.

"I love you guys. Coming here to see the old Wolf. If you guys ever need something, I'm there—a place to sleep or a drink or anything. I feel great with you guys here, and my whole family came from Connecticut and they brought meat-loaf and mashed potatoes and mashed potatoes. Oh it was *great*! I'm telling you, I should come here more often!"

"Yeah, that's great, Wolf."

"Don't worry, Lars, your painting made a lot of people smile. Some people even laughed, Lars."

"We'll have a big party in your honor, Wolf."

"You'll get out soon. The doctor says you're doing great."

"We miss you, Wolf. We're saving your place at the bar for when you get back."

There was one published poet at McGovern's who always made up limericks. He made one up for Lars in the hospital. He stood at the foot of the bed and recited:

"There once was a man from North Moore Street
Who liked to drink booze from his ma's teat
She said try a glass
And swatted his ass
And now he gets blood on the bedsheet."

"God, I love those," Lars said. "I love the way you do that right on the spot."

We all said goodbye to Lars.

46

LARS DID GET out of the hospital. The bleeding had stopped. He went straight to McGovern's and sat on his stool. "Vodka and orange juice, hold the orange juice."

"How about just the orange juice, Wolf?"

"No, come on, I'm taking it easy. Just one good pour. It's the Fourth of July."

"It's the sixth of July."

"I *know*, but I was in the hospital on the Fourth."

"All right, buddy. We're glad to have you back."

Lars drank. "Where is everybody?"

"They'll be here in a coupla hours." It was only three in the afternoon. Hank Williams was playing. "Take off your sunglasses, Wolf."

"Oh yeah, thanks. I thought it seemed dark in here." There was a picture light illuminating Lars's self-portrait. Lars hadn't gotten the shape of his face quite right, but the pale pink color of it was accurate.

"I feel very sad," the bartender said.

"What?"

"Nothing."

"That's a hell of a thing to say, Peter. You feel sad. You feel sad? What does that mean?" Lars asked.

"It doesn't mean anything."

"Well fuck you."

"All right, fuck me."

"No thank you, I'll stick with Vivian. You know what I missed most in the hospital? Being able to get up and take a nice long leak whenever I want to. I think I'll exercise my right to take a leak right now, Peter. So don't be sad."

"We all love you, Wolf."

"You guys are my family. My own family didn't come to the hospital, but you guys did."

He got off the stool and walked to the men's room. Past the jukebox, past the Michelob Christmas sign, past a man asleep where Lars had been when the *New York* magazine photographer came, past the one mysterious beam of sunlight on the floor that no one could figure out, past the chalkboard with the day's lunch selection written on it. Today was meat-loaf with mashed potatoes and gravy, $6.95.

He stopped in front of the men's room door. "I'll have a plate of that," he said. He opened the door and let it bang shut.

"He must be taking one good leak," Peter said to the man who worked in the kitchen.

"Hey guys, there's no ass-wipe in here, dammit! Get me some A.W." Lars opened the door a crack and Peter handed him a roll. "Jesus Christ!"

Peter put Lars's plate at his place at the bar, with a spoon instead of a fork. "Lars likes meatloaf with a spoon so he doesn't lose any gravy or any peas." The gravy congealed on the meatloaf. There was a loud thud. Peter knocked on the bathroom door and then tore it open, breaking the metal hook.

"Well it's not a bad way to go, old Wolf, in the john of your favorite bar, with a brand-new roll of ass-wipe." He called an ambulance, flushed the shit and blood in the toilet, and picked Lars up off the floor and held him.

Lars never really had a funeral. The hospital notified his family, but they didn't want anything to do with it, and Vivian refused to claim the body. Nobody in McGovern's had a grasp of the situation. The Judge hosted a big party in Lars's memory and everybody thought about him a lot. There would be silence and then someone would say, "I was just thinking about the Wolf," and then the other person would say, "Yeah, me too." Vivian told everybody he was buried in the rented tuxedo, but no one was sure he was even buried.

Vivian sat on Lars's barstool facing his portrait and cried every day.

"I am a widow," Vivian wept. "A wid—ooow." The Judge comforted her with money and compliments, with money and drinks. Everybody missed Lars. Everybody was very kind to Vivian. Adam was very sad about Lars. "If you think about it, it was because of the Wolf that we met," Adam kept saying to me. Of course I had thought about it. I thought about Lars and Vivian on Martha's Vineyard, so out of place, yelling and scraping, in their wedding clothes.

> There once was a drunk in black tie
> Who liked to eat chicken pot pie
> He also ate pussy
> He wasn't a wussy
> And now six feet under he'll lie.

GOING DOWN

PART 4

47

ON THE DAY Lars died, my brother called me from my father's country house. "Annie's dead," he said.

For a moment I had no idea who he was talking about and then I realized it was the dog. I had just been thinking about that dog over the Fourth of July. How she was so afraid of fireworks.

Once someone set off a firecracker on Sullivan Street and Annie bolted, her leash trailing behind her like a kite string. My father searched until three in the morning and found her in front of his building, where she had been waiting for hours.

"One can't live one's life scared," my father would say. "One can't be afraid to die." Shouldn't one be afraid that one's kids could die?

At times my father did show concern. He came with me to elementary school one morning, carrying an enormous green fan which he plugged in right behind my desk. It was very hot in the classroom. He explained to the principal that the lack of air was killing my brain cells.

Recently my father had taken me out to dinner and told me how good his moving upstate had been for Annie. "She loves it so much, Annie, I mean Benny. She's so happy. I should have done it years ago. She's outside for hours and hours, just running."

My father laughed. He had installed a birdhouse on a low

branch. Annie killed bird after bird all day long. "I should really take that down," he said.

My father grimly told me about a time in the apartment on Eighth street when he had punished Annie for going in the house. When people tell pet stories, I never listen, but my stomach clenched when he told me that it wasn't her fault, she was sick with diarrhea. "Oh, and she felt soooo terrible," my father said, his forehead crinkled, corners of his mouth down. "I felt such shame, such severe remorse, after I had rubbed her nose in it. I'm still suffering terribly, terribly."

How about my nose? I wondered. I got up to use the ladies' room.

"Do you still have that bladder problem?" my father asked. "You're not on another one of those crazy diets?"

My brother told me Annie had run off during a big thunderstorm upstate several days before. My father called the pounds in all the neighboring counties and filed a report with the ASPCA. He called radio stations and had descriptions of Annie broadcast on the air. Every time he called the local pound he got an answering machine, so he left message after message.

"He did everything he could," Dylan said sadly.

"He can't even take care of a dog," I said.

"What are you talking about, Benny? He was a very good father to that dog. Why do you always have to be so hard on him?" My brother sounded as emotional and serious as if he were defending an innocent man on death row. Dylan was always defending my father even though he was trying to talk Dylan into joining the Air Force when he finished high school. At least I tried to retain a sense of humor about the whole thing. I had to drag the rest of the details out of him.

On the second day after Annie's disappearance, my father started to get worried. Annie could get so disoriented in a storm, and the rain would wash away familiar smells. He knew that if a pound found a dog, they were supposed to call other pounds to see if a dog had been reported missing.

"On the third morning Dad freaked out," my brother said.

He got in the four-wheel drive that Siobhan's father had given them, and without even telling Siobhan where he was going, he sped to the local pound to see if anyone had gotten his messages.

"Dad got pulled over for speeding and they gave him a ticket. He got so mad he almost punched out the cop," Dylan said proudly.

When my father finally got to the pound, he saw Annie on the table. "Come on, Annie," he said.

"Is that your dog?" the voice that had been on the answering machine said.

"Yes."

"You're too late."

My father lunged at the man but he locked himself in the back room. He carried Annie to the car in his arms. She was still warm, he was an hour too late. They buried her in their yard under the birdhouse tree.

I was really shaken up after I heard all this. Dylan told me that Annie's name had been added to the plaque in the Cauldron. It said "Those Who Have Left Us For That Big Bar In The Sky." There were four names on the plaque, and five blank spaces. Annie was the only dog. I felt bad thinking about her in a big bar in the sky instead of a big meadow. I thought of Lars. I couldn't help but picture my father's name on the plaque in one of the blank spaces.

"Well, he's only a dog," I told Dylan.

"The best dog," he said.

"Is Dad there?" I asked. Dylan went to get him. He had just gotten back from a town meeting where he was preparing a lawsuit against the pound.

"I'm sorry about Annie," I said.

"I miss my girl. Oh, I miss my girl so much," he said. "I

have so many regrets." His voice was tight, stuck back in his throat like mine gets when I talk to him. "It shouldn't have happened. They're supposed to wait. That son of a bitch did it for the money. They get thirty bucks for each dog they murder. Oh, I miss my girl. I can't bear it. Oh, I miss my girl, my good girl."

"Maybe we can have dinner some time, when you're in the city, Dad."

"I won't be down there for a few months," my father said.

48

ON SEPTEMBER 29 of what would have been my sophomore year, Adam and I celebrated our three-month anniversary. We went to a Japanese restaurant on University Place.

I had just read in *Cosmo* that the three-month mark was the most precarious point in a romance, because that was when men decided whether or not they wanted to continue the relationship. The article said that most break-ups occurred in the third month, and there were scientific studies and plenty of testimonials to prove it.

I got to the restaurant first and told the waitress that I wanted to sit at the little table behind the delicate screen. I had to sit there. I was deep in some kind of Japanese fantasy world. I wanted to slip off my cork platform shoes, sit on the floor in my socks, behind the screen, at the short-legged lacquered table under the paper lantern.

"How many are you?" the waitress asked.

"Two," I said proudly.

It is such a treat to take off your shoes in New York City. A Japanese restaurant is the closest you can get to being at the seaside. There is the smell of fish and getting a mouthful of seaweed. I wrapped my hands in the small hot towel. It felt good on the back of my neck.

I ordered green tea and waited for Adam. He came a few minutes later and struggled to take off his shoes. His socks were gray with a paisley pattern and he looked self-conscious, rocking back and forth on the square cushion on the floor, trying to get comfortable. We sat with our legs stretched out under the table and our feet in each other's laps. His had a slight odor, but I loved him so much I didn't care. Shivers of love ran through me.

He told me he loved me and that I was the best thing that ever happened to him.

The waitress came over and I ordered chicken teriyaki and he made a disapproving sound. "Why don't you at least try one bite of fish," he said.

I loved him so much, I almost considered eating the squid he held in front of my mouth. I felt like I could do anything for Adam.

We ate, dodging scallions in our miso soup, and talked and laughed.

He suggested I skip dessert but I ordered green tea ice cream anyway. He scrutinized the check and paid. We stood up, put on our shoes, and took a cab to his apartment on the Upper East Side, eager to begin our fourth month together.

49

I WENT TO a diet doctor's office and sat next to a fat man on the couch. The waiting room was packed. I love being in these fat situations because I am always the thinnest person there. The fat man asked me if I had the time. I could tell he liked me.

On the coffee table in front of us there was a display called "What Five Pounds of Fat Looks Like." It was a large yellow and green plastic object that looked like molded vomit.

A nurse with a diamond ring said, "Dr. Label will see you now," and she led me into a room with pictures of frozen entrees and a chart of a man shrinking, as if someone had tied a ribbon around his waist and was pulling it tighter and tighter. There was a photo of Dr. Label in a military uniform, and one of him with his arm around Sally Jessy Raphael. He was a short German man with a toupee.

Dr. Label weighed me and took my blood pressure. His face was tan with a bright patch where a mustache must have been. He sat behind a big desk.

"You have trouble with your thyroid," he said.

"Really?"

"Absolutely."

"Interesting." He gave me a diet plan for five hundred calories a day and some pills for my thyroid problem.

"Just one peanut could ruin this diet."

"Really, one peanut?"

"Okay, now take your jeans down."

I hesitated.

"Take your jeans down so I can show you how to give yourself the injections."

I wanted to be thin for Adam. I unzipped my jeans and pushed them down to my knees. I looked over Dr. Label's diplomas, which were all in German. He rubbed alcohol on the top of my thigh with a cotton ball, grabbed a handful of flesh, and shot the syringe into me. It hurt. My skin started to bruise. "You give yourself a shot twice a day. Keep the syringes refrigerated. Pay the receptionist."

I had a feeling that Dr. Label was not a nice man. A woman at Blanche's had highly recommended him. She had a thyroid problem too. It turned out everyone who went to Dr. Label had a thyroid problem. I shouldn't have taken her advice. She was forty-five and lived in the Bronx with a man who wore a peach-colored nightgown and was her slave. She also had a rabbit-puppet with whom she would have long conversations in the living room at Blanche's. Blanche fired her after a couple of days.

I left Dr. Label's office with my bag of pills and my syringes. The fat man was still sitting on the couch trying to lose weight. I walked to East Forty-fourth Street. I had an interview at Gail's. It was supposed to be the best house in New York and the hardest to get into. They only hired very young girls who had never worked before. My interview was with a man named Dan. I felt nervous and sad. When I made the appointment I didn't plan on keeping it. Adam and I had had an argument. It was one of those masochistic days when you try on jeans at The Gap, go to a diet doctor, and then have an interview at a whorehouse.

Adam thought I should get a job where I made good money. He thought I should work out at a gym. He thought I should learn how to drive and cook and appreciate the country. Work harder, be more disciplined, less wild. More serious. Meditate, get acupuncture, go to the dentist and eye doctor, do laundry, start a garden upstate, be more punctual, get up early, not watch Oprah Winfrey, read the newspaper, wear Timberland hiking boots and a Patagonia rain jacket, never eat butter. I thought he was right about getting a job where I made good money. It would be interesting just to see the place even if I didn't get the job, or didn't take it. If I got the job, I could just work for a week or two and put a little money away so I could look for a real job. Adam was buying me so many presents, I wanted to get him something. I really wanted to buy Adam a fishing rod.

I walked up the brownstone steps and rang the doorbell. I was buzzed in and stood in the vestibule. I waited next to recycle bins: Glass, Plastic, Paper, Aluminum. I felt trapped. I was buzzed through another door, walked up a flight of stairs, and stood facing Dan. We were the same height. He looked like Dr. Label without the toupee, and had eyebrows that slanted upwards to somehow give the impression of horns. When he turned to lead me into a room, I noticed a bulge in the back of his pants, as if he had a tail coiled up and kept in a pouch there.

I followed him into a large living room, elaborately furnished with antique chairs, four-foot urns, and huge stereo speakers. Dan asked me where I went to high school, where I lived, what my parents did. "Have you ever done this before?"

"No never, my father's a math professor."

"Do you think you can handle it?"

"I think so." I was being very careful not to slip, I was trying to act like a virgin. I looked around wide-eyed. "What exactly do you have to, you know, do?" I asked.

"You spend time in the room. You have to do oral and intercourse." He spoke in a whisper. I strained to hear him.

"Do you use a condom?"

"Yes, always. Let me see you."

"What do you mean?"

"Undress." He sat on the edge of the overstuffed chair.

I unzipped my jeans before taking off my cowboy boots, and then had to kick them off awkwardly. I stood in a bra and panties.

"Take everything off. What's that?" He was pointing to the bruise on my inner thigh.

"A doctor gave me an injection today." He came over and looked at it, putting his cold hand on my leg.

"You could stand to lose a few pounds but we can use you."

"I can only work days," I said. Adam went to his office at eight-thirty every morning and he usually got home by seven. I wanted all my nights free to be with him. If I worked days I'd be able to go home and shower before meeting him at his apartment.

"Come back tomorrow then, at ten-thirty."

"Okay."

"Bring a few outfits."

"Okay."

"I won't be seeing you again, I just do the interviewing. It was nice meeting you. I'm glad you decided to take the plunge. Goodbye, Bennington."

"Goodbye," I said.

I walked to La Fondue on Fifty-fifth Street and had cheese fondue and a chocolate fondue sundae with peanuts. I wrote a letter to Perry Shepherd on Martha's Vineyard. I told her all about Adam, all the things we did and how much I liked him. I missed her high voice, bursting out in tears, nervous laughter, false statements, spending all her money, jealousy, faulty lamps, and gifts of torn lace dresses. *I miss you*, I wrote. The waitress cleared my gold pen away with the silverware.

50

I NEEDED STOCKINGS for my first day at Gail's, so I went to the lingerie store where I bought Vivian's nightgown. I brought a dozen pairs of black stockings up to the counter. I knelt and reached my hands into a tangle of garter belts, panties, G-strings, and bras in a sale basket. It was luxurious and messy like the top drawers I snooped through when I used to babysit. What a wonderful place this would be to work, better than a flower shop. I chose a lavender garter belt with black lace and a tiny rhinestone. I could hide my scar with a little makeup.

The drag queen behind the counter stopped arranging the pajamas and picked up the garter belt. "Isn't it pretty? I have the whole set myself." He counted the stockings. I never know how I'm supposed to act around those people, am I supposed to pretend that I don't know he's a man? I gave him a knowing look.

"You know, these are size A-B," he said.

"Yes I know."

"You know these are stockings, not pantyhose."

"Yes, I know what I'm buying."

"Oh I see you're a real pro," he said. I didn't say anything, I didn't feel a need to justify myself to a drag queen. "Cash or charge?"

"Cash."

"Of course."

I grabbed the shopping bag and took a cab to Gail's.

I waited a long time in the vestibule to be buzzed up. I stood there wondering what to do—push the buzzer again? Was it broken? I noticed that the Queen of Hearts was clothespinned to my bookbag from some store's bag check. I was sweating. Finally, I heard a click and I pushed through the door and up the stairs. Leaning against a large formal desk was a thirty-two-year-old girl, I can always pinpoint a person's exact age, wearing tight black jeans and a white cotton blouse with big flouncy sleeves. She had shoulder-length chocolate-brown hair with bangs trying to cover her forehead. The French doors to the living room where I had had my interview with Dan were closed.

"My name is Courtney," the girl said. "You've probably heard of me. Change in the bathroom there and put your things in the first cubby on the bottom."

I walked into the bathroom and shut the door. I took off all my clothes and pulled the new garter belt out of the plastic bag. I ripped the tag off but the plastic wire stayed. I heard my mother's voice telling me to use scissors. I put on the garter belt and felt the plastic wire digging into my waist. It felt good. As long as I felt that stinging pain I was in control. If I wanted to stop it I could get a pair of scissors and cut it right off. I pulled on a pair of stockings and clipped them to the garter belt. I put on lace panties, a new Betsy Johnson halter dress, and red high heels.

You have to spend money to make money.

I left the bathroom and found my little cubby. I remembered my cubby in nursery school with my name written in black Magic Marker on purple construction paper: BEN-NINGTON B. I lined up eleven pairs of stockings and a box of Ramses Unlubricated. I took my grandmother's delicate beaded purse out of my bookbag and put a strip of condoms and a lipstick in it.

"Let me see you," Courtney said from the reception area.

I walked through the door. "You look Spanish. I think we'll call you Marguerita or Juanita."

"I'd like to use Daphne," I said.

"That sounds quite hookerish."

"I don't think I would feel comfortable using the name Juanita."

"I think I know a little bit more about this business than you do, Bennington. I think I know what sells."

"Well, I'll use whatever you think," I said. I wouldn't work here if I had to be named Juanita. I tried to tell myself not to let my ego get in the way of a good job at the best house in New York. The only whorehouse with cubbies.

"No, use Daphne. I really don't care. The last thing in the world I care about is what names you girls use. Please empty the dishwasher. Glasses go in the cabinet above the washing machine and, well you'll see where everything else goes."

I walked into the kitchen. Off the kitchen was a small room with cushioned benches built into each of the four walls. A beautiful girl sat on one of the benches reading a paperback.

"Hi, I'm Daphne," I said.

"I'm Alana." She turned the page of her book and kept reading.

"Today's my first day."

"Today's my last. I finally saved enough."

"For what?"

"A nose job." She looked up at me for the first time, and I could see that a nose job would be a good investment.

"You have a great nose, Alana." It's always good to say a person's name a lot.

"I hate when people say that. Would you like to see a picture of my car?"

"Sure." She got up and went to her cubby. In the business Alana would be described as tall and willowy.

A woman, fifty, dressed very shabbily in black clothes and paint-spattered sneakers, appeared in the doorway. She had white blond hair tied into a severe twist on top of her head. She had small piercing eyes under invisible eyebrows and lashes, high cheekbones, and a very stern expression.

"Who are you?" she asked. Her voice was soft, which surprised me. I had expected her to yell, maybe in German. "Oh, you're Bennington, the new girl."

"Yes, I'm using the name Daphne."

"Oh that's lovely. Dan was pleased with you."

"Thank you."

"I'm Gail, this is my place. It's the nicest place in New York. I have the best clients. The rules are you do whatever I say. If I ever catch you giving out your phone number, seeing clients behind my back, or stealing money, I will kill you. I'm sure you'll do very well here, don't cut your hair. You have an appointment in ten minutes." She left the kitchen and I put away the few glasses that were in the dishwasher. I went into the "breakfast room" and sat across from Alana and tried to read a magazine.

Gail walked into the kitchen again and screamed at the top of her lungs. "Whose piece of shit is this?" I sat up straight. "Whose fucking piece of shit is this?" Gail was standing in the doorway screaming and cursing at me and Alana. She raised her hand above her head and hurled something at me. My beaded purse hit the side of my face and fell on the cushion next to me. I picked it up. "Whose ugly piece of shit is that?" She spoke slowly now, emphasizing every word.

"It's mine," I said.

"Don't you put your cheap little piece of shit on my beautiful brand new washing machine, you little whore. That machine is worth more than you'll ever be." She stormed out of the room and down the stairs and I sat there red-faced and shaking.

I wanted to call Adam.

"Daphne, please come meet your client," Courtney said. I stood up. "Don't forget to get paid up front, one hundred eighty for the hour." I followed her into the living room. "Styx, this is Daphne, Daphne this is Styx, one of our favorite clients."

"Very pleased to meet you." He held out his hand and I shook it carefully. He was very old and looked like he was made out of shards of glass.

"You're in the first room at the top of the stairs." It took us fifteen minutes to climb the stairs and get into the room. It was painted dark red and had plush carpeting and a king-size bed with a fitted sheet and two pillows. Styx spent a long time peeling two hundred-dollar bills from a big roll of what looked like wet leaves. Every time I walk down a street after it rains I have to stop every few seconds because the wet leaves under my feet sound like dollar bills. I keep looking down and getting that slight disappointed feeling.

Styx finally handed me the money and asked for change. "Please hurry," he said. "I'm ninety-four years old, I haven't got much time."

"You're ninety-four?"

"How old did you think I was, Daisy?"

"Daphne. I don't know. Early sixties?"

"Aren't you a little flatter." He was too old to finish the word. "You're a cutie."

I walked down the stairs and stood in front of Courtney's desk. She was on the phone and looked at me with a condescending deadpan expression, as if I were crazy. "What?" she said.

"Styx paid me," I said.

"Imagine that!" She quickly covered the mouthpiece and said, "You give me the money." I handed her two hundred-dollar bills and she handed me a twenty. "If he tips you, you bring it to me at the end of the session, and I give you back all your money at the end of the shift."

"Okay."

"Grab Alana and tell her to show you how to do the light test."

"What's the light test?"

"Alana help Daphne with the light."

Alana came out of the room carrying a lamp with no shade. I followed her up the stairs and into the room where Styx was sitting on the bed wearing a shirt and tie with no pants or underwear. They were lying in a heap under the hook on the wall. Alana plugged the lamp in and told me to hold it over Styx's dick. I held the lamp and she slowly and methodically started looking through Styx's pubic hair, parting it with her long red fingernails.

"We always check for crabs, or any other visible diseases." I was horrified.

"How am I, nurse?" Styx said, laughing and coughing. "My favorite kind of check-up."

"You're just fine, sweetie," Alana said, unplugging the lamp. "'Bye. Have fun." She left the room and I put his twenty on the bedside table.

"Why don't you take your shirt and tie off," I said.

"I leave it on. It's too much trouble. But take your clothes off, please." I peeled my dress off, over my bare breasts. "I like it slow," he warbled. "Daisy, do me one favor. Before you show me the rest of you, tell me what you call it."

"What I call it?"

"You know, what you named your virgina, pussy, snitch-snatch, honeypot."

"What I named it?"

"Yes, I call my thing Twiggy. Everybody has a name for theirs."

"Oh, mine is named Tribeca. That stands for the triangle below Canal Street."

"I love Tribeca! I knew Tribeca before anybody else did. Before the Tribeca Griddle Restr'nt. I spent the happiest days of my life there."

He lunged at me and kissed my neck, his lips shaking. A moment later he was done. I didn't think anything had happened but he explained that he had had an operation. "No white stuff comes out. No fuss, no muss. That's why all the girls love me here," he said.

I lay on the bed and watched him get dressed. I had watched Adam get dressed that morning. Wiping the shaving cream from his neck with a towel, cursing a broken button, selecting a tie. I was spending most nights at his house now, then going back to my mother's in the morning to change my clothes.

Styx had sneakers that fastened with Velcro. I bent down to help him with them and he patted me on the head. We then began the long, slow descent to the front door.

51

AFTER STYX I saw six more clients.

"I hope I didn't work you too hard," Courtney said in a moment of kindness. I leaned against the wall with my high heels in my hands.

"When I'm here I want to work as much as possible."

It was almost six-thirty and I was supposed to have been able to leave at five but Courtney had asked me to stay later and I didn't think I should say no on my first day.

She was lying on the floor doing sit-ups with her toes hooked under the desk.

I tried to think of something I could compliment her on

but I couldn't. "What are you working on?" I asked. I had seen her working on a laptop computer.

"I'm writing my thesis on women in literature who drown." She unhooked her toes and rubbed her hand over her stomach to test for flatness, then stood up and turned her back to me. I noticed she had little black pieces of lint all over the back of her white blouse. I walked over to her and touched her back with a quick brushing stroke. Her entire body became rigid. Even the pleats in her blouse became more pleated. "You have lint."

"Oh."

I brushed a few more times.

"Thank you." She sat down at the computer, and I went back into the room where the girls waited. One had a very small body and a big head like Vanna White. She said her name was Melissa.

"Thank God today is almost over." She was walking around in a pair of pink thong panties. She pulled on a pair of jeans and a T-shirt with no bra. "I have to teach two aerobics classes and then meet my Strasberg partner. Today was torture. I met a nice guy a few weeks ago and it was really hard to concentrate on work today. I really feel like taking a break from this and giving him a chance."

"A chance for what?" Courtney said, standing in the doorway. "Melissa, I want you to do one more. Steve Doctor for a half hour."

All the clients gave a first name and a code word, like Mike Mercedes, Charles Tennis, etc.

"My shift is over Courtney, I'm finished. I've already changed."

"No one told you to change."

"I don't see Steve Doctor. He's a psycho. I want to go home."

"Melissa, we're very flexible with you. Steve wants to see you. You have to."

"I'm not going to."

Courtney stormed out of the room.

"Steve Doctor is awful," Melissa said. "He writes on you in lipstick. He's sick and he's a pediatrician. Isn't that disgusting?"

Courtney walked back in. "Daphne, you will see Steve Doctor for a half and then you're done for the day. And Melissa, Gail says you're fired, and if you want your money for the day you have to come by tomorrow and talk to her personally. Lynn, help Daphne do the light test."

Lynn grabbed the lamp. She was a plain girl from St. Louis. She hadn't seen any clients. She had been sitting on one of the benches all day writing in a Hello Kitty notebook. I was dying to know what she was writing about me, so when I was alone in the room for a few minutes I opened her notebook and read: *I want to do something with my life I want to do something with my life when will Conrans deliver my couch.*

By now I was a pro at the light test. I had even come up with some cute things to say during the examination. Steve Doctor was ready for us. He had taken a shower and he was wrapped in a towel on the bed—clean, clean-cut, and not bad-looking. I collected the money and brought it down to Courtney. I was tired. My legs hurt. My hair hurt from being pulled in a clip.

"Daphne, don't pay any attention to Steve Doctor, he just likes to play mind games," Courtney said. "Oh, and didn't your mother ever teach you how to make a bed? The pillows should be standing up against the headboard."

After every client I had to change the fitted sheet and both pillowcases and spray air freshener into the room. I went back up to the top floor.

"Did they tell you about me?" Steve Doctor asked.

"No."

He looked disappointed. "Take off your clothes," he said. I took off my Betsy Johnson dress and lay on the bed. "Stand up." He took a new red lipstick out of a brown paper bag. The receipt floated down onto the rug. He handed me a paper hospital gown. "Put this on with the opening in the back and leave it untied." I put it on and he grabbed the front and ripped a big hole down the middle. "That's good. Turn around." He opened the lipstick and I felt it on my back. "You're a whore. Say it."

"I'm a whore."

"You're a slut."

"I'm a slut." He was writing words on my back. The lipstick felt like a tongue, and I stiffened. I have a very sensitive back.

"Suck my cock."

"I have to get a condom out of my purse."

"I said *suck* it."

"I know, I need a condom."

"You put a condom on to suck? No one else does."

"Well I do and everyone's supposed to."

"Fuck you, you little whore. You think you're a smart whore, don't you?" He was jerking off holding the lipstick in his other hand. He came all over himself, tore the hospital gown off me and cleaned himself with it. He got dressed and walked out of the room before I could get myself together to escort him down the stairs. I looked at my back over my shoulder in the full-length mirror. He had written *I am a slut Fuck me here* with a big arrow pointing to my ass.

Courtney knocked on the door. She came in holding towels. "These are old towels we use when he comes because they get stained with the lipstick. Take a shower. I'll fix up your room for you."

I got into the shower. I scrubbed my back with Softsoap and a towel, but the lipstick wouldn't come off. I rubbed baby oil on my back and the words became illegible but you could still see lipstick. I wouldn't be able to see Adam until I got it all off. I would have to call him and tell him I was sick or something. I went downstairs and put on my clothes.

"Tough day?" Courtney asked.

"Very."

"Go home." She handed me a roll of money. I sat down and counted. Nine hundred and ten dollars.

"Wow," Alana said.

52

I HAD TOLD Adam that I was working for a catering company. All the girls I knew at NYU were either call girls or caterers, which is how I got the idea. It seemed like such a vague occupation, working for a catering company. "What do you do again?" Adam would occasionally ask me, and I would say, "I specialize in children's birthday parties," or "I take the bookings." Once I even said, "I'm usually in the field." I used my theory of nonchalance.

It seemed like the perfect cover-up. It explained why sometimes I made a lot of money and sometimes I didn't. It explained why I couldn't call him from work because I was out in the field. There was no particular bar or restaurant where he could visit me.

But Adam started asking a lot of questions. Where was the "office" I had talked about? Where were these late-night parties? What was the phone number?

The answers came as easily as the men who paid me. I was a good liar. I bought business cards that said *Executive Caterers*, and *Junior Executive Caterers* for the children's parties. I got a voice mailbox and paid for a year in advance so I wouldn't receive any bills.

My friend Yuki helped me. She was the girl I had seen behind the desk at the Jane West Hotel and then in the living room at Blanche's. I had been calling her from time to time to find out the gossip at Blanche's. When Yuki had to quit Blanche's because the IRS was auditing everyone there, I got her a job at Gail's.

Yuki did my voice-mail tape to fool Adam. "Hello," she said on the recording. "You've reached the Executive and Junior Executive Catering Company," with music in the background.

The whole thing was very convincing. I left the business cards lying around all over Adam's apartment. I also had some note pads made up with the company logo and occasionally called Yuki and pretended to write down an order: a fake address, *pick up 40 party hats, 20 lbs lasagna, Mrs. Shapiro, apt 2B.* I called the voice mailbox constantly but there was never a message from Adam.

Sometimes I thought Adam seemed suspicious.

"Where's your office again?" he asked.

"Midtown."

"Where?"

"In the fifties."

"Is it in an office building?"

Finally I told him it was in a woman's apartment.

"Can I pick you up there?"

"No, she doesn't like people to know where she lives. She hates men. She's eccentric. She's an eccentric lesbian. She has two full kitchens. She's a millionaire."

Whenever Adam asked me about my job, I just made up more crazy things about my boss. I was even beginning to believe it myself.

I was walking down Fifth Avenue with Adam, after he

dragged me to an antique rug exhibit at the Metropolitan Museum. I told him I couldn't stay too long because I had to go to work.

"Where's your uniform?" he asked.

"I left it at work." When I was living with Andre Singh, I had worked for one day as a waitress at the Stage Deli on Seventh Avenue. I had spent a hundred dollars for a uniform and black shoes. I was trailing, and I only made five dollars and spent fifteen on a cab back to Roosevelt Island. My feet hurt so much that Andre rubbed them while I sat on the couch crying. I never went back, but the uniform came in handy now.

It was nice standing on Fifth Avenue with Adam. I was wearing sneakers and I bent down to tie my laces. My jeans cut into my stomach. I had almost sprained my hand trying them on at The Gap.

"Let me hold your bag for you," Adam said. He grabbed my bookbag and put it over his shoulder.

"Thanks."

I was telling him some long story, undoing the knot, tying the laces, standing up, when I looked over at him. He was staring at my open bookbag.

"What's this?" He pulled a red spandex dress out of my bag, and a black high heel rolled onto the sidewalk. He stood straight holding the dress out in his finicky fingers. The dress was still in my shape.

"What the hell is this? Just what do you serve up at this catering company?"

"What the hell are you insinuating?" I said. I had never used the word "insinuating" before. It was a terrible word and a terrible mistake.

"What are you, a hooker?"

"I'm lending this dress to a friend at work."

"Is she a hooker, too?"

"She's in a show. It's a costume for a play."

"What play?"

"Genet's *The Balcony*."

A boy on a skateboard made a too-fast turn around the fountain and his skateboard flew out from under him. I covered my head. I have very bad depth perception.

I kissed Adam on the cheek.

"I'm sorry, Benny, I shouldn't have insinuated that." Something in his tone had changed. He kissed me hard on the lips. He held me in his arms for a long time. I was surprised because he usually didn't like "P.D.A." as he called it, public displays of affection. "I'll get you a cab," he said. "What's the address?"

I got into the back of a cab, pulling my bookbag in after me. That night, there was a message from Adam on the voice-mail tape.

53

I DECIDED TO give Adam the Persian carpet I had inherited from my grandmother ten years before. It was worth thousands of dollars and I had it in my closet, rolled up in garbage bags. I wanted him to have it. He had given me so many things and was talking about taking me to Italy after Christmas.

Adam was excited when I told him about the carpet. It needed to be cleaned and he told me to call his friend Hashim, who sold antique rugs. Hashim said I could drop off the rug and he would get it cleaned for me as a favor to Adam.

I brought the rug to the shop and a cabdriver helped me
drop it in the middle of Hashim's beautiful wood floor. There
were rugs everywhere on the walls and ceilings, ancient rugs
and kilims. Hashim showed me around the store and ended
the tour with a rug from the fourteenth century. He beamed
at it. It was his prize possession.

"It's perfect," he said. "Perfectly preserved. It is almost
impossible to have a rug of such age in such pristine condition." We stood in front of it for a long time. "Shall we open
up your rug and take a look at it?" he asked.

He was very handsome, tall and slim, in a silk suit and gold
cuff links. Adam told me that Hashim slept with two or three
women every night. He was only twenty-eight but he looked
much older, with a receding, Draculean hairline. He was a
millionaire. He had been to Elle MacPherson's birthday party
the night before. His father was some kind of king in Leba-
non. He went to L.A. or Monte Carlo on weekends. He was
unbelievably charming, saying, "That is magnificent!" or
"That is bullshit!" in a Lebanese accent.

"I'm afraid I'm taking you from your work," I said.

"That is bullshit!" he said. "It is no problem."

We walked over to my garbage-bagged heap, and he
opened it up using amber-and-jade scissors. It had been mag-
ical talking to Hashim, with beautiful Indian music playing
and all the rugs and bronze and ivory. He cut for several
minutes and peeled away layer after layer of black and then
green garbage bags. Then he unrolled the rug.

A cloud rose into the air. At first I thought it was dust
mushrooming up and filling the room. I couldn't see for a
few minutes but I could feel the dust hitting me like a wind-
storm in the desert.

Finally the dust settled and I looked down at my rug on
the floor. In the center of the rug was an enormous hole. All
that was left was the border of deep red wool.

"Take your filthy bag of moths and get out," Hashim screamed.

Moths! They were swarming in my face, burying themselves in my hair. They were everywhere, tiny and brown.

"This is live larvae! This will ruin me. Who sent you here?"

Hashim picked up the remains of the rug and bellowed at it in Arabic. He opened the heavy glass door and threw it out onto the sidewalk. It was so strange to see my inheritance, my beautiful gift to Adam, lying on Madison Avenue.

"Get out!" he screamed. "Get the fuck out of my store."

I stood frozen.

There were moths all over the back of his suit jacket. Every rug in the store was covered with a layer of tiny moths. An army of them swarmed to his fourteenth-century rug, the one in pristine condition.

"I didn't know. I'm sorry." I was clapping my hands together, trying to kill some of them, but I couldn't catch any.

"Just get out!" He tucked a small pillow under his shirt to protect it.

I was in big trouble.

I called Adam from a pay phone.

"Did you meet Hashim?" Adam asked. "Isn't he a great guy?"

"Well, there was a problem," I said.

"What kind of a problem?" Adam said slowly.

A bag lady examined the rug fragment and put it around her neck, poncho style.

I have nothing, I thought.

The bag lady struggled to double it like a long strand of pearls and walked away with my rug dragging after her on the street.

54

ADAM WAS INVITED to a black tie wedding in Summit, New Jersey, by a partner in his law firm. He bought me a black velvet gown trimmed in silk, and an evening bag that looked like a Fabergé egg. He carried the gown home in its Bendel's zippered case, in his arms, triumphantly. I followed him out of the store as if I were the one in his arms.

Once when I was seven, my nanny, Pierette, spilled a pot of boiling tomato soup on my neck and chest. It looked like blood pouring down my shoulders, my nipples, and stomach. We lived five blocks from a hospital and my father carried me there in his arms, while I watched as if from a distance. I watched myself being packed in a tub of ice, being bandaged, my father covered in tears and tomato soup too.

"You got here just in time to save her pretty white skin," the doctor said. My father loved me when I was seven.

Adam was very proud when we dressed for the wedding. We arrived in the middle of the ceremony and sat down quietly in the back of the church. The priest was talking about divorce. I waited for a moment to feel some sort of guilt, a prostitute, in a church, in black velvet. But it was just a dramatic notion and I felt nothing. Adam, on the other hand, looked panic-stricken at the idea of a wedding.

When the priest asked if anyone objected to the union, I wondered what would happen if I said, "I do," and rushed down the aisle.

My thoughts were interrupted when I noticed a familiar pile of blond curls, three rows in front of me, on a long slim neck. They had a sort of wet look which I recognized vaguely.

At the reception Adam and I danced, and he introduced me to a lot of people. When I met the bride I said she was wearing the most beautiful wedding gown I had ever seen. If I want to, I can say exactly the right thing to someone, exactly what they want to hear.

Across the room two blue eyes were staring at me under the blond curls and over a man's tuxedoed shoulder. It was Georgy, the girl I had done a double with at Le Tight Rope.

Adam was talking to a tall Frenchwoman wearing a tall black hat.

"It's a small world," Adam was saying, when a man waltzed over to me and said, "Daphne, I've been trying to get an appointment with you but you're never on anymore."

I felt my pantyhose rip between my thighs and run down the back of my leg. My barrette pinched my scalp. I wore a necklace of tiny hives.

Adam turned from the hat lady.

"I'm sorry, did I say the wrong thing?" the man said, and put his hand on my velvet puffed sleeve.

I stepped back. I looked at the man's face, but it looked like all other men's faces—shaved, nicked, round, chapped.

"You must have me confused with someone."

"Yes I must," the man said awkwardly, and fakely, as if he were winking.

Adam said nothing.

"My name is Bennington," I said and put out my hand, elbow bent, wrist limp, palm down, like Marilyn Monroe.

"I'm sorry, I thought you were someone else," he said, and walked over to two other guests.

"That was weird," Adam said. "What did he call you?"

"Daisy, I think."

"I think it was Daphne," Adam said.

"Weird. People always mistake me for someone." I told him the story about the time I was followed into the ladies' room of a coffee shop near Lincoln Center and asked for my autograph by a whole busload of old ladies from New Jersey.

"What did you do when they asked?"

"Signed my name."

We danced to the last two minutes of a song.

"You are the most beautiful woman here," Adam said. "And the best dressed." He was drinking champagne.

"I'll be right back," I said, and went to look for the ladies' room. Georgy followed me in.

"Do you remember me?" she whispered.

"Georgy."

"I'm here with a trick," she said.

"You're kidding. You two look like a married couple."

"We've practiced. He takes me to all his family and business events."

I couldn't get the image of her in the hot tub at Le Tight Rope, bouncing up and down on the fat Texan, out of my mind, his bald head between her breasts. I remembered her pulling away when I kissed her arm. Since then I had done many two-girl sessions. They were easy and lucrative. One girl would put her face between the other's legs and drape her hair over the girl's thighs so the man couldn't see that nothing was happening. "Oh we can do it with each other all day long, we want to concentrate on you," we would say to the man and stick him in between us like a hot dog.

"What have you been up to?" I asked her.

"I finally got that dog, can you believe it?"

I had no idea what she was talking about. "That's great. I'm here with my boyfriend. He doesn't know. Don't give me away."

"I won't, Daphne. I'll say I know you from the gym, or the bridal shower or something like that."

"Don't call me Daphne. My name is Bennington."

"Okay, I'll say I know you from Bennington."

"I think it's better if we just pretend not to know each other."

"All right," Georgy said, but she seemed a little insulted.

When I entered the dining room, Adam was seated at a large round table deep in conversation with the man who had called me Daphne.

55

AFTER THE WEDDING, Adam and I went to his apartment. He was quiet and drunk. It was two in the morning and I wished I could call someone to talk about what had happened. I wished I could call Andre Singh and say, "Meet me at the Gemini Diner at four A.M."

We were waiting for the elevator while Eddie, the doorman, made rude polite comments about how dressed up we were and how he hoped we had an enjoyable evening. His image appeared many times in the multipaned mirror over the brass table with the faux flowers next to the waterfall. Adam was absorbed in his mail. He was reading every word of a Learning Annex catalogue. The *New York Observer* pressing against his chest was leaving newsprint on his white tuxedo shirt, and he had a small newsprint goatee. Going up in the elevator I had pretty much decided to quit. I had to. Before Adam found out. After I had saved a little money.

As soon as we got into his apartment, Adam sat in his green

leather chair and read. I went into his bedroom and looked in the bag of stuff that I kept at his house. I unzipped my gown and pulled off my shoes and shredded pantyhose. There was a buzzing feeling in my ears like when I was little and God was watching me.

I pulled on some fishnet stockings and clipped them to a black garter belt. Holly always said, "Fishnets catch fish." The seams were twisted all around my legs like seaweed in the ocean. My mother always tried to get me to bunch up my stockings like a Chinese paper fan and then put my foot in the middle and pull them up straight, fingers working a mile a minute tugging and smoothing, but I never mastered the technique. Holly used to say that she would be out of business if women wore garter belts at home, so I wore them for Adam even though he always told me to take them off and so did all my clients. I think women like them more than men.

I walked into Adam's living room and straddled him in his chair. I reminded him that it was our four-month anniversary. He put down his paper reluctantly. He kissed my neck and my nipples, pulling my breasts out of my black lace bra. I started to moan a little and he stopped and said, "Stop acting. You're always putting on a big act. Women with large breasts don't have sensitive nipples."

"They don't?"

"No. Just be quiet and do what I tell you to do."

Maybe he was right. There was a copy of *Our Bodies, Our Selves* at the brothel which I had been meaning to read. I'm not even really sure where my vulva is.

"Just be yourself," Adam scolded, "you don't have to make all those crazy noises. Now just relax and be yourself." I got up and he grabbed my hand. "Don't get mad."

He pulled his hard penis out of his tuxedo pants and I knelt on the floor in front of him. I was using a special technique I had read about, where you keep moistening the man's cock with extra saliva while you're licking it.

"Do me a favor," Adam said. "Don't spit all over my dick. It's disgusting."

"I'm not spitting."

"Don't make all those slurping sounds. You sound like you're in a porno movie."

I got up and walked over to his stereo. I plugged in his headphones and put on a Madonna CD.

"What are you doing? You're so aggressive."

I placed the headphones on his balding head and proceeded with the blowjob, slurping and sipping and sucking and spitting.

56

THE NEXT DAY I saw a client named Richard, also balding but a good deal taller and richer than Adam, who said I gave the best blowjob he had ever had. He gave me a three-hundred-dollar tip. He said I had great instincts, that it was as if I knew just what his cock needed. I was the sexiest woman he had ever met, with the best mouth, the best tongue. The trick to my great blowjobs was the chanting I did in my head; *ninety dollars ninety dollars ninety dollars*, over and over again. He was still going on about it as I escorted him down the stairs and out the door.

Courtney was standing frozen in the corner next to the coat rack.

"Courtney, what's wrong?" She didn't say anything, just stood in the corner and then started rocking back and forth on her feet. I went over to her and shook her a little. "What's wrong?" I asked.

"You don't have time to get your coat. Just leave. I think there's a cop in room number two."

I grabbed my bookbag and pulled my jeans and T-shirt out of my tiny cubby.

"Go!" Courtney whispered. She was stuffing a stack of money in the clothes dryer.

I put my fishnetted feet in my cowboy boots and ran out the door, one black satin high heel flying out of my bookbag on the stairs. It had a bright silver lining that said Shoe Biz on it. I wondered if the cops would find the shoe and search the city far and wide to find the hooker whose red polished toes slid right in.

I ran three blocks and stumbled into an empty diner. The door to the ladies' room was locked and I had to ask the hardened caricature of a waitress for the key. The key was attached to a huge piece of wood, a two-by-four. "Are you a customah?" she asked. She looked at my red cocktail dress. I ordered a diet Pepsi and let myself into the bathroom. I unzipped my dress and tried to get my jeans on over my cowboy boots, and looked at myself in the mirror. Son of Sam could be chasing me and I'd still take a moment to look at myself in the mirror. Son of Sam went to my high school. Whenever there's an article or a documentary about him they always stress that he went to Bronx Science. I tried to stuff the dress into my bookbag but it had a mind of its own.

I paid for the soda and walked back towards the brothel. A big crowd had gathered in front of the brownstone. I stood across the street and watched six men in black pants and white T-shirts lead Courtney down the front steps. She was crying. Her hands were in handcuffs behind her back and she was wearing her little white crocheted slippers. She must not have had time to put on her shoes. The cops opened the back doors of a red van. "Join your friend in there, whore," one of them said. He was Chinese, the only one without a mustache. I wondered who else was in the van, who they got in room number 2.

Courtney saw me and started to mouth words that I couldn't make out. I have very bad vision. I moved forward but the cops started looking across the street in my direction. Somebody was tapping my shoulder and I turned to find myself face to face with my mother. She was carrying a Bloomingdale's shopping bag and trying to hide its contents.

"Don't look in the bag," she said. "It's a Christmas present for you."

"I'm not looking."

"It's a hat!" she said, pulling out a forest-green hat with beautiful green and black feathers all over it. White tissue paper was sailing across the street towards the van and the crowd of people. She put it on my head.

"It's beautiful," a woman said, who was just standing and staring at us.

"This is my daughter," my mother said to the woman. "She's an actress."

In her own way, my mother always knows just what I need. Under all those feathers I felt protected and safe, like Heidi in a big goose-down bed. The van turned the corner and I maneuvered my mother up the street. We walked with her clutching my arm which I hate. She wanted to know why I wasn't wearing a coat and insisted on going to the diner where I had just changed. She was drawn to it like a magnet.

The waitress came over and said, "Are you going to order anything this time?"

"What does that mean?" my mother asked.

"She just changed from a princess into Cinderella."

"What on earth is she talking about?" my mother asked.

"Mom, I just came from an audition."

"For what?"

"Genet's *The Balcony*."

My mother beamed with pride.

57

ADAM CALLED ME at my mother's as soon as he got to the office. He said he was meeting Hashim after work for a drink. Hashim had just found out that his fiancé, a runway model from Paris, had been working the whole time as a call girl. The engagement was off. Hashim was furious.

"Can you believe she lied like that?" Adam said. "She must have been really beautiful to be a call girl. You have to have a great body to do that. She must have a really great body."

"Maybe they'll work it out," I said.

I had been worrying more and more about what would happen if Adam found out. At Gail's I would sit in the living room with the other girls and we'd talk about our fears. Like girl scouts telling ghost stories around a campfire, we scared ourselves to death. We talked about getting robbed, raped, shot, murdered. We talked about AIDS. Night after night we rehearsed getting arrested, what we would do, who we would call, what we would say.

One girl suggested that we all make a list of the worst things that could happen to us working at Gail's. Hookers play the most interesting parlor games.

I picked up my jeans off the floor next to my bed and put them on, patting down the legs to make sure yesterday's socks and underwear weren't still in them, making big lumps. I started to call Gail's, not knowing what would happen. Would the phone ring and ring, or did Courtney have time to make a tape for the answering machine before they took her away?

Before I finished dialing I hung up. The place was probably padlocked and empty. I wouldn't be working tonight or tomorrow, I would need to find a new job. I counted my money. I had four hundred–dollar bills.

The phone rang and I answered it quickly.

"Hi, Benny." It was Yuki. She never said, "This is Yuki", she just said, "Hi," leaving me to figure out it was her. "Did you hear that Forty-fourth Street got busted?"

"I was there," I said.

"You're kidding, what happened? Can you talk?"

My mother and Tad were out somewhere and Dylan was at school, so I was able to talk freely. I felt really bad for Dylan when I thought of him at school, because he was going to the same high school that I went to.

I started to tell Yuki what happened.

"Who did they get?" She sounded terrified.

"Courtney and one other girl, but I don't know who."

"We're so lucky it wasn't us. We have to find another place, and it couldn't have come at a worse time. I need eight hundred dollars."

"I don't have it, Yuki, or I'd give it to you. I thought high-paid call girls were supposed to be rich. Why don't we have any money?"

"I've been seeing someone and he proposed. He's not a rocket scientist but he treats me right. His dog ate my gold sandals, and he bought me a new pair. I want you to meet him."

I listened skeptically. I told her I was very happy for her.

She sighed. "Oh poopie."

I closed my eyes. I hated it when Yuki said, "Oh poopie." She said it constantly.

"Marty is so sweet," Yuki said. I heard her taking a deep drag. "I've been thinking about working in a massage parlor.

I have an interview at one. Two crazy sisters own it. They're freaks. You get to keep fifty for the hour and then they pay for extras. Nude is forty-five, topless is thirty extra, and if they want to touch you they pay another fifty. Supposedly there's no sex, just hand jobs, and you get to wear a rubber glove. You should have heard them on the phone. I had to talk to both sisters and they were talking all this crap about how when we bring a man to orgasm we are bringing him to a point of pure spirituality and bringing him closer to his own enlightenment and what a wonderful healing service we are providing. I practically had to vomit the whole time. When I got off the phone they said, 'Goodbye, sister healer.' Oh poopie. I think it will be easier for me to lie to Marty there. They have a private phone line that's only for personal calls. I could give him the number."

"Maybe I should do massage," I said. "How did you meet Marty?"

"When I was working on Forty-fourth Street, a couple of days after I started, Courtney asked me to work the phones for a few minutes, and this nice guy Marty called and asked if we needed a new vacuum cleaner. He sells vacuum cleaners. We started talking and we made a date. He thinks I'm a receptionist. Oh, by the way, some guy called the other day and asked a lot of questions about you."

"What kind of questions?"

"If someone named Daphne worked there and what you looked like, and your shifts. I think he said he was referred by a friend or something."

"What was his name?"

"I don't remember, but he sure asked a lot of questions. At first I even thought he called you Bennington, but I think that was just my imagination."

I shuddered. "Did you give him an appointment?"

"No, I told him it takes a while for a new client to make an appointment, but he sounded nice. Only Courtney's allowed to book new guys. Marty asked me how many men I've slept with, and I said five.''

"Five or five thousand?"

"I gave him five names. He's so naive."

"You shouldn't lie to him about your past," I said. "He's going to find out. I think you should be totally honest with him if you're going to marry him."

"Am I supposed to tell him that I'm a whore, that I've had six abortions? I'd be a fool to pass him up. He's a nice Jewish boy from Long Island. He doesn't know about these things. Oh poopie. You're such a hypocrat! Stop being so hypocratical."

I told her I was sorry and I got off the phone, a little stunned. She was right to reprimand me. She was happy. Marty had bought her shoes. A man had probably never bought her anything before. But I would never lie to Adam if we were married. I was going to quit.

I wondered who the man was who called and asked so many questions about me. Personal referrals were the best clients because they came to the session already appreciative and almost in awe of me. I would pretend to remember who the friend was that had recommended me and then I would say how nice he was and how gentle and what a great tip he had left. Then his friend would feel competitive and try to outdo him.

I dialed the number at Gail's. I was looking forward to not working. I loved waking up and not taking a shower, not shaving my legs. Gail answered immediately. I was surprised because she never answered the phone. She was always saying it was tacky for the madam to push the business.

"Hi, it's Daphne," I said.

"I don't care if you have a hundred and four fever, you're coming in tonight or I'll kill you. I'm very busy here, Daphne."

"So we're open?" I asked.

"Alana charmed the cop, and my attorney is down there now. He said it's fine for us to stay open."

"Nothing happened?"

"Alana quit, but that's good riddance as far as I'm concerned. I want to ask you a question. How would you like to work on the phones. Courtney may want to take some time off, and I was considering training you. You're probably the least stupid of all my girls."

"Working the phones is a felony."

"Thank you so much for bringing a little sunshine into my day."

"I'll have to think about it, Gail."

"You know, Bennington, if there's one complaint that clients have about you it's that you think too much."

I hung up and lay back on my bed. I had to get another job. I had a feeling that Adam was going to ask me to marry him.

58

I GOT TO work that night a little early and took my time getting changed in the bathroom. I accidentally knocked over a bowl of potpourri and carefully picked up every crumb. I put on a garter belt, stockings, and my red cocktail dress. I put on red lipstick and improvised with a black eyeliner. My red shoes were in my cubby with condoms stuffed in the toes.

Gail knocked on the bathroom door. "Bennington, there's a Will Choose coming in five minutes. He's new."

I put on my shoes and went into the living room to sit with the other girls. All the seats were taken, so I had to prop myself up on the arm of the couch. Gail shut the large curtained French doors and the five of us sat silently, rolling our eyes at each other, waving Hi, smiling.

"What happened to Courtney? Is she out?" I whispered.

"No way, she'll be in there for at least three days," a girl named Judee said. She had new breasts like balloons resting underneath her chin. I couldn't stop looking at them.

I suddenly got an intense urge to get out of there, but the doorbell rang and I could hear Gail greeting the client, telling him how lucky he was to get an appointment with us on such short notice, that it usually took new clients three months.

I felt strange. Everyone was spooked by the police having been there. It was Halloween and Gail had decorated the living room with paper ghosts and a badly carved jack-o'-lantern with a flashlight in it. There was a dish of candy corns on the coffee table.

"Okay, Jack," I heard her say. "Okay, Jack."

Judee zipped me up the back. I looked at the framed poster over the empty client's chair. It said TAKE OFF YOUR MASKS! and had a picture of a couple dancing at a masquerade ball.

"Go right on in, Jack." The French doors opened and Gail walked in. "Ladies, I would like you to meet Jack."

And then, sitting down in the client's chair, was Adam. He was wearing a suit, and holding the briefcase I had bought him with the initials A.B. I had spent hours choosing that briefcase and those letters. Gail took his briefcase and looked at the letters. She pointed to them and said, "Jack must be a nickname." His eyes were watery and his lips were pursed. His chin was down and he stared at me.

I looked down at the floor.

"I see Jack has fallen in love with Daphne," Gail said.

Adam looked up, startled.

"Would you like to see Daphne?" Gail asked.

I started to stand up.

"I don't know," he said slowly. "Maybe I'd rather see one of these other ladies."

The girls introduced themselves and Adam looked each one over very carefully.

I somehow stood straight up in my high heels. "Won't you please excuse me?" I whispered, and walked out of the room past Adam and Gail and the other girls. I walked into the bathroom and locked the door. I was walking with my eyes closed. I knocked the bowl of potpourri into the toilet and managed to fish the broken pieces of pottery out of the bowl before throwing up all over the potpourri. I wiped my face with a towel.

Then I realized I must have made a mistake. It wasn't Adam. It couldn't be him. I was nervous and my mind was playing tricks on me. Once I had thought a client was Adam's brother and I ran out of the room, and when Gail dragged me back in I saw that the guy didn't look anything like Adam's brother.

Adam was starting a big case today. He was in court with six other lawyers on his team. He was having drinks with Hashim after work. Then we would have dinner and sex and watch TV.

I thought about having sex with Adam. How I would sit in the tub first and get that slight nervous feeling when he started to go down on me. Could he tell that I had been with other men that day? Did he somehow know? But he didn't know, and I would kiss him with my lips that I only kissed him with, and I would forget all about the clock, and counting, and condoms.

I could stay in the bathroom and the man would pick someone else or just go away. New clients were often walkouts. I would tell Gail I was sick and then leave and never come back.

"I love you, Adam," I said out loud and then I knew he

was sitting in the living room with the other girls and Gail would be coming for me any minute and I would have to get up off the bathroom floor. I had to decide what to do. I could kill myself, I thought, but I almost burst into tears thinking about how much Dylan would miss me. I had really made a mess of things.

"What the hell do you think you're doing in there?" Gail said through the door. "He wants to see you."

I came out of the bathroom and escorted Adam up the stairs to room number 4.

"They always pick the one who doesn't want to see them the most," I heard Judee say.

59

WALKING UP THE stairs with Adam following me, I felt like a mermaid growing legs. It was over. My double lives had become one life. It was excruciatingly painful, but at the same time strangely satisfying, and I had a sudden feeling of wholeness. My breathing was normal, my back was straight, my hips swayed.

I would explain everything when we were alone in the room, I thought on the first landing. I could tell him how much I needed the money and how sorry I was. Adam would hold me and cry, and I would comfort him.

And if he doesn't like it, he can go to hell, I thought when we reached the second landing. I can do what I want.

He's awful to do this to me, evil to do this to me. Trapping me like this. I hate him, I thought on the third.

The door to room number 4 was in front of us. We walked in and stood next to the bed.

60

I HAD BEEN in this room dozens of times, but Adam being here made me notice it for the first time. It was painted dark red and had carpeting that Gail was always vacuuming and calling "The French Wool." There was a black satin bed up on a platform that she'd bought at Jennifer Convertibles. The bed had the words "Jennifer's Fantasy" embroidered on the mattress in pink script. There was a small gray loveseat with a huge ceramic otter, or groundhog or something, standing on its hind legs next to it.

"What did you just do, go in the bathroom and throw up?" he asked.

"Yes." I sort of mouthed the word. My chin was trembling like a child's. I wished I could lock the door. There were no locks on the doors for the girls' protection.

"Are you going to spend your whole life throwing up in bathrooms?"

It seemed unlikely that I would live long enough to ever throw up again. "I'm sorry," I mumbled.

"You *should* be worried."

"I said I'm sorry."

"I don't care what you said." Adam put the heels of his

hands over his eyes. I started to walk toward the door. "Where are you going?"

"I'll be right back." I scurried out of the room. Gail would be downstairs expecting a hundred and eighty dollars and then I would have to do the light test with another girl. I thought about Judee holding the lamp while I ran my fingers through Adam's pubic hair. I told myself that if I could just get through the procedures and into the room alone with Adam, I could work everything out.

I ran downstairs and grabbed my bookbag from the cubby.

"No running in heels," Gail said. I took my bookbag into the bathroom and transferred two hundred-dollar bills from my wallet into my beaded purse. Then I paid Gail with my own money.

"He said I should keep the change." I would get half of the money back at the end of the shift, when we got paid. Or I would leave the place with Adam. I would grab my things and leave with him in a cab. I would quit. It was over.

"Take Judee up with you to do the light test," Gail said. She was agitated and sweating. She picked up the phone. "Hello, can I help you? . . . No, she's not here today but I have six other lovelies for you to choose from. I have a new willowy blonde and Judee is back from vacation and she has a big surprise for you, Howard, or should I say two big surprises . . . That's right . . . thirty-six double D's, more than a mouthful . . . Howard, Marilyn Monroe wouldn't be good enough for you. I hate when you call here and waste my time . . . Fine, call back on Wednesday." She slammed the phone down and I stood frozen in front of her, about to quit. "What the hell are you waiting for?" she snapped.

Judee walked with me quickly up the stairs and grabbed the lamp at the first landing.

"Judee, I have to ask you to do me a big favor."

"What is it?" She looked annoyed. I must have taken her

away from the important task of staring at her new breasts in the mirror.

"I don't want to do the light test on this guy."

"Why not?"

"I think it will make him too nervous. He seems very shy. He's a nice guy."

"Do you know him or something?"

"I know his type." I had recently had a discussion with Judee about Adam. She had said all men were the same, that he would end up here one day. "If not your boyfriend, then your father. Or your shrink, or priest, or the family doctor. Someone will show, you'll see."

"Not my boyfriend," I had said.

"Well," Judee was saying, "we're supposed to do the lamp every time." This from a girl who broke every rule in the book, including having anal sex and being late for shifts. Suddenly she was the most proper prostitute in New York.

"Please, Judee, I'll owe you one."

"Well, okay. I'll wait here for a minute and then I'll go back down."

Then I heard Gail calling me. I went downstairs with Judee right behind me.

"Try to get this one out of here quick. There's another client waiting for you in the living room."

"What!" I practically shouted. "Gail, I'm sick. I just threw up."

"Daphne, just do one more, and then you can leave. Hurry up!"

I went back into room number 4. Adam was standing in the middle of the room. He had a terrible, sad look on his face.

"What took you so long? Where were you, doing another guy in the next room? Take your clothes off, the meter's running."

I didn't point out that he hadn't actually paid any money.

"You want me to take off my clothes?"

"That's what you do for everyone else, isn't it?"

"I don't want to take them off."

He sat down on the loveseat and I sat next to him. I had had sex on the loveseat once with a client who was too shy to lie on the bed.

"So, what's a nice girl like you doing in a place like this?"

"I could ask you the same question. Do you come to these places often? Maybe we both have secrets."

His eyes raged. His mouth opened wider and wider like a snake's.

"I found out you were working here weeks ago."

"How?"

"You talk in your sleep. I don't ever want to speak to you again. You make me sick."

"Adam, I'm sorry." I touched his hair. I put my arms around him.

"Don't touch me—you're disgusting."

I burst into tears. I cried so hard, I got my first nosebleed.

"Oh, this is really attractive," Adam said. "First I find out my girlfriend's a hooker, then she throws up and slobbers and bleeds all over herself."

I was trying to keep my head back.

"How long have you been doing this?"

"Not long."

"Bullshit. You ruined everything. You fucking bitch. I hate you so much. If you needed money, I could have given it to you."

He said the word "bitch" over and over again and then he started crying, too. Tears were streaming down his stone face. I was gasping and coughing, trying to keep my head back, trying to breathe.

"I love you, Adam." My voice was the size of a pea.

"Fuck you. I never want to see you again. You didn't have to lie to me. If you were in trouble I could have helped you."

I got down on my knees on the floor. "I'll never do it again."

"Get up and let me see you earn your money," he said. He grabbed my arm and threw me on the bed. He kissed me hard and bit my lip until it bled. He held my wrists together over my head and spread my legs with his knee. He unzipped his fly and took his penis out. He couldn't enter me, he was soft. His body pounded against mine.

"Adam," I whispered. "Stop."

Suddenly he was inside me, panting and grunting. My mouth was filled with blood. I couldn't see or breathe. My face was pressed hard into his chest. He collapsed on top of me, coming. He rolled over and stood up.

"I was going to ask you to marry me."

"I'm quitting here now." I could hardly talk. "Please don't leave me."

He got dressed silently.

"Please don't go. It's not as bad as it looks."

He looked at me and shook his head.

"I have to escort you downstairs," I said. "Please, I'll leave with you."

"You've got to be kidding." He threw open the door and ran downstairs.

"Was everything okay?" I heard Gail say.

I changed the sheet and the pillowcases. I put the tissues in the wastebasket. I locked myself in the third-floor bathroom and washed my face.

Gail knocked on the door. "There's a client waiting for you in room number three. He's all ready to go."

"I can't, Gail."

"Well, just do a half hour then."

I stood in the bathroom for fifteen minutes running water in the green shell sink. I poured mouthwash into a Dixie cup. Gail had put a pourer spout on the mouthwash so that no one could drink right from the bottle. Judee knocked on the door and said, "You better get in there." I opened the door and walked across the hall to room number three to find a short client changing stations on the radio. I hated when they tried to control the atmosphere of the room, changing the music and the lights. Then he spun around and said, "Guess who?"

It was Boyd, my first client ever and my date from the Personals.

"Bennington, it's so good to see you."

"This is amazing," I said. "You were my first client and you're my last."

"Was I really your first?" he said.

When I run into someone I haven't seen in a long time, even if they are my worst enemy, I get thrown off track for a moment. I run up to them and smile and say, "Hi," as if they were my only friend in the world. I am always happy to see someone from my past. It took me a minute to remember that I hated Boyd.

"It's a small world," he said.

"Yes, it is," I said, looking at his penis.

"You didn't have to run out of that restaurant so fast . . ."

I took the money that was lying on the faux mantelpiece and ran downstairs in the middle of Boyd's sentence.

Gail grabbed the money out of my hand. "Judee told me that you didn't do the light test on that client. You're fired. As soon as you finish Boyd, you're fired."

On the floor at her feet was a plastic bag filled with the contents of my cubby. She went into the kitchen and I lifted my coat off the rack by the desk and slipped out the door. I wondered how long Boyd would lie on the bed waiting for me with his tiny erection before poking his head out and asking where I was.

I had to make it to the phone booth on the corner. I had to call Adam. We would have dinner and talk. I could explain everything.

MANHOLE

PART 5

61

IN NEW YORK you can always buy a futon from a stranger. You can walk into any Korean laundromat and read descriptions of futons on a bulletin board. They are never described as an uncomfortable mat on the floor with old period stains. They are described as "like new, with a beautiful jade and ruby print." No one in New York has ever bought a futon in a store.

You tear off a tab from the sign on the bulletin board, or you take the whole sign so that no one will beat you to it and buy the beautiful futon out from under you. It is $50 or B/O. You used to wonder what B/O referred to until you realized it meant best offer.

You call the number and make an appointment to go to a man's house on Avenue A. He calls it Avenue AIDS. You laugh nervously. You want to make a good impression so you can get the futon and maybe even talk him into delivering it to your apartment in his friend's car or strapped to a motorcycle or something. You don't want to have to go through this again with another futon.

You go to the address and yell, "Steve," and he leans out of his window and throws you the key to the front door in a black knotted sock. You don't catch it and have to fish for it under a car. You climb six flights of stairs. A man answers the door. He has a nipple ring and knows you from Bronx Science. He remembers you from the debate team. He says it's a great futon but he wants to sell it because he just broke up with his girlfriend and there are too many memories. His friend is moving and is giving him another futon, so he is selling this one.

The futon is green with a few brown stains. There is a small slash in the material. He says he once slashed up his girlfriend's pillow and the knife slipped but he could get that sewn up. He says if you want it, it's yours for ten dollars and he can deliver it because his friend has a van. He is also selling a one-way ticket to L.A. which you consider.

You would never date someone who slept on a futon. *Cosmo* says it's a sign that a man can't commit. A man should have the works—mattress, box spring, frame, footboard, and headboard.

It will feel good to be so close to the ground. A mattress could never support your heavy heart. The box spring from Sleepy's would splinter and crack down the middle. The frame would creak terribly. The headboard would hit the wall and cause the bookshelves to crash down on you. On the floor you can feel yourself move and hear yourself think. You just try not to think about all the other people who slept there before you or about water bugs crawling on you all night.

You tell yourself how lucky you are that your father is letting you take over his rent controlled apartment because he is never in the city anymore. You go to the apartment every day and clean to get it ready for your new futon. You clean out the closet. Bags of your father's wife's clothes from before she was fat, her shoes with holes going straight through, her crushed wedding hat, rusted metal poles, bathrobes through the ages, a thousand old Combat roach traps which you heard become nests if not removed, books, an old coffee grinder, cables, newspapers, hundreds of hangers, and a ruby ring which you put in your pocket.

No matter how hard you scrub, the shower still smells of semen.

You answer the buzzer. Con Ed is there to take care of the gas leak. They tell you to open the windows, not to light matches, and to evacuate the premises as quickly as possible.

62

I CALLED ADAM'S answering machine every half hour and punched in his secret code to retrieve his messages. In three days he got ten calls from people who were trying to reach the Humane Society. The Humane Society had been accidentally listed with his number in the phone book. It was the bane of his existence. He also got a message from Delta offering him frequent-flyer miles. I listened to it over and over again. I cried every time the woman said, "You and your wife or companion . . ."

I moped all over New York.

I got in a cab to meet my oldest friend, Thisbe, for brunch. It seemed like just yesterday we had been hanging around on her bed under white netting, wearing our *pointe* shoes, discussing our divorces or the fact that her stepfather wouldn't let her date a boy she liked named Chip.

"Where you from, beautiful?" the cabdriver said.

"I don't give out personal information about myself," I told him.

"Is that because you look down your nose on taxi drivers in your country?"

"No, I wouldn't give out personal information about myself to the president of the United States," I said.

"What's your name?" he asked.

"I'm not going to tell you."

"Is it because I am taxi driver and you are beautiful girl?"

"Yes," I said. "I don't feel like talking about this." I cried in the back seat, at first silently and then loudly. He gave me a paper towel.

"We are friends now," he said. "We are both miserable friends. No charge. On me."

In the restaurant Thisbe tried to cheer me up about Adam. "I never liked him," she said, "but now I really hate him. I just hate him so much."

I wanted to tell her that she didn't know the whole story, that it wasn't Adam's fault.

"Don't bother trying to defend him," Thisbe said. "I hate him."

"My chest hurts," I said. "I feel like I have a hole in my chest." I made a fool of myself telling Thisbe about how I was in actual physical pain. "It's as if I have an uncovered manhole in my chest." I couldn't stop talking about manholes and holes and Thisbe kept looking around the restaurant. "It's as if I've fallen into a very deep hole . . ."

"You know, I like you like this," Thisbe said. "I always thought you were so strong, but you're not, you're a mess, you're like me." She had hacked off her beautiful curls over some guy. She was wearing a unitard with her bicycle chain across her chest like a pocketbook. "Only when it happened to me I lost twenty pounds."

"Great," I said.

"When it happened to me I felt like the tiniest summer breeze would knock me over."

"It's time you saw the writing on the lawn," a woman was telling another woman at the next table. "He's a pig."

I pressed the heels of my hands between my breasts where the hole was. I closed my eyes and sat like that for a long time.

Thisbe picked up a package wrapped in white paper that she had on the seat next to her. She untied the rope and opened it carefully. I had been wondering what it was. "I've been going to a Chinese doctor," she said.

On the table between us Thisbe uncovered a huge pile of dead bees. They were dried like potpourri. They were the color of dust with faint stripes and onionskin wings. "I have to boil them into a tea, and drink it twice a day," she said. "Maybe he could give you something for a broken heart."

"I need Adam," I said.

"Why do you think he dumped you like that? Right before your trip to Italy. It's easy to analyze, he must have been afraid of commitment."

"I don't want to talk about it anymore," I said. I wrapped my arms around myself and sort of cupped my breasts in my hands. "Let's get out of here."

Thisbe and I called our machines at twin phone booths across the street. I don't look at street lights anymore and I don't look both ways before crossing. I have an internal traffic signal and I walk or don't walk naturally. I had a pocketful of warm coins. I called Adam's machine and listened to the woman from Delta Airlines. Thisbe was holding a corkscrew in her hand. She had to bring her own with her to work. She got on her bike and unitarded off to her waitress job on Avenue A.

I got on the subway. There was poetry on the subway between Planned Parenthood posters and dermatologist advertisements. Adam used to read the poems to me in a poetic accent. Everything was blurry.

I got off at Seventy-seventh Street and walked into Adam's

building, past the doormen. The manhole in my chest had hot steam coming out of it. I thought it might be comforting to let myself into Adam's apartment and look around for a while.

63

FIRST THING I did was get myself a glass of water and sit on the couch. I looked at my watch. I noticed a strand of my hair on the carpet. I cried for about fifteen minutes, curled in the fetal position around Adam's Rolodex. "Oh no, oh no, I've ruined everything," I wailed. Thisbe said that when her boyfriend broke up with her, she cried so loud the neighbors called the police. Six cops came to her door and told her she was young, she would meet someone else.

A jar of foreign money, collar stays, cuff links in a black leather box, business cards with all men's names except for one mysterious K. L. Burke, broken watches, a video called *Down and Dirty Scooter Tramps*, a video called *My Sister Seka*, Astroglide lubricant, a letter from his mother with a list of all the members of his family and their birthdays, shirt buttons, photos of me wearing a paper crown. I put the photos in my bookbag.

Nothing was different from the last time I had inspected his top drawer. Nothing had changed. His bed was unmade and it looked like only one side had been slept in—the side near the humidifier and the Sound Machine, which simulated either waves or rain on a rooftop. One thing I would not miss was sleeping with that humidifier and the sounds of rain on the roof and waking up waterlogged and irritated as if I had spent the night in a puddle.

I picked up the book about architecture by his bed. I read a sentence about buildings in SoHo with identical "foot-prints" and "sperm-candle columns" made from the oil of sperm whales. He must have thought about us when he read that.

In the drawer of his bedside table I found a stack of photos of me taking a shower, wearing a light blue showercap. First my back is to the camera and I am bent over shaving my legs. Then I'm turned toward the camera and my breasts are soapy and my eyes are closed. Then my eyes are open and I'm furious. I took the photos and put them with the others in my bookbag. I went around looking for every picture of my-self I could find and took them all. I didn't want some woman to come across them and say, "Who's that?"

Looking in the medicine chest, I realized I was lucky to be rid of him. I never saw a man with so many Band-Aids and prescription drugs. Tinactin for athlete's foot. Hotel sham-poos and mini soaps. A big bottle of Prozac was proudly dis-played on the glass shelf. Looking in the mirror I realized I should focus on myself. I weighed myself a few times on his scale. Even though I had eaten every meal at La Fondue since the break-up, I was still pretty thin. The waitresses were so kind there, bringing me tissues and sitting with me while I cried.

Adam's phone rang and I picked it up without thinking. I used to love answering his phone, hoping it was a girlfriend from his past who would be jealous when I said hello and make all kinds of assumptions about me from the sound of my voice. This time I didn't say anything, I just listened, concentrating like a criminal.

"Hello? Hello?" a man said.

I didn't say anything.

"Hello?" The man sounded anxious and I suddenly wanted to talk to him. I felt anxious too.

"Hello, is this the Humane Society?" he said. He sounded familiar.

"Dad?" I said without thinking.

"Benny?" His voice was grave, as if he were calling from six feet underground. I had spoken to him only twice since his dog died, once to say I was sorry about the dog and once about the apartment.

"Dad, this isn't the Humane Society, this is my ex-boyfriend's apartment."

"I looked it up in the phone book," my father said. He recited Adam's number.

"You have the right number, Dad, but it's not the Humane Society. The phone company screwed up."

"Oh my," he said, resigned.

I had gotten into Adam's bed. The down comforter that we'd shopped for together was all fluffed up in its striped Ralph Lauren cover. I pulled it up to my chin. My mouth was turned down like a mask in a Greek tragedy, like my father's. I imagined myself crying at his funeral. Eating a corned beef sandwich afterwards. Listening to all the people from the Cauldron of Clams tell me he was the greatest guy, the nicest man, the warmest individual.

"I've missed you, girl."

I turned on the Sound Machine and listened to the rain on the roof. I felt like I was ten years old, talking to him from camp. "I miss you Ben-Ben, I miss you, girl."

My father started talking about how Dylan had told him I had dropped out of NYU. He said I could finish my college education at the City University. I could apply my credits from NYU and get fifteen extra credits for "life experience" with an essay.

"Working as a call girl should get me more than fifteen

credits of life experience," I told him. I could just imagine the essay.

"Stop kidding around, stop being such a wisenheimer, I'm serious about this. I think this would be very good for you. I want you to use yourself, girl. ALL I've ever wanted was for you to use yourself. Use your BRAIN. USE yourself. USE yourself, girl."

"I'll use myself up, Dad," I said.

"Good, use yourself UP. You know, I love you."

I didn't say anything. With my father I am always telling him I hate him when I love him, and I love him when I hate him.

"It would make me very happy if you said you loved me too." There was a long pause while he waited for my answer. He made a little sound like a pained sigh.

"I love you too, Dad," I said.

"You know, Benny, I've never felt anything but the deepest connection with you. When Dylan called and said you had dropped out, I sensed something was wrong."

I thought about my father sensing something about me.

"I feel I know you better than anyone else in the world, and when something is troubling you I can feel it. Even when we haven't spoken, I have always felt close to you. Soooooooo close. I know I didn't handle the problems between you and Siobhan well. I just didn't know what to do. Am I a bad daddy? A bad daddy?" His voice was serious and begging. He slurred his words but I wasn't sure if he was drunk or if he had his dentures out. Dylan told me that he had recently gotten dentures and didn't always wear them.

"No, Dad," I whispered. "I love you too," I said again. For a brief moment I felt like a different person, like I had a father. "I hear you got dentures."

"I hate the bloody things. Vanity, vanity, who needs it? How's your mother?"

"She wants to get back together with you. She told me."

I laughed. I loved saying that. It was like telling him she had been abducted by aliens.

"Oh my." He laughed too, sounding like a bank teller who had to remain calm even though someone was holding a gun to his head. "That's not true. You're a wiseguy."

"Would you like to spend Thanksgiving with me, Dad?"

"I can't, there's a town fair and everyone has volunteered to do something. I'm reading *The Legend of Sleepy Hollow* to the kids." I pictured my father sitting on a pumpkin, reading. I wanted to go and hear the story, sit on a pile of leaves at his feet in front of all the other children. But Siobhan would probably be there running the raisin booth, winning the pie-eating contest.

"How about Christmas?" I asked him. "I know it would mean a lot to Dylan for us all to have Christmas together."

Tears started to pour down my face thinking about Christmas without Adam. And without my father and brother. I knew my mother would be at her millionth annual Bennington reunion/Christmas party.

"Maybe I can come down for Christmas," my father said. "I'll call you."

I got off the phone and put my shoes on. I washed and dried my water glass and put it away. I left half hoping I would bump into Adam.

64

THE ONLY THING I took from Adam's apartment, besides the pictures of myself, was a ticket to the Matisse show that I found on his dresser. There were two tickets in a Ticketron envelope but I only took one. I had bought them ages ago to surprise him, so it wasn't really stealing. They were my tickets.

When the Saturday after Thanksgiving finally came, I took a cab to the Museum of Modern Art. I decided to go so I could say I had seen it and to maybe meet a man.

I had heard on Sally Jessy Raphael that I wasn't going to meet a man sitting around at home.

I went straight to the museum cafeteria and had lunch. Then I strapped myself into headphones with an audiotape of a guided tour of the exhibit. I like to be told exactly what to think about a piece of art. There were hundreds of people in every room, plugged into headsets, walking like zombies, hushing complaining children. Benches filled to capacity. People looked around proudly.

I realized this was the last place in the world I wanted to be. I stood in front of a painting called "Parrot Tulips" that didn't have a horde in front of it because it wasn't featured on the audiotape. Crazy parrot tulips flopping around. I stood there for several minutes deciding what to do next. Be brave and continue on to the dreaded second floor, or go to my first movie without Adam. Ever since Adam had broken up with me I always needed a plan before leaving anywhere.

I walked from room to room thinking I was seeing people from my past. Any odalisque on a divan or female security guard in a blue uniform. The rooms were crowded with every man who had ever rejected me. Josh Lesh in the sixth grade, sitting next to me in the movies while I rolled bubble-gum-flavored lip gloss on my lips continuously. Russel Cedarholm, who invited me to his high-school prom and spent the whole evening crying in his car because he was leaving for Princeton the next morning. And Adam. In every room. In every room I saw Adam leaning against a wall watching me. He had the other ticket.

That morning I had awakened from a dream. It was my wedding day and I had plates of chocolate break-up every-where. White chocolate break-up piled high on plates. I used to get a piece of chocolate break-up at Munchmaker with my friends every day after school. It was cheaper than the stacks of perfectly shaped homemade chocolate bars. I was on a diet and I only allowed myself five fattening things a day. I had a mouthful of break-up when my father told me he was moving out.

The museum was overheated. I got very dizzy and the tulips jumped out of the painting onto my face and hair and jeans and I was wallpapered.

I had to get out of there. I would just get on the escalator and leave the building. My rich cousin, Pepper, broke both her legs running up a down escalator when she was a child. She was almost sliced up like a seedless rye.

"I've missed you," I thought someone behind me said.

"What?" I turned around, fumbling with my heavy coat and the headset. A group of Japanese tourists surrounded me, listening to the translated audiotape.

I saw Adam heading toward the escalator.

"It's an illusion," the woman on the headset said.

"It's him!" I said out loud. "I love him and it's my heart."

"Matisse loved the light in New York," the tape said.

I walked out of the room and saw Adam. He got on the escalator to the second floor. He was stuffed into a new sheepskin coat with big buttons. It looked like it was a size too small. I glided up behind him.

I followed him into a room called The Swimming Pool. The room was too crowded for me to make my way over and hold his hand. There were hundreds of people in the little room listening to their headsets.

"I've missed you," I said. He was too far away from me to hear. He fumbled with his headset. "I've missed you, Adam."

"He missed swimming," the woman on the audiotape said. "When Matisse became an invalid, the thing he missed most was swimming in the ocean, so he transformed his dining room into one of his greatest works of art."

Blue cutouts danced on the four walls. Shapes of waves of ocean and spouting whales lit by the New York light.

I pushed my way through to Adam and kissed the back of his sheepskin coat. "I miss you," I said.

He turned around and Matisse's pool emptied. Everyone disappeared. We were all alone and he turned to look at me, but he wasn't Adam.

65

ON DECEMBER 12 I called Perry Shepherd and cried that it had been one month and two weeks—six weeks, exactly forty-two days—since Adam had left. "And I'm broke," I said. I'd told her that I had been fired from my catering job. I burst into a new storm of tears. After an hour of listening to me cry she suggested that the only way to get over Adam was to try to keep myself occupied.

She told me that I could make a lot of money working as a coat-check girl at the Russian Tea Room on Fifty-seventh Street. She said that Barbra Streisand ate there every day and she wore two fur coats and checked both of them, a white one, and a black one over the white one to protect the white one from getting dirty.

"You can wear velvet dresses even at lunch and you'll meet people like Lucille Ball," Perry said.

I thought about the last time I had worn my velvet dress, at the wedding with Adam.

When I got off the phone I realized that I couldn't meet Lucille Ball because she was dead.

I walked to the corner to get a cab. My jaw was locked shut from crying so hard. Talking sent shooting pains into my head. My chest hurt. It had been six weeks since Adam had left and I still couldn't go fifteen minutes without crying. I thought about him every second. Why didn't he love me? Why didn't he love me enough?

I had to keep talking myself through things.

I talked myself into the cab.

I figured nothing could make me more miserable than I already was so I might as well try a regular job. I applied for the exalted position of Coat Check Girl. I was wearing a lipstick called Russian Red and my hair was in a bun because the pain in my chest hurt more when I tried to brush it. I was perfect for the part. I was so pathetic, trying to pretend to myself that it was a part instead of a part-time job.

They took me to the little room and I sat on a stool. A girl handed me her coat and I put it on two hangers the way I had seen Perry hang up heavy costumes. Her lining was all ripped up like mine. I handed her a tag.

"How do I look?" she asked. She was wearing a lumpy green knit suit with a button missing.

"You have a button missing," I told her.

"Yes, but it is not so noticeable," she said angrily.

I tried to think of what Perry would do. "I have a needle and thread," I said.

"Yes, well, I don't have a button."

"You look very nice," I said. She headed for the dining room, trying to smooth herself down.

I was already beginning to regret this job. I didn't like sitting in a coat closet all day and I hadn't met any celebrities, just a lot of smug happy couples. Then a handsome man gave me a ticket and I found his coat and handed it to him. He put a hundred-dollar bill into the slot of the wooden box on the counter.

"I wrote my phone number on it, I hope you don't mind," he said. I could barely muster a thank-you.

I worked there for five hours and everybody slid money into the slot. This isn't so bad, I thought. I saw Tony Randall. I couldn't tell how much he had put in the tip box, so I tried to open it. The box was locked. I pulled and pulled at the lid but I couldn't get it open. I called the manager and told him that my box was locked.

"You don't get the tips," he said. "We keep the tips. I told you the pay is six dollars an hour." There was $411 in the box, not including whatever Tony Randall put in. The manager left and I tried to pry the box off the counter but it was nailed down. I took out my Swiss army knife and struggled to pull the little saw out. I hacked at the box for ten minutes but it barely made a dent.

A man came to get his coat and I grabbed the tip, a one-dollar bill, in my fist. "Don't put it in the box," I said.

The manager came back into the room and fired me. "We have the whole thing on videotape," he said. A coat slid off its hanger onto the floor. "And I looked over your résumé and made a few calls. I don't think you ever were a personal assistant to Helen Hayes or Lucille Ball." I ran out holding my dollar and wearing a woman's fur-lined raincoat that I had tried on. It was the nicest coat I had tried on all day.

I called Perry Shepherd and told her about the manager at the Russian Tea Room keeping my tips and how I got fired. "How could you recommend a job like that?" I asked her.

"It's still nice to get those big tips even if you don't get to keep them," she said. "I know a great restaurant where you should work. Grand Central Station!"

"That's just a bar."

"No, they have soup and chicken pot pie and stuff. You get a lot of regulars who take the same train every day and you make great money. I really liked working there until I passed out on my birthday because I had a high fever and they forced me to work even though I was really sick. You know in the summer how it gets really hot in there?"

I decided not to take any more job advice from Perry Shepherd. I bought a *Village Voice* with the dollar I made at the Russian Tea Room and turned to the regular Help Wanted section. I noticed an ad that said, "Women Against Pornography, $10/hr, must be willing to yell at passers-by on the street." I always thought those women holding up pictures of naked legs and meat grinders did it for the love of it. I didn't know they were being paid. I called the number to set up an interview and a woman answered.

"What's your name?" she said.

"Ben," I said. I wanted to sound tough.

"Where are you calling from?"

"I'm on Fifty-seventh Street. I'm on a pay phone."

"Let me hear you yell at a passer-by right now," she said.

"You want me to yell at someone?"

"Yeah, just find someone and yell anything."

A tall man walked out of the Russian Tea Room and was heading towards me. "Pornography equals rape!" I screamed at the top of my lungs. He walked right by me. "Woman hater!" I screamed after him.

"That was good," the woman said. "We'll put you in front of Saks Fifth Avenue. Can you come in for a training session?"

I wrote down the information. I figured I could be a woman against pornography during the day and do phone sex or something at night. I would still have time for auditions and it would help me keep my mind off of Adam.

66

I WENT TO an audition for an off-off-Broadway play about an ingénue who overcomes obstacles to get everything she ever wanted. The ad in *Backstage* called out to me. I was sure I would get the part since I was the only one in New York out in the biggest snowstorm of the century. I was the only one who showed up. The director was impressed by my dedication, coming out in such a storm on Christmas Eve. I stood in the small office and cried. I was private in public, I was in the moment, I was totally in touch with my emotions.

He said I gave a good reading and I realized that an actress has to have known pain and now I had known it.

The audition was on the third floor of the Empire State Building and I was the only one in the lobby, the only one in the elevator, the only one in the ladies' room. I wanted to go up to the top but it was closed.

Afterwards I was alone on the street being blown all over the place. The sky had big puffed-out cheeks, spouting. The snow made me feel better. It was so harsh and outrageous. It reminded me that things could be a lot worse. I could be shoeless or I could have to move.

I had moved into my father's apartment on Eighth Street. He was living in the country full time and said I could have the apartment as long as I didn't tell Siobhan. He said I could throw out anything I wanted. After I got rid of all of my father's stuff, Perry came over and sanded and painted the floor. She carried all my boxes and the duck chest up the five flights of stairs and made up my futon. She dragged a huge Christmas tree in and decorated it with ornaments she made out of clay. I just sat on the couch.

On the day I moved into my father's apartment the streets were jam-packed with moving vans. New York was an ocean of them. Everywhere you looked you saw trucks—Moishe's, Mazeltov, Schleppers, Van-Gogh. You saw people sitting on their couches on the sidewalk outside of their new buildings, crying. The doormen yelling. Most people in New York have to move every two or three months.

Now my big audition was over and I was all alone on Fifth Avenue in front of the Empire State Building. There were no trucks, no cabs, no people. Anywhere. Everything was quiet. The snow was coming down like confetti in a school play.

It was Christmas Eve. One year ago I was at the Chelsea Hotel introducing myself to Holly, watching my father through the beveled glass at the Cauldron, sleeping in Jennifer's dorm room. I hadn't met Blanche or Gail or the girls. I hadn't met Adam.

I walked down Fifth Avenue. I walked right in the middle of the street, creating the only footprints. I was starting to get over Adam. The wind was pushing against me and I felt like I was running through a car wash, being whipped by black rubber strips.

I was myself again, lugging my wet bookbag, all alone on Fifth Avenue, walking down the middle of the street. I was on my way to the Cauldron to see my father and brother. We had Christmas LOBster plans. My father had sounded cheerful on the phone. I wished I had gotten him a present. Dylan got him a glass beer mug with a bell on the handle that you ring when the mug is empty.

I had never seen anything as beautiful as this snow. My heart was pounding. What do you have to be so excited about? I asked myself. Why do you just keep smiling every minute? I usually try not to smile or cry when no one is looking, it seems so pointless.

I made my way to Sixth Avenue and saw the subway entrance. I decided it would be my only hope of getting to the Cauldron. The stairs were slick with ice so I had to grip the banister with both hands and climb down like a small child, making sure both feet landed safely on a step before attempting the next.

There was no one in the token booth and the whole station was deserted so I ducked under the turnstile without paying. I knew a woman who did that once and got arrested. There was a long line to buy a token and she was late for her shrink appointment so she waved a twenty-dollar bill at the woman in the token booth. She wanted to show that she *had* the money, she just didn't have the time to wait on a common line. They kept her shackled to six homeless men for five hours until they had accumulated enough vagrants to meet their quota and then she spent a night in jail. They showed her on the news and she was humiliated because she was a millionaire. It cost her thirty thousand dollars to fight to have the charge removed from her permanent record.

I went to the edge of the platform to see if there was a train coming. There was slush and ice everywhere. I leaned over to look for rats. It's safe to look at them from way up on the platform for short periods of time and watch their seven-foot tails drag along the tracks. They never look up at you. I noticed a metal pool ladder at the end of the platform.

I stood there for about half an hour singing at the top of my lungs. I always sing in the subway but only when there is a train coming so no one can hear me. I was singing a made-up song about how much Adam would regret dumping me when I became a famous actress. Still singing, I did a half pirouette and saw a man slide right down the steps and land on his butt. We stared at each other, mortified.

"Are you okay?" I asked him.

"I guess," he said. He sounded annoyed. He didn't make any move to get up. I went out through the turnstile and walked over to him. I put out my hands and he grabbed them and pulled himself up. His hands were ice cold and scraped.

My teeth started chattering like a jackhammer. He put a token into the slot and walked through the turnstile. I followed him without a token, ducking under.

"Don't you have any gloves?" I asked. I sounded like my mother.

"That wasn't exactly my most flattering moment," he said. He spoke slowly with a soft, hoarse voice. He cleared his throat.

He took a pair of huge blue gloves out of his jacket pocket and put them on. We stood several feet away from each other for a long time. He was staring at me. It looked like two fires burned under his cheeks.

"When I heard you singing I started to fall . . ."

The train thundered into the station and I couldn't hear the rest of what he said.

The doors opened and we got on the train and sat across from each other. His legs stretched out in front of him. We were alone on the train. We sat there forever, staring at each other, the train doors still open, the train not moving.

I wanted to join him on the tiny orange seat for two and kiss him. Kiss his hands and lips, his burning cheeks.

He stood up and leaned against the metal pole in front of me, looking down at me.

"This is crazy," he said, "We've been here twenty minutes and nothing is happening. Maybe we'd be better off trying to walk."

I couldn't believe he said "we." I got up and started to get off the train, when the doors slammed closed on my arm. I had been holding my bookbag out in front of me and now it was hanging from my wrist outside the subway car while the rest of me stood inside. He tugged on my arm and tried to pry the doors open with his foot. I dropped my bookbag and heard it land on the platform.

The train started moving slowly and my arm got numb. Suddenly the doors opened. My arm fell to my side. The doors crashed shut.

"I'm sorry about your bag," he said. "We can go back and try to get it."

"There's nothing in it I need," I said. I thought of it lying abandoned on the platform with its straps and buckles flailing in the slush. Its sad contents spilling out. Tampons, loose change, pens, some overdue NYU library books, the address book I'd had since fifth grade, pictures of myself from Adam's apartment, scraps of paper, condoms—all over the platform.

We sat back down across from each other. I smiled at him and he smiled back. He was tall and thin with light blond curls sticking out from under a red and white hat that said "Winston" on it. He seemed to be a normal age, around thirty.

His face was flushed. His eyes were icy blue. He had a sweater wrapped around his neck like a scarf.

We rode in silence. I rubbed my arm. He came over to my side of the train and sat down next to me. He took off his gloves and touched my back. I have a very sensitive back.

At West Fourth Street I stood up and told him that I had to have dinner with my father. I felt strange, explaining my dinner plans to a stranger on the subway.

He stood up too. I wished the doors would close and we would be left alone together. "I have to get off the train now," I said.

"I want to go with you," he said.

"Do you like lobster?" I asked him.

"No, I hate it."

He followed me off the train and the doors banged shut behind us.

ABOUT THE AUTHOR

JENNIFER BELLE is an editor at the literary magazine *Mudfish*. She lives in New York City. *Going Down* is her first novel.